LANDSCAPE

LANDSCAPE

A Novel
by
Donna Cousins

iUniverse, Inc.
New York Lincoln Shanghai

Landscape

iUniverse books may be ordered through booksellers or by contacting:

iUniverse
2021 Pine Lake Road, Suite 100
Lincoln, NE 68512
www.iuniverse.com
1-800-Authors (1-800-288-4677)

ISBN-13: 978-0-595-35660-7 (pbk)
ISBN-13: 978-0-595-80138-1 (ebk)
ISBN-10: 0-595-35660-5 (pbk)
ISBN-10: 0-595-80138-2 (ebk)

Printed in the United States of America

For

Dirk

"Yes, the soil gives us more than flowers that are beautiful to look at or fruits and vegetables that are good to eat. It gives us hope, courage, patience, and quiet joy. It anchors us to something solid, fundamental, timeless, and constructive."

Elsa Uppman
Visual Garden Manual

CHAPTER 1

▼

Fog crept across the trim green lawns of west Los Angeles as a battered van made its way along a block of graceful stucco houses. At each property, the van stopped next to the four or five trash cans clustered on the parkway between the curb and the sidewalk. While the driver sat behind the wheel, a lone passenger stepped out to peer inside the receptacles. Leaning over, he poked a gloved hand among knotted plastic bags, damp garden clippings, and neatly folded cardboard boxes. When his quest yielded nothing of interest, he quickly turned to reenter the waiting vehicle. At some stops, however, the scavenger hit it big.

Recycling had put a dent in the amount of trash left near the curbs each Friday morning. Fewer wine bottles, soda cans, and jumbo plastic water jugs rattled within the large receptacles. Newspaper bundles had almost disappeared. But plenty of glass, aluminum, plastic, and paper still turned up for a free ride out of town.

The pink house on the corner regularly produced a sack of tins labeled "Feline Spa Cuisine Lite." The people next door liked their beer in bottles, their chicken in buckets, and their baby in disposable diapers. The city would pick up almost anything. All a resident had to do was leave it near the curb before six in the morning on collection day, preferably inside a thirty-five gallon container. Boxes and tied-up trash under sixty pounds and four feet in diameter were acceptable too. The rules permitted a lot of garbage. And the pair in the van wanted to see it all before the big sanitation truck rumbled through the neighborhood.

They had come across some interesting items: expired passports, scuba gear, a dilapidated dollhouse. One morning they found a flawless satin evening bag containing a brass key and two Founders passes to the Disney Center. Another dawn yielded an old collection of *Playboy* magazines and a case of floppy disks. There were four-page credit card bills, rumpled scorecards from The Riviera Country Club, and essays in binders labeled "Harvard Westlake School."

But the fancy flotsam that surfaced curbside each week held little appeal for the couple in the van. They were searching for something far more valuable. And they had to hurry.

The fog had vanished by the time they rounded the corner to Palm Street and parked near the curb where four black trash cans marked 701 sat in a row. A newly mown lawn sloped from the sidewalk to a bed of azaleas bordering a silent white house. A bicycle with blue tassels hanging from the handlebars leaned against the front steps.

The gloved man looked up and down the vacant street before exiting the van. The sky still glowed with the warm colors of early morning. Songbirds were making a racket, but other than a newspaper truck about three blocks away, he saw no sign of human activity.

He took a step toward the receptacles, then stopped. Turning, he beamed a wide grin at the woman behind the wheel. "Bingo."

She shifted the van into gear and inched forward until the rear of the vehicle drew even with the garbage cans. Leaving the key in the ignition, she set the parking brake, pulled on thick rubber gloves, and leapt out. Her partner was already opening the back door.

"Five units. Maybe four to be safe," he said in a low voice as he reached inside the van. Hesitating, he swept his eyes once again up and down the quiet street. Satisfied that they were alone, he handed out a plump sack twisted into a knot. The woman took it in one hand and a second, identical bag in the other.

She glanced at the dark windows of the house across the street, then turned and lowered the parcels deep inside one of the cans. The container had been nearly empty. In one fluid motion she pulled a handful of paper from a pile at the bottom of the can and dropped it over the new additions as she straightened up.

Her companion had already hauled two more black bags from the van. He stuffed one of them into a second can under a low layer of garden clippings. She took the other bag and hoisted it in place beside a solitary bundle of kitchen garbage.

"Not bad for one stop," the man said in a low voice, brushing moist greens from his sleeve. "Three more units and we're done for today."

The woman ducked into the driver's seat and checked her watch. The drop had taken less than thirty seconds.

CHAPTER 2

▼

Andrea Blair Grant stood in the middle of her studio sipping from a ceramic mug. A lanky brunette in slacks and a cream-colored shirt, she swallowed her coffee and savored the silence. Both house and garden seemed utterly still in the wake of Lindsey's departure with Mark.

Andrea and Mark's daughter, Lindsey, was an ebullient seven-year-old who talked the same way she swam—in breathless bursts that propelled her, lickety-split, to the deep end of long sentences. Lindsey awoke with her mouth in motion. She talked while she pulled on white tights, a plaid jumper, and five beaded friendship bracelets. She chatted between gulps of granola, coming up only for air, orange juice, and the occasional time-out to pick some dreaded morsel from the mixture in her bowl. She babbled to Wiggles, the Wheaten terrier, while Andrea and Mark shared an affectionate kiss good-bye. On her way out the door, Lindsey launched a merry monologue, craning her neck to look up at her father's tall form.

"If I took your briefcase and you took my backpack, well, when you got to your meeting and looked for your papers you'd find a turkey-baloney sandwich." Giggles. "Uh, Boss, what this bank needs is mustard. Here, have a Gummy Dinosaur." More giggles, plus a chortle from Mark. "And guess what I'd have for lunch—Tick Tocks."

"Tic *Tacs*," he corrected her.

"Tic *Tacs*. Gross."

While Andrea enjoyed the combined effects of caffeine and solitude, the first rays of sunlight stole across the cool white surfaces of her office. A former porch wrapped on three sides by French windows, the studio held a drawing board and swivel chair, some file cabinets, and against the solid wall, a built-in desk and shelves laden with equipment: computer, printer, copy machine, and fax.

Above the desk, a bulletin board revealed older habits in a riot of checklists and reminders handwritten on multicolored squares of paper. Centered on the board like the eye of a storm were a neatly typed deadline schedule and a row of crisp newsletters Andrea designed and ushered through the heavy metal of offset presses every month of the year.

That morning in early April seemed as fresh and promising as the damp lawn outside her windows. Her drawing board faced a thick carpet of grass that led across the yard to a border of jasmine laced with bobbing stalks of blue and white agapanthus. Behind the border, an ivy-covered wall marked the edge of the property and wrapped around each side. On Andrea's right, near the garage, stood a quartet of shiny-leaved lemon trees and the end of a dense hedge that began in front by the street. Across the lawn, to her left, masses of white roses still dripped from an automated morning shower.

Her gaze lingered on the pale blooms. Mark had presented the rose bed to her on their ninth anniversary, the same year she quit corporate life to begin her own graphics business. He remarked that Blair Graphics' new studio had more windows than his corner office at American Coastal, and he had worked at the bank for sixteen years. But Andrea's view, they both agreed, could use some improvement.

Happy for the mission, Mark made a trip to Hancock's, where he examined rose bushes with the intensity of a breeder choosing a race horse. Hancock's Landscape Services was to Mark what a good hardware store is to widget enthusiasts—a source of endless fascination and discovery.

Along with six prize-winning rose bushes, he purchased three sacks of fibrous peat moss, a set of rustproof zinc plant nameplates, and a new pair of thorn-resistant cowhide garden gloves. Then he surprised Andrea by having the acclaimed French Lace Floribundas planted while she attended a computer graphics seminar at UCLA.

That was two years ago. Since then both the roses and Andrea's business had blossomed, though neither grew without problems. Drought, snails, mildew. Lean budgets, cranky editors, careless printers. As sweet as the planting had been, Andrea knew the roses in her garden celebrated pest control and perseverance as much as love and wedded bliss.

Somewhere nearby, the sanitation truck thundered a load into its depths, right on schedule. Andrea set her coffee cup on the desk. She faced one more chore before her official work day began.

Wiggles followed her through the house and out the front door. Overjoyed to be free, the dog ran an excited, loopy route from tree to bush, sniffing like a bloodhound on the trail of a serial killer. Lindsey had left her bike out again. Andrea wheeled it from the front steps around to the driveway, then walked back for the empty garbage cans.

The barrels contained nothing except the usual residue of sticky grass clippings. By stacking the containers in pairs, she could manage all of them in one trip. A lazy man's load, her mother-in-law would say. But after eight years on Palm Street and how many garbage details? Three, four hundred? Andrea could haul those cans back to the house in a coma.

She noticed that the numerals she had stenciled near the rims were still visible. The neat white 701s gave the familiar black bins a slim advantage against theft plus the panache of 72-point Helvetica Bold. Designer trash cans. She plunked the barrels down in their usual place by the back door and called Wiggles. The dog had sniffled all the way around the hedge to Mrs. Woodley's new patio planter boxes, where, at Andrea's second and louder summons, he reluctantly abandoned his frenzied digging.

Three hours later, the phone on Andrea's desk rang for the eighth time that day. However, this call was not from an editor, a freelance designer, or someone who dialed a wrong number. It was Mark.

"Can you get a sitter for tonight?" he asked casually, yet with an edge she couldn't identify.

"I can try. What's the occasion?"

"Something I want to discuss. Make a reservation at a place where we can talk."

"You won't give me a hint?"

"Uh, no. It can wait." He hesitated. "I love you."

Startled, she raised her eyes from the desk. Mark's calls during working hours were normally pure business. "I love you too."

He hung up.

She stared at the receiver, then slowly put it in place. A tiny seed of unease took hold within her as she turned to find the sitter's number.

*   *   *   *

The restaurant Andrea chose featured deep booths attended by moonlighting waiters who were too busy to hover. She and Mark talked inconsequentially on the way there, and exchanged few words over the menus. They ordered from a young man with slick hair who appeared to be practicing a rare, East European accent.

"Tenk you. Tenk you wery much," he chirped before rushing away. Andrea watched his back disappear through a door. She sipped her wine, placed her glass on the table, and eyed her husband expectantly.

He cleared his throat. "Tenks for arranging the sitter and everything at the last minute." He waited.

She let the joke go.

"I wanted the right time to tell you—if there is a right time."

"Tell me what?" Her eyes locked on him.

He took a deep breath. "Well, it seems I've lost my job."

She sat perfectly still, torn between this stunning news and the creepy sensation that some vital fluid was draining from her head. Mark plunged onward, businesslike.

"You know the bank has laid off hundreds of people recently." He looked at her.

She managed a nod. Or had her neck simply failed?

"I was told today they're going to cut even more. And I'm on the list."

"But there was no warning." Andrea located her voice an octave higher than where she had left it. "You were promoted again only a few months ago."

He put his hand over hers on the table. "I served on the planning committee that recommended workforce reductions, remember?"

She swallowed hard, taking in the irony.

"In fact, I was among the most outspoken about the need to trim our overgrown bureaucracy. Old-fashioned, top-heavy commercial banks can't compete in a shrinking market. American Coastal has been one of the worst offenders in my opinion. Many people agree."

A reduction in forces. Riffed. Andrea took his hand in both of hers. His palm felt damp.

"If it's any comfort, I'm in excellent company." He named three other senior executives who, like he, had worked a decade or more with American Coastal and that day received termination notices.

"No one is immune. It's happening throughout the industry. First West announced two thousand layoffs over the next three months."

He withdrew his hand from hers and ran it through his sandy blond hair. A few gray strands graced each temple.

"I'll receive my regular pay for the next nine months, plus outplacement services. Fortunately, I'm fully vested. My pension won't be affected. Medical benefits will cover the family until I'm employed again. It's a generous severance package."

He was working hard to reassure her, and his effort wrenched her to the core. Here was a man who followed the rules. From a football scholarship at Northwestern, Mark had advanced through the Kellogg School of Management to the bank without a pause. He had worked hard to pay his way since freshman year, when his father died. He put in long hours. He was diligent, loyal, and effective. He hadn't been unemployed a day in his adult life. The sturdy way he held his shoulders as he spoke and the sheer cheeriness of his delivery made her want to take him in her arms.

"Mark, you know you're one of the people American Coastal should keep. You understand what needs to be done and you've got the courage to say so. If those qualities aren't valued, you're better off leaving." She gulped. "You really are."

The waiter reappeared with her salad and Mark's plate of carpaccio. "Pippaire?"

"Pardon?"

He waved a wooden pepper mill over Andrea's salad. "Pippaire?"

"Oh, yes, please." She met her husband's glance. This cockeyed waiter could be just what they needed.

When the waiter departed, she began again. "I know how disappointed you must be. You-we...never thought this would happen."

Mark broke a crust of bread and dipped it in a saucer of dusky olive oil. "Everyone's security is at risk in a major downsizing. I knew that. I hoped I would be part of the team that fixed the problems and moved forward. Yep," his voice cracked, "it is a blow."

That was better, she thought. He was acknowledging the hurt, letting off steam. "You know what I think?"

"What?"

"I think they're fools," Andrea said, resting her fork on her plate.

"You're prejudiced," he said without looking up.

"Of course. I also know you very well. And it's clear American Coastal isn't right for you anymore."

He stabbed a slice of beef and grinned. "Yeah. Because I just got canned."

"Because you can do better." She leaned toward him. "It's time you tried something new." Mark used to dream about heading his own business. Where had that dream gone? Warmth had returned to the planes beneath her cheekbones. Her skin burned with excitement, fueled by a combustible mix of love and grit.

Mark was watching her intently. "Does bad news always turn you on like this?"

"Maybe it's good news."

CHAPTER 3

▼

Saturday morning. The mulch smelled earthy and soothing as Mark worked the fertile mixture into the hard soil between the surface roots of the azaleas. He stopped to wipe his brow on the sleeve of his T-shirt. Wiggles regarded him from a shady spot near the hedge, too hot to venture into the afternoon sun. After a moment, Mark lifted his shovel and began digging again.

Despite the heat, he felt better with every foot of ground he tilled. He had spent the last two weeks plumbing the depths of his psyche in the chilly embrace of Webb, Watson, Latour and Meeks. They were consultants in state-of-the-art job search strategies for executives who had succumbed to large-scale downsizings. Winston Latour himself had handed Mark his homework assignments.

At first the ream of imbecilic questions separated by wide blank lines reminded Mark of Lindsey's second-grade workbooks. "What activities give you the most pleasure when you are not at work?" He sneered. They're asking a healthy forty-year-old, the husband of a stunning brunette, what activities give him pleasure?

But he soon realized that the self-assessment was serious business. Finding a job had become his full-time occupation. And Latour, with his Italian suits and his name in brass on the door of an antique-laden office suite, evidently knew something about the process.

So Mark dutifully listed his interests. He rated his abilities on a scale from one to twenty. He searched his memory to name two accomplishments from every four-year period of his life beginning in childhood. Latour's buffed henchmen plied him with multiple choice tests from which they could supposedly deduce the kind of job he could do well—brain surgeon, for example.

He dumped a bag of lumpy mulch between the bushes, and attacked the chunks with his shovel. After eighteen years in banking, he was supposed to figure out what he could do well. The thought depressed him.

The test results came back in the form of a dozen annotated charts and graphs neatly packaged in a loose-leaf notebook. When Andrea saw his personality profile, she got that gleam in her eye again. He, Mark W. Grant, was allegedly a born businessman, the kind who liked to run the show. Team-building. Goal-oriented. Persevering. A moderate risk-taker with the brains to ask for help and the gumption to master his fate. He was also supposed to be highly creative, but no test is perfect, as Andrea had noted.

Latour promptly handed Mark another thick binder, hot off the busy desktop presses of Webb, Watson, Latour and Meeks: *The Entrepreneurial Handbook*. These guys don't skip a beat, Mark had thought. What happened to the days when a person simply polished a résumé and sent it around?

He had to admit, however, the handbook interested him more than a little. He scored high on the Entrepreneurial Self-Rating Scale, which advised, "Get going, you have what it takes!" He breezed through the risk-assessment worksheets, aided by financial statements that he regularly updated on the computer in his study. Andrea's business was still modest, but in the black and growing. Their careful program of savings and investments, including a small trust fund for Lindsey's education, was paying off. And now, for the short-term at least, they could count on his severance income.

He pried a small piece of glass from the earth. Wiggles raised his head, interested. Mark looked at the dog. "Don't get excited. It's inedible."

Wiggles yawned and hung out his tongue. Mark tossed the chip into a trash can and returned to his thoughts.

He recalled the day he had entered American Coastal's training program, a newly minted MBA who saw the giant money center bank as the first step in a legendary business career. He would be, he believed, a salesman making rounds with a briefcase full of financial services. But his customers—they would be something else.

American Coastal's blue-chip clientele included corporate decision makers from all the major industries, even industries he had never known existed. Treasurers and CFOs with decades of business experience would usher him and his colleagues through heavy doors, open multimillion-dollar ledger books, and reveal management secrets he would never find in textbooks. What better way to get started?

He yanked a deeply rooted foxtail from the dirt. The plan made sense. Fresh from business school he had been pumped and primed to become a captain of industry, but uncertain about where to start. Like most kids his age, he needed time to look around the real world.

What Mark had not anticipated was the challenge he found in commercial banking. Lending, he soon discovered, was more than selling financial services. It was major-league problem solving. Every deal involved a new set of business goals, and often an entirely different industry. The customer wanted a new factory, warehouse, laboratory, or theme park. Whatever the customer wanted, he needed capital to make it happen. Mark's job was to help that business grow and prosper, and to stimulate the growth and prosperity of American Coastal at the same time. With a well-crafted loan agreement, everybody won.

An ancient, four-wheel drive Scout rattled up the street. Mark raised a gloved hand to Helen Woodley, the retired nurse who lived next door and supplied the whole block with zucchini from a prolific plot she maintained near her fuchsias. Mrs. Woodley tooted the horn of her vintage car and disappeared around the corner.

Mark sank the spoon of his shovel deep in the dirt. Aside from getting sacked, he had to face the fact that the business of lending to major corporations was virtually dead. Commercial-paper financing, in which large companies raise cash by selling notes directly to investors, had drastically reduced the loan demand from big business. That meant fewer jobs. And one important bank had just told Mark that its jobs were not for him.

Could he go to work for a different financial institution? Sure, probably. And set himself up to get whacked all over again.

He hardly saw the ground in front of him as he wielded the shovel and unearthed his soul. By the time he reached the end of the azalea bed, a simple truth had dawned on him. The idea of starting over at another bank—whatever job they offered—left him cold.

He stood very still as the realization washed over him and finally sank in. After eighteen years, he didn't want to be a banker. The truth was, he didn't want to be an employee. Working for another person who made all the key decisions had the appeal of a gig in San Quentin.

This new reality—so obvious and radical, it had seemed obscure—struck him with the profundity of a religious conversion. Andrea was right. Latour and his fat binders were probably right too. He, Mark W. Grant, former banker, could make his own company grow and prosper. Well, why not? Just thinking about running a business jumped his circuits like a generator.

Andrea's Volvo pulled into the driveway. Wiggles forgot the heat, and ran to leap on Lindsey who bounded from the car with wet hair and news.

"Daddy! Guess what, I dove headfirst from the diving board, and it was so fun. I think I dove three or maybe five times."

"Good for you, champ."

"I thought I might get water in my head through my nose but I didn't except that one time—maybe two. Did you mend the soil?"

"Amend. Yep, all done."

She flashed him a dimpled smile, and raced toward the house with Wiggles on her heels and a turquoise towel trailing from her shoulders like a cape.

Andrea walked over, but wouldn't touch the grubby cheek he offered. "You look hot."

He let the shovel drop. Perspiration traced grimy rivulets down his forearms and plastered the old Kellogg emblem to his chest.

"Better get used to it, gorgeous." He grabbed her in an exuberant embrace, and planted a salty kiss on her lips. "We'll both be sweating bullets pretty soon."

CHAPTER 4

▼

Frederick Dunn watched a bushel-sized chunk of cement fall from the long arm of the backhoe into the dump truck. He did not recognize the operator, a man with meaty forearms and reflector sunglasses, who controlled the heavy earthmover from a cab above the tractor. The fellow sure knew how to rip out old pavement.

Fred had seen enough excavation jobs to appreciate the finer points. He was a landscape contractor whose work graced some of the choicest real estate on the west side of Los Angeles. Fred's father, Hancock Dunn, had built Hancock's Landscape Services on a reputation for quality that helped the company prosper for fifty years. What began as a small retail nursery had grown to include a profitable landscape construction business that Fred managed under his father's watchful eye. Since Hancock's retirement more than a decade earlier, Fred had worked hard to maintain the company's high standards. So far, he had succeeded.

But anxiety lined the younger Dunn's deeply tanned face as he surveyed the site of his newest project. Worry had pounded through his head all morning, a jackhammer of a headache that made rubble of his normally reliable ability to think through and solve problems. Fred had a problem, no doubt about that. He also had schedules to keep, customers to please, and estimates to complete. Worry and indecision—

the skull-thudding duo that had harassed him since dawn—weren't going to stop Fred from putting in a full day's work.

He squinted in the sun and forced himself to concentrate on the job at hand: a Bel Air nuke-it-style renovation. The heavy-handed client readily approved the Russian olive trees Fred proposed to frame the redesigned driveway, which curved up a recently graded hill to a totally rebuilt house. Properly chosen and installed, the gnarly evergreens would mature into a neighborhood landmark. If someone didn't trash them first, Fred thought, shaking his head. People around there had a bad habit of tearing everything out and starting over again.

The methodical contractor glanced at his preliminary estimate. Twelve trees installed twenty-five feet apart on each side of the driveway. He made a note to prescribe good-sized specimens, say four caliper inches with forty-two inch boxed root balls. Such a tree, Fred calculated, would cost his clients about fifteen hundred dollars planted, pruned, mulched, wrapped, guy-wired, and backfilled with planting mix. The bill for twenty-four of them came to more than thirty-six thousand dollars. Fred wasn't cheap, but he was fair and conscientious, and his crews completed jobs on schedule—a rarity. Well-heeled west-side customers lined up because they knew they could count on Hancock's to do a first-rate job.

His head hurt less when he kept his mind busy. He gripped the clipboard and doggedly paced the route of the new drive, counting his steps and keeping watch for the relentless backhoe out of the corner of his eye. The road crew presumably knew who he was.

A trim fifty-nine-year-old in hard hat and work shoes, Hancock's second-generation owner looked official enough to walk onto a job unannounced if he had to. But Fred preferred to keep things aboveboard and cordial. He greeted the foreman on his way through the chain-link fence that guarded the work site, and received a nod of acknowledgment in return. Some of the old-timers used to mistake Fred for his father.

They didn't anymore, of course. Since the stroke, Hancock Dunn had grown increasingly frail, and spent most of his days wrapped in an afghan in a chair by a window. Agility had not fled his mind, however. Hancock's founder still asked pertinent questions about the business, and pored over its monthly sales figures like a politician reading exit polls. In recent months, Fred had shielded his father from the thornier issues of running the business, and the younger Hancock certainly intended to protect the elder from the shocking bit of news that sent his own throbbing system into overdrive. If his dad tried to process that information, he would burst an artery.

Fred barely noticed the wildflowers that grew through cracks in the doomed pavement at his feet. Normally the plants would interest him. But as he crushed a white pygmy poppy beneath the sole of his work shoe, all he could see was the demise of Hancock's Landscape Services.

Hancock's best customers were real estate developers, savvy operators with a keen sense of self-preservation dressed up as community responsibility. Some of them, like the developers of Glenwater Place, conducted high-profile environmental impact studies before they uprooted poison oak. How would those bellwethers react to the storm of publicity that would sweep the West Side once Fred's news became known? Fred knew the answer. They would take their business elsewhere, at least until the commotion was over…maybe forever. As for the others who counted on him—the weekend gardeners, his friends and neighbors—would they ever trust Hancock's again?

Twelve yards away a load of broken cement crashed into the truck's deep bed. Dunn grimaced. On top of everything else, he had to worry about going deaf. Mowers, trimmers, blowers, and all the other ear-splitting tools of his trade had taken a toll on his hearing. He could almost feel the tiny receptor hairs in his ears wither under the punishing vibrations of that last drop.

He fumbled in a pocket for his earplugs. He never remembered to wear the darned things until some auditory assault nearly knocked him over. He pressed a plastic plug into one ear, and listened to the racket leap to the other side of his head. Then he repeated the procedure on the other ear, and the clamor of the excavation faded to a muted rumble. Now he could relax a little.

Muffled from the noise and distracted for a moment from his worries, Fred watched the hoe operator manipulate the rig. Years in the landscape trenches had taught Fred three simple rules for loading earth into trucks. Load from level ground. Park the truck bed ninety degrees from the loading position. And approach the truck squarely, keeping the rig far enough from the truck bed to land the load smack in its center. This backhoe jockey did it exactly right, Fred noticed with satisfaction. Unlike some of the yahoos he had seen, the guy hit dead center every time.

Turning resolutely to his calculations, Fred counted fifty-two more paces to the top of the drive, and stopped to mark his tally. Painters were busy on the house, a multi-gabled, over-built mansion that shimmered on its barren lot like a mirage on a burning desert. Shielded from public scrutiny atop an exclusive hill, the builder had ripped every plant from the property. Dunn shook his head. Defoliation was good for his business, he supposed, but totally unnecessary.

He crossed the road and began to count his strides back down the other side. Inside the ear plugs he could hear the rhythmic murmur of his own healthy pulse. As he walked he studied areas of shade and sun, patterns formed by scarce running water, and the quality and texture of the soil. Occasionally he leaned over to poke the earth with the blade of his pocketknife. Every finding confirmed his opinion. Olive trees would thrive here.

The drone of the earthmover seemed a barely audible hum by the time Fred paused to write a summary on his pad. Squinting at the paper, he failed to see the backhoe's mammoth jaw gouge a clod of rock from the roadbed behind him and lift it high into the air. He did notice a shadow cross his clipboard as the arm of the hoe swung between his back and the bright midday sun. He looked up at the same moment the gaping bucket tipped its weighty contents fifteen feet above his head. By then it was too late to run. All Fred could do before the rocks crashed down on him was register surprise that this load would miss the truck by quite a long way.

In an instant, surprise gave way to a reeling series of images that flashed across Fred Dunn's popping mind like lightening in a midnight sky. Slammed to the Earth by a still-settling mass of rock and road debris, he saw vividly his first bicycle…his old college dorm…his wife, Beth, with Natalie in her arms. And finally, just before the life ebbed out of him, Fred saw in his mind's fading eye the sight that had preoccupied him all day—a tiny stick-like hand, half buried in potting soil in a tub of pink petunias.

CHAPTER 5

▼

Ginny Grant knew she was right, as usual. Her convictions tended to amuse or irritate Mark depending on his proximity to the crux of the matter. From a distance, Mark found it easy to smile at his mother's world, at the whiteness and blackness of the place, where no predicament seemed too subtle or too foreign to escape her knowing nod and pithy platitudes. Close up, however, when the chestnuts fell at Mark's own feet, he found her declarations harder to take.

"A penny saved is a penny earned," Ginny liked to tell Lindsey, shaking her granddaughter's pink ceramic piggy bank. Ginny was dedicated to doing a good deed daily. She also tried to do unto others as she would have them do unto her, which is probably what saved her from being a total pain in the ass. Andrea often reminded Mark that along with her affection for annoying clichés, Ginny possessed, well, a heart of gold.

Today Ginny's subject was Mark's intention to go into business for himself. "The grass is always greener on the other side of the fence," she told him, placing three jars of his favorite tomato salsa in a row on his desk.

Mark was working in the study when Ginny had shown up bearing gifts from her kitchen. Andrea had gone to oversee a job at the printer's, so Mark found himself alone and stuck. He looked at his mother warily.

"I've been thinking about your situation, dear." Ginny perched herself on the edge of a leather chair and arranged her tightly zippered purse and tote bags around her like disciples. "You built such a fine career in banking. I'm very proud of you. Your father would have been too, rest his soul."

Oh, oh, the big guns, Mark thought as he laid his pen on the blotter. This was going to take a while.

"At your age, with your obligations…," Ginny's sentence trailed off as she gestured around the oak-paneled study. "Wouldn't it be wise to find another job in your own field? In a nice bank or treasurer's office? Taking on a small business is a very risky proposition."

Mark eyed her and waited for the punch line.

"What I'm saying, dear, is that a bird in the hand is worth two in the bush."

He suppressed a smile. "There is no bird in the hand, Mother. I lost my job, remember?"

Ginny plucked at a handkerchief stuffed under the wrist of her cable-knit sweater. "I understand why you have to leave American Coastal. I really do. But you do not have to abandon the entire financial services industry for some crazy scheme that could send you and your whole family into bankruptcy." Her eyes grew wider as she spoke. She was scaring herself. She was scaring him.

He got up from his chair, circled the desk, and wrapped an arm around her shoulders. "I appreciate your concern, Mom; I really do. Please don't worry. You know I'll consider any decision I make very carefully."

Does a clematis climb the wall? Mark had sat at that desk and considered until his legal pads began to curl. Yes, taking on a business *is* a very risky proposition. He could fail. He could lose his life savings. He could even go bankrupt. Ginny was irritatingly right, as usual.

He patted his mother on the back while steering her toward the door.

Extended family living nearby was rare among West Side Angelenos because so many residents of Los Angeles grew up back east. "Back east," in local lingo, meant anywhere beyond the Sierra Nevada Mountains, a region so vast—nearly nationwide—it excused the geographical uncertainties of the natives, and made newcomers feel like one big, happy gene pool. New Yorkers, Floridians, North Dakotans, even Coloradans arrived from "back east."

"You're from Wisconsin?" people asked Andrea. "Ah, back east."

Friends often reminded the Grants how fortunate they were that one of Lindsey's grandparents lived not back east, but practically in the same neighborhood. Most of the time, Andrea and Mark agreed.

"Thanks for the salsa, Mom." Mark pecked Ginny on the cheek. "Were the tomatoes from your own plants?"

Reluctantly resigned to the change of subject, his mother gave him a look, and then nodded. "A bumper crop. Tomatoes and all the plastic junk that keeps turning up in my yard." She fished a ring of keys from a compartment in her purse, zipped up the compartment, zipped the top of the purse, and snapped a fold-over flap. "Hug Andrea and Lindsey for me. And please remember my advice."

"I'll remember," Mark said. The phone on his desk began to ring.

"A fool and his money are soon parted."

"Bye, Mom."

*   *   *   *

He reached the phone on the fourth ring. "Hello."

"Hi. It's Rick." Rick Edwards was a former Northwestern teammate and one of Mark's closest friends.

"I dug up some interesting material on buying a business," Rick said. "Can I fax it to Andrea's studio?"

"Sure."

Mark and Rick went way back, over both smooth and rocky terrain. Rick was dating Andrea when he introduced her to Mark. The classmates' three-way friendship managed to survive the ensuing tangle of heartstrings, and when Mark and Andrea eventually married, Rick performed impeccably as their best man. He even charmed the older generation, including Mark's mother, by dancing with all the ladies. "A regular Fred Astaire," Ginny Grant called him, watching the handsome young man in a gray cutaway steer his Gingers through the crowd.

Later, at the hotel where the wedding party was staying, Rick allegedly got drunk, and jumped fully clothed into the swimming pool with two bridesmaids wearing long linen dresses. Luckily the soused trio managed to ditch their soaked clothing before it drowned them, but hotel management frowned on skinny-dipping, not to mention clogging the delicate pool filtration system with diaphanous lingerie and abundant amounts of a substance resembling oregano.

Blotto as he was, the silver-tongued best man managed to talk the authorities out of arresting all of them by agreeing to pay damages and promising to check out at dawn. Rick later became vice president of marketing for a multinational pharmaceutical company, and vice chairman of the local United Way fund-raising campaign.

"I've got an article about owning a fortune cookie franchise. Any interest?" Rick inquired.

"What do you think, pea brain." Mark answered. "Send it anyway."

"I thought so."

Under the smooth veneer of a born operator, Rick possessed a finely tuned sense of understanding that was never more apparent to Mark than since he lost his job. Rick seemed to fathom the way unemployment socked him deep in the gut with unfamiliar and wrenching issues—self-doubt, loss of identity, fear of failure. Rick, remarkably, had all of those feelings pegged. But unlike people whose good intentions fall heavily, like sacks of rice that crush the hungry, Rick produced a jocular brand of empathy that nourished both heart and soul.

"I'll also include a list of recommended reading," Rick said.

Mark heard papers crackle.

"Here's a title for you—*Entrepreneurial Terror: The Psychic Toll.*"

"No thanks. I'm still on *Outplacement Gut-Spilling.*"

"Ah yes, the peptic toll." There was a pause on Rick's end of the line. "Uh, Mark. Did you hear about Fred Dunn?"

"Of Hancock's? No."

"Oh. I'm afraid it's not good. I've got the article right here." More crackling paper. "Dunn was killed Tuesday. In an accident, apparently."

"Fred Dunn? I just saw him last week," Mark said, incredulous. He had purchased five sacks of soil amendments from Fred Dunn himself.

"I'll fax the clipping to you along with the other articles."

Stunned, Mark leaned back in his chair. He could picture the kindly, knowledgeable man with whom he often chatted among the leafy greens and colorful flats of Hancock's nursery. He would miss him.

"Mark, are you there?"

"Yeah."

"I'm sorry about the bad news."

"I know. Me too. Listen, can you send that stuff right away?"

The fax machine was spewing paper when Mark reached Andrea's studio. He took the stack back to his desk and found the brief article about Fred Dunn. Metro section, page eight.

"Frederick H. Dunn, 59, of Pacific Palisades, the second-generation owner of Hancock's Landscape Services, died of injuries suffered Tuesday on an excavation site in Bel Air. Mr. Dunn sustained the injuries when a load of cement rubble fell on him from the scoop of an earth-mover. He died instantly.

"Investigators said Dunn was wearing hearing protection at the time of the incident, and probably did not realize how close he was to the heavy equipment. The machine's operator is in seclusion and could not be reached for comment.

"Dunn was the son of Hancock M. Dunn, founder of Hancock's Landscape Services on West Clarrington Boulevard. In addition to his father, Dunn's survivors include his wife, Beth, and a daughter, Natalie, of San Francisco.

"A memorial service will be held at 1 PM on Friday at Grace Church, 642 Los Rios."

*   *   *   *

The church was packed with mourners and orchids when Mark arrived shortly before one o'clock on Friday. He was accompanied by Andrea and their tearful neighbor, Helen Woodley, who owed her bountiful zucchinis, her espaliered fuchsias, and her newly landscaped patio to her old friend, Fred Dunn. The three squeezed into a pew near the back from which they occasionally glimpsed the white-haired Beth Dunn seated in front between a young woman, presumably her daughter, and the frail Hancock Dunn, who was wrapped in a shawl and slumped in a wheelchair at the side of the wide center aisle.

At the end of the service Mark, Andrea, Mrs. Woodley, and the rest of the congregants filed into the afternoon sun, where they lingered on the lawn in twos and threes. Mark spotted several of Fred's employees and a contingent of Folees from Folee's Nursery, Hancock's chief competitor. After a few minutes, Beth Dunn and her daughter emerged from the church. The two women moved among the mourners, thanking everyone for their sympathy and support.

At the appropriate moment, Andrea stepped forward to introduce herself, her husband, and their neighbor. Beth Dunn nodded in appreciation and presented her daughter, Natalie, a professor at a small women's college outside San Francisco. Natalie spoke.

"My father would be pleased so many of his customers are here today," the attractive young women said in a low voice. Natalie Dunn solemnly shook each of their hands. Mark found her poise and her red nose indescribably touching.

"We'll miss your father," he said when she extended her hand. "He was a fine man."

She met his eyes and managed a small, sad smile. Then she tucked her arm under her mother's elbow, and the two women turned away.

"Such a tragedy," sniffed Mrs. Woodley, dabbing a handkerchief behind her spectacles. "Every time I look at my plants I think of that sweet man. What do you suppose Beth will do about Hancock's?"

Mark stared in the direction of the Dunn women. The question had occurred to him too. Andrea put an arm around her neighbor's shoulders and started toward the car.

"We'll just have to wait and see, Helen."

CHAPTER 6

▼

They didn't have long to wait.

The next morning Mark drove his Jeep Cherokee up West Clarrington Boulevard and found the nursery gates wide open. Not surprisingly, Hancock's Landscape Services was back in business. Fred's death left three full-time employees who were perfectly capable of running the day-to-day operations until Beth and her daughter made further plans. Mark knew all three of them.

There was Maggie McBride, Hancock's bookkeeper, who probably understood the business better than any other single person. She had crunched its numbers and organized its files for more than twenty years. Maggie was efficient, smart, and colorful, with a preference for big hair and small clothes. She wore an abundance of bleached curls that looked more like a nesting habitat than a hairdo. But she dressed down a size or two, in tight, bright things that moved the focal point of her body from her friendly smile to a bosom the shape of a planter box. Mark wondered if Maggie's personal style startled auditors who studied the meticulous records she kept. To him, she was as unexpected as a sonnet in the tax code.

Carlos Hernandez, Hancock's second key player, was a college student who worked full time while studying at night for his Associate degree in horticulture. When Fred Dunn hired Carlos several years earlier the boy was a skinny, bright-eyed beacon of light who had recently arrived in Los Angeles with his parents and seven siblings from a small town outside Mexico City. In those days Carlos knew only one English phrase: *okey-dokey*. The syllables served him well. Eager to learn, the enthusiastic apprentice took on any task with gusto, crying, "Okey-dokey!" as he leapt into action.

Carlos's English improved as quickly as his understanding of the landscape business, and soon he became Fred's indispensable assistant. Still only in his early twenties, the likable young man virtually ran Hancock's retail nursery.

Rudy Vale, the third full-time employee, was the first person Mark saw when he drove into Hancock's parking lot. Rudy was an experienced foreman who focused almost exclusively on off-site landscape contracts negotiated and signed by his boss. He had been with Fred about two years or so. Once Fred and a client agreed on a project's specifications, Rudy would hire a crew of day laborers and go to work. He was a hands-on foreman, a real gardener, who liked to dig in the dirt and handle the plants right along with his workers. Mark guessed Rudy had his hands full on Glenwater Place, a six-acre mixed-use development for which Fred, with some fanfare, had won the landscape contract a few months earlier.

Mark waited in his Cherokee while Rudy backed out of a parking space. The foreman drove a shiny Toyota Land Cruiser with license plates that read PLANTS2. Rudy spotted Mark and waved. Mark waved back, then eased into the vacant place.

Hancock's looked exactly the same, yet seemed entirely different without the warm presence of Fred Dunn. Mark made his way down a slim gravel path that cut through a checkerboard of bright impatiens arranged by color in flats. The walkway led to a narrow paved area under a striped awning in front of the open window where Maggie McBride rang up retail sales. He peered inside. The blond bookkeeper sat at her desk behind a large box of Kleenex, sorting letters of condolence.

"Hi, Maggie," Mark ventured.

She turned a ravaged face toward him and broke into a smile, looking like a teargas victim who just won the lottery.

"Mr. Grant. How nice of you to stop by." She rose from her chair and stepped to the window. Black plastic hoops dangled from her earlobes. "I saw you and your wife at the funeral yesterday. It meant a lot to all of us that so many people came."

"I'm sorry about your loss," Mark offered. "How is everyone doing?" He looked around. A few customers were examining plants. He could see Carlos helping one of them.

"We're holding up okay," Maggie said, leaning her elbows and chest comfortably on the counter. "Fred's death was such a shock." Tears welled in her eyes. "I don't know what we're going to do without him."

Mark nodded sympathetically. "You could run the place yourself if you had to."

"Hello there," came a low voice behind him.

He turned. It was Natalie Dunn.

"Didn't we meet yesterday?" she asked.

Mark was pleased Fred's daughter remembered him. She was wearing blue jeans, a white T-shirt, and a baseball cap with a ponytail hanging out the back. Without the voice he wouldn't have known her.

"Hello, Professor." He shook Natalie's hand and reintroduced himself with help from Maggie.

"Mr. Grant is one of our regular customers," Maggie said to Natalie. "Your father was quite fond of him."

Natalie's smile encompassed them both. "Please call me Natalie," she told Mark. "Are you a developer, Mr. Grant?"

"Mark. Uh—no." They stepped away from the window to make way for a shopper carrying a pot of ferns. "I was a banker until recently—American Coastal. Gardening is my hobby."

She led him a few paces to a wide aisle where filtered sunlight fell on a dozen varieties of fuchsias. "You're between jobs then," she said conversationally.

"You could say that." Under her visor she had deep blue eyes. Purple, almost, the color of iris. "Actually I'm looking for a business to buy."

Natalie stopped abruptly and regarded him. "Is that why you're here? To find out if you can buy Hancock's?"

Mark felt heat rise in his face. "I'm here because I respected your father and I honor his memory. Yes, I do care what happens to Hancock's." Annoyance had crept into his voice. She had read him like an essay. "Why? Are you planning to sell already, a day after the funeral?"

"Forgive me. I didn't mean to question your sincerity." She turned a troubled gaze on the verdant inventory around her. "I am hoping to help Mother settle some things before I go back to San Francisco. Naturally, Hancock's is one of them." She looked at Mark. Gray circles framed her azure eyes. "Remember, this is all new to me."

An ancient stab of pain cut through him. He recalled his own father's death more than two decades earlier when he was a college student. An only child racked with grief, he stayed home for three weeks, determined to put his widowed mother's affairs in order. He couldn't, of course. It was way too soon.

He looked at Fred's daughter and softened. "Natalie, may I give you some advice?"

"Of course."

"Take your time," he said gently. "Sit down with your mother and her advisors and evaluate your situation very carefully. Don't make hasty decisions."

She was listening intently. Should he say more?

"If, and this is a very big if, the two of you do make up your minds to sell Hancock's...." He stopped and swallowed hard. "Call me."

He took a nominally obsolete American Coastal business card from his wallet and jotted his home phone number on the back. "I might be interested."

*   *   *   *

While Mark visited Hancock's, Andrea and Lindsey spent a productive, soggy morning bathing Wiggles. They had perfected a grooming strategy that worked wonders on the lively dog. Lindsey simply chatted

Wiggles into submission. The Wheaten Terrier gazed adoringly at his pint-sized mistress, who knelt next to Andrea by the tub and talked incessantly. She discussed the pros and cons of cleanliness, wondered out loud where shampoo came from, recalled great, sloppy bubble baths of her past.

"And afterwards, we'll play catch in the backyard," she promised her soaked and forlorn pet. "Won't that be fun?"

Meanwhile, Andrea soaped, rinsed, and soaped again the acquiescent animal, whose paws and muzzle showed the grubby signs of interesting garden dirt. She never minded this chore; Lindsey's imaginative monologues entertained her too. When at last the dog was clean, Andrea squeezed excess water from his coat and stood back with Lindsey to let him shake.

With two large towels and four quick hands, they rubbed him nearly dry. Then the three of them went outdoors to wait for Dr. Broder. Like many savvy Los Angeles professionals, Wiggles's veterinarian made house calls. Today she was coming to check the dog's teeth and look him over in general. Wiggles trotted obediently to the back steps where Andrea sat in the sunshine to trim and brush him. Before long Dr. Broder's station wagon turned into the driveway.

As soon as the examination was complete, the immaculate and certifiably healthy dog sprang like an overwound toy across the grass toward no particular destination and back again, insistent upon a reward for his patient suffering. Lindsey was happy to oblige.

She threw an old yellow tennis ball across the yard. Wiggles almost beat the high curve to the edge of the lawn, where he snatched the ball between his teeth before it bounced into the jasmine. In an instant he dropped his quarry between Lindsey's small, bare feet.

"Good dog!" She tossed the ball again.

Andrea and Dr. Broder watched for a few minutes before they said good-bye and the doctor departed. Andrea gathered the grooming tools and went inside.

"Good Wiggles! What a good boy!" Lindsey enthused as the outdoor game continued. This time she threw the ball backward over her shoulder. Wiggles raced past her. On the next throw she spun around with her eyes closed and underhanded the old Penn 3 straight up into the air. Wiggles nearly burst with joy at her inventiveness.

Airborne with glee, he flubbed the catch. The deflected ball shot toward the driveway and bounced high into the hedge. Undaunted, the dog dove headlong through the dense greenery toward Mrs. Woodley's. Rapid panting could be heard from the other side.

After a moment Wiggles squeezed back through the bushes and ran toward her with something gripped tightly in his teeth. Not a yellow tennis ball, but a bone.

CHAPTER 7

▼

Driving north on Sawtelle, Mark tried to control his excitement. Since the moment he handed Natalie Dunn his business card, a delicious sense of—daring?—had risen within him. He felt juiced, risky, like a diver on the edge of a high platform.

He sat at a red light and wondered if his excitement signaled some serious character flaw. Was he hoping to gain from Fred Dunn's tragic death? Or had he brilliantly identified the opportunity of a lifetime? The words *ambulance-chasing opportunist* came to mind, and then the stoplight turned green.

He stepped on the gas, and told himself to be sensible. Beth Dunn was hardly a defenseless widow. Her daughter was a competent professional with no apparent interest in taking over the family business. And Fred, rest his soul, had liked him. Mark had already advised Natalie to take her time. If she and Beth decided to sell Hancock's, he would do them all a favor by negotiating a fair deal, a win-win transaction.

Most pertinent to both the Dunns and himself was the importance of a sound business decision. What was Hancock's worth? Could he afford to buy the company? Was he qualified to run a landscape business? Fred's shoes would be tough to fill. Nevertheless, Mark admitted as excitement churned within him, he would love to take on the challenge.

He followed Ohio Street to Westwood Boulevard. Traffic was light for a Saturday. On an impulse he decided to drive past Glenwater Place, the new development whose landscape contract Fred had won but not lived to complete. Mark picked up his cell phone and called home. Andrea answered almost immediately.

"I've been thinking about you," she said.

"Would you and Lindsey like to go for a ride?"

"Sure. Where?"

"Glenwater Place."

"The construction site?"

"The landscape site."

A pause. "Come and get us."

*   *   *   *

Andrea, Lindsey, and Wiggles were barely settled in the Jeep when Mark edged into a parking space next to Glenwater Place. The prestigious, six-acre parcel was located east of Brentwood, not far from Westwood Village, and less than a mile from their house on Palm Street. Wiggles poked his newly shampooed head out the window, disappointed that the ride had been so short. Lindsey chattered in the back seat, a new story about Wiggles and a bone. Mark interrupted.

"Let's go for a walk." He snapped a leash on the dog's collar and handed it to his daughter with instructions to stay in the block.

Nearly finished and scheduled to open in June, Glenwater Place included a small hotel, several luxury town houses, space for specialty stores, sidewalk cafes, restaurants, and two movie theaters. What tied the elements together was the best in Spanish-style architecture: graceful arches, spacious squares, and an abundance of pale stucco, terra cotta tile, and custom wrought iron.

The design called for generous amounts of greenery. Terraced gardens, tree-lined colonnades, and a central public plaza, Camellia Court, gave a landscaper plenty to work on. The much-publicized development was the perfect showcase for Hancock's Landscape Services. When Fred's proposal beat all the other bidders—including Folee's Nursery chain—the second-generation businessman had launched his company to a new level of recognition and success.

The Grants piled out of the car. Wiggles took off with Lindsey in tow. She yanked the leash to remind the dog who was in charge. He eyed her and resumed his sniffling at a slightly less frantic pace.

Mark took Andrea's hand and walked in the opposite direction, to the middle of the leafless block. The damp clay odor of plaster, cement, and recently turned soil wafted from the sparkling buildings. Brilliant in the midday sun, the stucco walls and arches looked like new toys in a sandbox. Between the structures stretched bare earth, rich with the promise of growth.

Andrea spoke first. "This place could use some plants." Behind her sunglasses her expression was unreadable. "The project is a coup for Hancock's, isn't it?"

Mark nodded. "The zenith of Fred's career. Only he didn't live to break the soil."

They turned a corner and stopped at the wide entrance to Camellia Court, a handsomely tiled plaza still roped off for construction. The buzz of a saw echoed between the buildings. Several men with hand hoes and shovels were bent over black soil in the broad planting areas surrounding the courtyard. One of them was Rudy Vale.

"That's a Hancock's crew," Mark said, pointing. "The big guy in the plaid shirt is the foreman."

"Working on a Saturday," Andrea observed. "They're not wasting any time. Could Fred's death have altered a major contract like this one?"

"Not likely. To win the bid Fred was required to submit a detailed proposal, one that specified nearly every blade of grass and cubic foot of potting soil he planned to install. An experienced foreman like Rudy Vale knows how to implement such a plan. He's no doubt ordered the materials already. There might be a question of quality control but, again, Rudy's work is known. I doubt the developer would pull this job from Hancock's now."

"A lot of people will be watching," Andrea said.

Mark knew she was right. The project could make or break Hancock's. Rudy Vale seemed to know it too. He was working the crew hard as they prepared the soil, giving rapid instructions, keeping everyone busy.

"You want Hancock's, don't you," Andrea said matter-of-factly. "If the business is for sale, you want to buy."

He felt his pulse jump again, a rush. "I saw Natalie Dunn at the nursery this morning. I gave her my business card." He waited. Andrea had encouraged him to take a risk, strike out on his own. Was she going to back down now?

"You need more information," she said flatly. The curves beneath her cheekbones remained as cool and expressionless as her voice.

"Of course." He could hardly contain himself. "Hancock's may not even be for sale."

"But if it is, and the numbers are right," she turned to face him. "And you really do want to get up every morning and go to work at a nursery...." she slipped off the sunglasses. Her dark eyes sparkled like lamps in a well. "You'd better go for it."

He exhaled. He couldn't have said it better. Wrapping an arm around her he landed a kiss on her smiling lips. "If it is and they are, I will. Because I really do."

The sound of a dog barking and a man's angry shout undid their embrace. Wiggles had pulled the leash from Lindsey's grip and was running free across the soil at the far side of Camellia Court. Rudy Vale yelled, "Scram!" and waved a shovel while the distraught Lindsey stood behind a pedestrian barrier opposite with her hands pressed against her cheeks.

Locked on a scent, Wiggles paid no attention to the ruckus he was causing. Rudy brandished his shovel like a Louisville Slugger and went after the dog. "Scat!" he yelled menacingly. "Git!"

Mark scrambled over the tape at the far side of the plaza and ran across Camellia Court toward the oblivious animal. He knew Wiggles wouldn't be diverted from his intriguing quest until danger practically severed his head. "Wiggles!" he called in his most authoritative voice.

Rudy Vale stopped in his tracks. The dog raised his head. Mark scooped up the trailing leash and pulled the unwilling pet from the dirt onto the courtyard. Rudy lowered his shovel and broke into a broad grin.

"Mr. Grant. Hello. Is this dog yours?"

"Sorry, Rudy. He must have gotten away from my daughter." Rudy followed Mark's glance toward Lindsey.

"No problem, really. As long as he's on a leash. We have to protect the property you know."

"Right," Mark said agreeably.

Lindsey, who finally summoned the courage to cross the barrier, ran to Wiggles and threw her arms around his neck. "I'm sorry I let him go, Daddy. Wiggles went on a rumpage."

"*Ram*page. It's all right, honey. Next time, hold on tight."

Mark would have liked a few words with Rudy about Glenwater Place, but Lindsey was visibly upset and Rudy had already turned away. Wiggles strained at the leash, restless, a total pain. Mark understood why his fifty-two-pound daughter had lost control of him.

"Let's take this wiggly critter home," he said, offering Lindsey his other hand. They trotted the frisky, unrepentant terrier across Camellia Court, rejoined Andrea, and headed for the Jeep.

CHAPTER 8

▼

"A watched pot never boils," Ginny said cheerfully when she walked into the kitchen. Andrea stood by the stove, poised to dump penne pasta into a large, steaming vessel. Ginny put a container of fresh basil and eight ripe tomatoes on the speckled granite countertop. "I'm so glad you invited Rick. He's a rascal, isn't he?"

Andrea smiled and nodded. "Uncle" Rick Edwards was at that moment in the living room explaining to Lindsey the intricacies of the saline breast implant he had brought as a hostess gift, along with six white tulips and a bottle of Ruffino Chianti. Burton-Abbey, the pharmaceutical company where Rick was vice president of marketing, had recently acquired a large medical supply division that produced surgical and patient care products. Rick usually showed up with something new: an artificial heart valve, a set of doll-sized petri dishes, a plastic syringe ("Like a squirt gun, see?"), state-of-the-art, head-to-toe, non-woven scrub apparel. Lindsey loved Rick's show-and-tell routine, but didn't seem too sure about tonight's squishy, gelatinous saline implant.

"I have one of these on my desk," Rick assured his suddenly shy listener and her startled parents. "For a paperweight."

While the pasta boiled, Andrea took a sprig of basil from its container and wiped the leaves with a damp paper towel. She piled up several leaves, rolled the stack into a cylindrical shape, and used scissors to snip off a fragrant mess of fine green curls.

"Where did you find this unusual little jar?" she asked her mother-in-law. Ginny delivered her home-grown basil cuttings in water, like a bouquet. They stood in a clear glass bottle with sloping shoulders and a narrow opening at the top.

"Perfect for herbs, isn't it," Ginny replied. "I own several. Can't think where they came from." She futzed distractedly with a wedge of Romano cheese. "Rick has done well, hasn't he? I mean professionally."

Rick was divorced, a failing in Ginny's mind. But lately Mark's mother never missed a chance to applaud the fully employed.

Andrea replied, "Yes. Rick has done well."

She was working fast now; the pasta would soon be ready. She pushed the basil strips to a corner of the cutting board next to a mound of minced garlic, then quickly chopped the tomatoes from Ginny's garden.

"Please tell Lindsey to wash her hands, will you? And call everyone to the table?"

Andrea hoped Ginny wouldn't press Mark further about his professional future. Opposed to most forms of risk-taking, Ginny became apoplectic at the idea that her son, after eighteen years in a big solid bank, might invest his future in a small slippery business. Stories of entrepreneurial failure stuck in her mind like Post-it Notes. Most of her acquaintances, it seemed, had already stuck some there.

Rick knew that Mark and Andrea were waiting to hear whether the Dunns would sell. Otherwise they had told no one, including Mark's mother. Enough competitors would be after Hancock's without advanced notice of the sale via Ginny's bridge group and garden club.

Mark walked through the swinging door. "Smells delicious. May I help?" He pressed a kiss on the back of Andrea's neck. While he dressed the salad, Andrea sautéed the minced garlic in olive oil and stirred in Ginny's tomatoes. In rapid succession she added the home-grown basil, two handfuls of toasted pine nuts, some black olives, and the hot, drained pasta. Four shakes of red pepper flakes, a toss, and it was ready.

They carried steaming plates to the table, where Rick seated Andrea at one end, and a giggling Lindsey next to Ginny. Mark poured dark red Chianti into wine glasses. The men sat. Andrea passed freshly grated cheese and a basket of warm, crusty bread. Forks were lifted. Appreciative murmurs sounded around the table. Andrea regarded her family and friend with pleasure. One of life's finest moments, she realized, was the very start of a meal.

Mark raised his glass. "A toast. To Mother's excellent produce, Andrea's formidable pasta, and Rick's—er—interesting new products."

They clinked glasses and drank. Lindsey's milk left a white line on her lip. "I like the siren squirt gun best," she said to Rick.

"Syringe," he corrected her. "Disposable products are interesting, all right. The future of health care. Sterile, easy to use, then," he backhanded an imaginary item over his shoulder, "out of there."

"You throw them away?" Lindsey looked confused.

"Not the implant I brought tonight, Tunafish," he said affectionately. "That's meant to be permanent. But many other products Burton-Abbey makes are used one time only by a doctor, nurse, or some other health care worker, who then tosses it."

"That way they don't have to clean and sterilize so many things," Mark explained. "It's healthier."

"Out of sight, out of mind," Ginny blurted.

Andrea swallowed a savory mouthful of pasta. "When I think of disposables, I think of tongue depressors and Q-Tips," she said. "Evidently there are many more."

"Yep. Syringes, of course. And the needles that go with them. Catheters, suture removal trays, sterile dressing trays, surgeon's gloves and scrubs, urological products, oxygen and intravenous delivery systems, pressure monitoring systems, diagnostic kits, blood filters—" he took a breath. "Want more?"

"I get the picture," Andrea said, impressed. "I had no idea." One of her most lucrative design jobs was a newsletter for health care professionals. Readership numbered in the tens of thousands. She wondered if subscribers read *Healthy Times* once, then threw it away like a disposable. Probably.

"It is an enormous business," Rick said. "Americans spend over sixty billion—with a *b*—dollars a year on drugs and disposable health care products."

"Where do the disposables go after they're used?" Mark wanted to know.

"Incinerators, medical waste treatment and storage facilities, landfills; disposal differs for toxic or biohazardous waste and nonhazardous medical waste. Every state has its own code."

Ginny sat with her lips pursed, looking like she wanted to change the subject.

"Toxic waste?" interjected Lindsey, alarmed. "Isn't that pollution?" She wrinkled her nose.

"Well, yes," Rick affirmed. "That's why the state of California makes sure disposables and other medical wastes are handled carefully. The code, or rules, on this subject are quite detailed. About thirty pages of fine print."

Lindsey relaxed. In her enlightened young lexicon, the word *pollution* ranked on a par with horrors like *stranger*, *graffiti*, and *saturated fat*.

"My company tries to be responsible, too. For example, we figured out we could reduce our patented IV bottle by half an inch without compromising utility—that is, reducing the bottle's usefulness." He looked at Lindsey. "Guess how many pounds of plastic waste we saved our customers."

"A hundred?" she guessed, wide-eyed.

"Eight hundred thousand."

"Cool."

"You certainly are in a fascinating business," Ginny said, dabbing her lips with a napkin. "I do hope Mark finds work that interests him as much." She shot a look at her son.

"So do I, Mom, believe me." Mark poured the last of the Chianti into her glass.

"Have you told Ginny about the outplacement service you're using?" Andrea prompted. A red herring.

"I don't think so. Have I, Mother?"

Ginny said he hadn't.

"Then here's my chance." He glanced gratefully at Andrea.

While Mark extolled the virtues of Webb, Watson, Latour and Meeks, Andrea and Rick cleared the table. Lindsey carried her plate to the kitchen where Wiggles looked up from his plaid cushion in the corner. She ran to nuzzle him.

"No news on Hancock's, I take it," Rick said quietly.

Andrea lifted a bowl of fresh fruit from the kitchen table. "Not yet. The Dunns know Mark is interested. They said they'd call if they decide to sell." She selected five ripe nectarines and rinsed them under the tap. "Mark is trying not to appear too eager, but the truth is, he wants Hancock's more than anything. He spends most of his time studying the landscape business and taking five-mile runs to work off his anxiety."

She sliced the nectarines into glass bowls and squeezed a wedge of lemon, fresh from her own backyard, over the top. Rick picked up Ginny's container of basil from the counter and turned it in his hand. "Where did you get this vial?"

"Vial?" repeated Andrea, amused. "Your job has affected your vocabulary. Ginny brought it."

She took two of the bowls and a plate of biscotti and backed through the swinging door to the dining room. In a moment Rick and Lindsey followed carrying the other three bowls.

"...but headhunters," Mark was explaining to his mother, "are primarily interested in people who are employed and rising. That's why they're called executive search firms. Their business is hiring executives away from other companies."

"I see. So you would not interest a headhunter because you no longer work at the bank," Ginny said, disappointed.

"Right. Although some search firms keep files on unemployed job-hunters who have a strong background in their specialty. I sent my resume to a couple of those."

"Isn't Sloan & Barrett the best known in bank searches?" asked Rick, placing a bowl of fruit in front of Mark.

"Um-hmm. I've talked with Sloan & Barrett." Mark picked up his spoon. He did not want to raise his mother's hopes regarding a future in financial services.

"Well you reap what you sow," Ginny declared waving a biscotti in his direction. "Keep that in mind."

Conversation stopped while they pondered Ginny's pronouncement and spooned fruit into their mouths. In another room the telephone rang.

"I'll get it," Mark said hastily, folding his napkin. "Excuse me." He pushed back his chair and hurried to the study.

Ginny finished her dessert, got up, and began to clear the dishes.

"May I read a story to you, Grandma?" Lindsey asked.

"Go ahead," Andrea urged. "I'll take care of the dishes."

Hand in hand, Ginny and Lindsey left the room. Andrea and Rick remained seated, sipping the last of their wine. In a moment Mark reappeared at the dining room door wearing the dazed expression of a survivor pulled from a wreck.

"That was Natalie Dunn." He waited until the news penetrated various lobes and ganglia including, apparently, his own. "Hancock Dunn died last night."

Andrea placed her wine glass on the tablecloth. Hancock Dunn, dead. Less than three weeks after his son. She guessed what Mark was going to say next.

"Beth is ready to sell the business."

CHAPTER 9

▼ ——————

Folee's wanted Hancock's too, of course. Sam Folee, the head of the ubiquitous Folee's Nursery chain, owned garden centers from Pasadena to Palos Verdes, and was still expanding. Hancock's prime location on West Clarrington Boulevard, its affluent clientele, and the lucrative contract for Glenwater Place attracted Sam Folee like a thrip to a fig.

When Mark saw Hancock's financial statements, he understood the attraction even better. The figures supplied by Beth Dunn's accountant showed the business to be solvent, efficient, and profitable. Mark ran the numbers through his computer and calculated a dozen key business ratios. When he compared the ratios to industry norms, his respect for Fred and Hancock Dunn grew. The men had built an exemplary small company that would warm the coldest heart in business school.

It was terrible news, Mark realized. How could he, a mere mortal, compete with a big chain of nurseries for this juicy, wormless plum? When he pictured his loan application next to Folee's on a loan officer's desk, his heart sank. No contest.

The former banker despaired in his study amid the litter of an optimist: a dog-eared pamphlet titled *Paths to a Business of Your Own,* Dun and Bradstreet printouts on the landscape industry, brochures from the state contractor's license board, market research, competitive analyses.

The respectful business plan he prepared for Beth Dunn in a heart-pounding state of hope and naiveté. He had thought of every-thing…except the fact that Beth would be nuts to turn her back on a big, well-capitalized buyer like Sam Folee.

Beth did exactly that.

Folee's, it turned out, also submitted a plan—fifty slick pages detailing the chain's intentions for the small family business the Dunns had built from scratch. Beth told Mark she read the document carefully. She said she could swallow the office renovation, the rows of colorful flags atop the bright new fence, even the inevitable name change. Nevertheless, she balked at the section titled, "Management Functional Responsibilities," which clearly doomed to lesser jobs—or worse—both Maggie McBride and Carlos Hernandez, whom Beth viewed as members of her family.

A protective clause was running through her wary mind when she got to the "Product Innovations" the Folees had in mind for Hancock's: artificial plants, "everlasting" gift bouquets, whimsical garden art—including "whole families of colorful elves."

The elves, she explained, were the last straw. She thought of her husband and her father-in-law spinning like rototillers in their graves, and decided she had read enough. She informed Natalie and her advisers that she would sell to Mark Grant at a fair price and finance the deal herself if she had to. She had to, and she did.

*   *   *   *

The day Mark was to become the owner of Hancock's Landscape Services, the phone on his desk rang moments before he planned to leave for his final meeting with Beth and their respective attorneys. Andrea had already departed to drive Lindsey, and then go to the printer's. She promised him a celebratory dinner when he returned from his first afternoon as a CEO. He had lain awake half the night, reeling with ideas and excitement. The day felt like Christmas, his wedding anniversary, and final exams all rolled into one. On the second ring he picked up the receiver.

"Hello." He hoped whoever it was would talk fast. He was in a hurry.

"Mark Grant? Hi, this is Tad Bliss with Sloan & Barrett."

The headhunter. Mark stopped stuffing papers into his briefcase. "Yes. How are you?"

"Fine, thanks. I've got something that might interest you. A position that looks like a good fit."

Mark felt the hair rise on his arms. This couldn't be happening, not now.

"Senior vice president and group head in middle-market lending with a mid-sized financial institution. It would involve stock options. You would have about twenty direct reports. It's downtown. Our client is eager to hire, and we'd like to talk with you."

SVP? Stock options? Mark blinked. He thought jobs like that in banking had disappeared. "Well I, uh, appreciate the call," he stammered, sinking into his chair. The sudden onslaught of career riches rumbled in his stomach like a heavy, undigested meal. In a couple of hours he would become the head of Hancock's Landscape Services— now this.

"Actually, Tad, I'm in the process of buying a business." Getting the words out wasn't easy. His mouth had dried up. "The closing is today."

Was it sweet, telling this guy to take a leap? No. Closing was an apt word, Mark thought as his stomach churned—closing a deal and closing a door. "I wanted a chance to run my own show."

The headhunter said good for you, congratulations, let us know how it goes, and some other polite things Mark barely heard. Mark couldn't remember how he replied. Turning his back on about three hundred grand a year for the opportunity to dig himself deeply into debt was a novel experience. He hung up the phone feeling flattered, resentful, uncertain, alone. He was farther out than he had ever been on a bare and bobbing limb. His mother would commit him had she heard that conversation. Was he crazy? He poured himself a handful of Tic Tacs. He was about to realize a lifelong dream, and he felt like he had the flu. He snapped his briefcase shut, took a deep breath, and headed queasily toward his new life.

*   *   *   *

Natalie Dunn came to the closing too. She arrived with her mother, carrying a suitcase and a small box wrapped in shiny green paper. At the conclusion of the signing, Beth thanked the lawyers and said she was pleased with the transaction. Nevertheless, tears glistened in her eyes. Her husband's memory hung over the table like mist.

"I'm confident Hancock's will continue to thrive in your capable hands," she sniffed, looking at Mark. "Fred would be happy to know you are tending the business."

Mark regarded her fondly. "I appreciate your kind words, Beth. It won't be easy to operate Hancock's as well as your husband and his father did." He looked at Natalie. "But I promise both of you I'll do my best."

Sitting at the conference table with all eyes on him, Mark realized he had never, ever, felt so deeply the desire to succeed.

"Who knows," he added with an innocent smile. "I might even make some improvements. Like a brand new line of designer lawn art."

Beth rolled her eyes and laughed, visibly relieved he had brightened the mood. Mark's stomach fluttered. He shook Beth's hand, and the meeting was over. Hancock's belonged to him.

Natalie watched Mark pack his papers while Beth and the attorneys filed through the door. Sleek in a dark silk suit, Fred's daughter looked polished, taller than he remembered. She said little during the meeting, he noticed. She was hard not to notice.

"Congratulations, Mark." She held out the small wrapped parcel. "This is for you." Her hyacinth eyes met his.

He thought four or five different things at once. A present? Eyes can't be that color. She's glad I bought the business. Will I see her again?

"Open it, please." She pressed the box into his hand.

He ripped his eyes from hers, undid the wrapping, opened the box, and found a slender silver pocketknife engraved with oak leaves. It had one sturdy blade.

"It belonged to my grandfather," Natalie explained in her velvety voice. "Hancock carried it with him every day, until he retired. Then he gave it to Dad."

Mark weighed the handsome knife in his hand. He had seen it before, at the nursery, wrapped in Fred's thick brown fingers. Fred used the blade to take cuttings, test soil, open boxes and bags, and so forth. He probably had it with him when he died.

"Thank you, Natalie. I'll be proud to carry this."

She kissed him lightly on the cheek, causing erratic blips in most of his clinical measures. "I hope it brings you good luck." Then she was gone.

CHAPTER 10

▼

Mark stopped at home to change out of his business suit. Andrea wasn't there. Ten minutes later, he climbed back in the Cherokee. Twelve minutes after that he turned into Hancock's parking lot. Sitting at the old maple desk in the office Fred had shared with Maggie, the new owner of Hancock's Landscape Services found little time to celebrate his comfortable clothes, his ridiculously short commute, or his enviable new job. Maggie had his orientation all planned. She had honored him by dressing up more than usual, in a red-dotted miniskirt and nearly matching red shoes. However, the honeymoon would be short.

"The sooner you get up to speed," she told him briskly, "the sooner Hancock's can return to normal."

The bookkeeper led her new boss on a tour of the nooks and crannies that held Hancock's files, invoices, bank statements, and checks. Her systems were orderly, sensible, and hopelessly out of date. Mark sifted through an alphabetized stack of payroll slips and decided he would change nothing until he knew the business inside out. Computers, for instance, could wait. He needed Maggie on his team, and would take the time to earn her trust. Besides, he didn't have another nickel to spend.

She laid a heavy ring of keys in front of him. "Beth brought these over."

Mark fanned Fred's keys on the desk. The jumble of sizes and shapes, old and new, dull and shiny, assembled over the years like charms on a bracelet seemed personal, fraught with meaning.

"This one opens the front gate," Maggie said, fingering a round brass Yale. "Here's the greenhouse." An ancient Segal. "The potting shed." Another Yale. "The truck." A silver Schlage. She identified several more, then peered at a small silver key threaded on a dime-sized wire loop. "Made in U.S.A. Steel Case. Grand Rapids, Michigan. I wonder what this one's for."

"A steel case I suspect," Mark said, eyeing her. "Have you got a locked file?"

"Only the ones I showed you. We haven't locked those in years."

He tried the key in the bright round lock on the file drawers behind him. It didn't fit. Maggie shrugged and turned to answer the telephone.

Mark guessed Fred hadn't culled his key ring in a while. The steel case was probably long gone.

Maggie put the phone on hold and tucked a stray shock of blond hair behind her ear. "It's George Alder, a friend of Fred's. He wants to talk to you."

Mark nodded.

She pushed a button that rerouted the call three feet to the phone on his desk. He picked up the receiver, thinking of the light years between this cozy room and his old executive office suite at the bank. "Hello. This is Mark Grant."

"Hello," said the voice. "I'm George Alder, a classmate of Fred Dunn's from way back. We went to U.C. Davis together."

"I'm happy to hear from you." Mark wondered if he should offer condolences to Fred's longtime friend.

"I didn't hear Fred died until after the funeral," George said. "I was fishing in Canada when it happened. Golly, what a blow."

Mark murmured sympathetically. George sounded like a decent guy.

"I wanted to call and wish you well at Hancock's. Beth speaks highly of you."

"Thanks. I'll try not to disappoint her."

"Fine. Uh, Mark. I do have another reason for calling. I wonder if you have any idea why Fred phoned me the day before he died. He left messages at the office and with my wife. Wanted me to call as soon as I returned."

Mark frowned in concentration. No, he had no idea why Fred called George. Should he? He opened the appointment calendar on Fred's desk and leafed back week-by-week to the Tuesday of the accident. "Olive Trees/654 Bel Air" was printed across the fateful day in Fred's neat block capitals. The preceding square was blank.

"Sorry, George. I don't know the answer. His agenda for that day is empty."

"I see. Beth doesn't know either. She said Fred spent the entire day at the nursery. Well, it just seemed odd, the timing and all. I hadn't heard from him in nearly a year."

The man sounded sad and regretful. Mark wished he could help. "Maybe Fred just wanted to catch up with an old friend. Give me your phone number; it's probably here somewhere, but just in case. I'll call if I find out anything else."

"I'd appreciate that." George recited his home and office numbers while Mark jotted them down.

"Where do you work?" Mark asked.

"Civic Center Plaza, First and Broadway. Department of Environmental Health."

Environmental health? That made sense. U.C. Davis was known for its environmental sciences department. "Interesting. Well, I'm glad you called. I hope you will stop by the nursery so we can meet in person."

George said he would, and they hung up.

Mark stepped outside and stood under the striped awning in the center of the nursery that now belonged to him. His lips curved into a smile. To his right and left stretched his very own inventory, a prosperous expanse of widgets that literally grew: yellow marigolds, Spanish bluebells, showy rhododendrons in pink, red, and purple. People said Hancock's colorful acre resembled a quilt, but anyone attuned to the great dramas of botany knew that beneath the placid patchwork lurked forces as wild as a New Guinea rain forest. In cellular terms, the place rocked.

He made his way down a neat gravel path, wise to the world of erupting buds, grasping tendrils, invading roots, and a million stealthy leaves committing photosynthesis in the sun. He was looking for Carlos, the keeper of the zoo. Mark found him bent over a menagerie of aggressive ground covers caged in four-inch pots.

"Cape week spreads fast, stays low, and is very tough," the horticultural student was explaining to an interested customer. "See the yellow flowers? If your hillside is shaded, you can use English ivy. Otherwise you might try gazania, right here, or ice plant, santolina, snow-in-summer...."

Mark eased away and went to speak with the others who were helping in the nursery that afternoon. Hancock's stayed open seven days a week, although Fred had toyed with the idea of a Wednesday closing. Maggie and Carlos usually took Sunday morning, Tuesday afternoon, and all of Wednesday off. They had reliable backups who filled in during their absences, and a long roster of full- and part-timers who helped haul, water, dig, load, stack, rake, and generally do the heavy lifting.

Rudy Vale, in supervising the off-site projects, let the work dictate his schedule, as had Fred Dunn. It was not uncommon for Rudy to labor ten straight days, take four days off, then work ten more. Rudy's single-mindedness when it came to completing landscape jobs was one of the reasons Hancock's—in a noted departure from industry norms—nearly always finished its projects ahead of schedule.

Carlos's customer chose cape weed. Carlos spoke rapid Spanish to one of the helpers, who quickly loaded three flats onto a cart and led the way to the cash register. Mark took the opportunity to approach his star employee; Carlos saw him coming.

"Mr. Grant, welcome to Hancock's."

"Thank you, Carlos. I'm glad to be here." Mark stepped closer. "I appreciate the fine job you're doing, and look forward to working with you."

"That goes for me too," Carlos beamed. "I also look forward." He cast an expert eye on the seven or eight shoppers browsing among the greenery. "Would you like me to show you around and tell you something?"

Mark smiled. Maggie must have clued him in about Orientation Day.

"I'd like that, Carlos. Let's do our tour first thing tomorrow, when there are fewer customers."

"Okey-dokey."

Mark poked his head into the office to sign off with Maggie, then walked to his Cherokee and departed for Glenwater Place. On his first day at Hancock's he wanted a few words with all the key players, including Rudy Vale.

Mark drove north on Sawtelle and then east on Ohio with to-do lists sprouting in his mind like mushrooms after rain. The anxious energy that had roamed his innards earlier found its way to more-productive paths. While his mind raced, his stomach, at last, felt calm.

He expected something different—more joy, perhaps—once the papers were signed and Hancock's belonged to him. But the tension of the last several weeks led directly to total absorption in his new responsibilities. His goals had already leapt forward.

Afternoon shadows were lengthening when he steered around a corner near Glenwater Place and slowed to cruise the block for a parking space. The complex would soon open an extensive parking facility of its own. Until then, he and his crews had to compete for curb rights with endless waves of west-side moviegoers, shoppers, students, and people with no identifiable business driving banged-up trucks.

One such vehicle, a dented white van, noisily vacated a spot just as Mark arrived. He nosed into the gap, acing out a red Miata that had made a sharp U-turn in the middle of the block. The Miata driver shrugged his shoulders, conceding defeat. A local. A person from back east would have honked.

Rudy Vale stood a little apart from four men and two women who were planting dogwood trees in a neat row next to one of the stately colonnades that bisected Glenwater Place. Mark stopped a short distance away to watch. He gave Rudy high marks for productivity. The guy knew how to motivate his crews. The six workers were filling holes with trees and planting mix like there was no *mañana*.

The foreman stood with his back to Mark, and he was holding his hand near his chin. Mark realized Rudy was speaking on a cell phone. Fred Dunn had not brought his office into the electronic age but his foreman, at least, was up to speed. Rudy turned, saw Mark, and nodded. Then he apparently ended his conversation and slipped the phone into the pocket of his overalls.

"Hello, Mr. Grant."

Mark greeted the foreman and complimented him on his progress. Rudy said the project was ahead of schedule. "We'll finish this section today," he said, pointing. "And tomorrow we can bring in the shrubs for Camellia Court."

"Good," Mark responded. "Because you know we have to start on those olive trees Fred chose for Bel Air. Maggie got the go-ahead from the client."

Rudy frowned. Mark guessed he anticipated at least two, maybe three more weeks of work on Glenwater Place. The grand opening was three weeks from Saturday.

"Let's let Carlos supervise this crew for a couple of days while you assemble another team to complete the job in Bel Air," Mark suggested.

"That way you can stay on schedule here without compromising the other project."

The foreman's brow wrinkled like the folds in a canvas sack. He had some problem with the arrangement, Mark could tell. Rudy probably felt a sense of ownership about Glenwater Place and didn't want someone else getting involved. Mark liked that. He cleared his throat and tried again.

"Rudy, on big projects you need an assistant foreman. It's the only way to keep your crews working when you have other business. Assign Carlos a specific, straightforward task, say, planting the camellias in Camellia Court. In a few days you'll be back to finish the job yourself."

Rudy looked at Mark, considering, then slowly nodded. "Whatever you say, Mr. Grant."

"Good. I'll speak to Carlos tomorrow."

Hoping he hadn't mortally offended his foreman, Mark walked away. Until he could earn his own landscape contractor's license—a whole year from then—or get Carlos licensed, he would have to lean on Rudy.

Like other states, California required a license for any business or individual who constructed or altered a building, road, parking facility, railroad, excavation, or other structure. That included specialty contractors and those engaged in the business of home improvements. Landscaping was a Class C specialty license, one of forty separate classifications for contractors whose work required special skill in a trade or craft. Mark had practically memorized the regulations.

Fred Dunn's landscaping license expired right along with Fred. The credential could not be included in the sale of the business unless Fred, the qualified individual, still worked there. Fred, however, had the good sense to hire another licensed landscaper, Rudy Vale, under whose supervision Hancock's landscape business continued to function even in the owner's absence.

Fred also made a smart move when he took Carlos under his wing. His able protégé now had more than enough work experience and related schooling to qualify for a license. Carlos simply hadn't taken the exam. Getting the young man prepared, tested, and licensed would be one of Mark's top priorities.

Rudy, in the meantime, had put his credentials to excellent use, Mark noted approvingly as he strolled through Glenwater Place. The tile sidewalk on which he walked skirted a bevy of recently planted jacaranda trees, expertly staked and mulched, their fern-like leaves already sprouting lacy new growth. The hardy jacs would grow to nearly forty feet and bloom reliably several months of the year in a spectacular shade of lavender. Against the white stucco walls of Glenwater Place, the trees would be a knockout.

Mark entered Camellia Court, where another stand of matching trees faced the pavement like a line of leggy Rockettes. These were *Washingtonia filifera*, California fan palms. Sturdy, fast growers to about sixty feet, the trees were popular with designers for their showy fronds and dramatic vertical effect. They looked dramatic, all right.

Landscaping generally went top down, like painting a room from ceiling to floor. Although Glenwater Place was divided into more than a dozen discrete planting areas, Rudy—correctly—treated the entire site as one project. He planted the sky-scraping fan palms in Camellia Court first, then the mid-sized jacarandas that edged parkways throughout the project, and finally the dainty dogwoods along the colonnades. When he finished the trees, he would have a wide choice of shrubs to plant in the five to ten-foot range. Fred's design called for dense hedges of glossy-leaved *rhaphiolepis*, neat boxwood borders on all the terraces, and, here in Camellia Court, sixteen varieties of *C. japonica*. The camellias would bloom alternately from October to May in lip-smacking pinks and reds.

Mark circled the courtyard next to the dark, bare borders that rested in readiness for their new occupants. Partially sheltered from sun and wind by the fan palms and the high white walls of the surrounding buildings, Camellia Court provided the ideal habitat for the flowering shrubs.

He crouched down, scooped up a handful of soil, and let it sift through his fingers. Dark, organic material—perfect. He plucked a couple of stray chips of plastic from the mix and pocketed them until he found a trash can. He examined another handful. Clean and rich as fresh ground coffee, the particles fell from his hand like rain. A translucent—worm?—caught his eye in the soil he had disturbed. No, not a worm. He carefully brushed away the earth and extracted twelve grimy inches of plastic tube.

CHAPTER 11

▼

Home run, bases loaded.

Andrea pinned to the bulletin board above her desk four newsletters printed that afternoon on the busy offset presses of Alphaprint and Pico Press, neighboring establishments on Pico Boulevard that produced most of the publications she designed. She spent much of the day rushing back and forth between printers while the four newsletters passed through the final stages of production.

Andrea was a stickler for quality printing. The cleanest layout, the most compelling photos, the snappiest, liveliest, boldest look could be ruined by an indifferent print job. Quality control at press time was as basic to her business as pulp is to paper.

She stood back from the bulletin board to consider her work. *Healthy Times,* her biggest client, was distributed to a hundred and fifty thousand medical professionals in southern California. Eighty-pound stock, black ink, blue accents. Plenty of white space. *Healthy Times's* twelve neat pages looked as crisp and authoritative as a doctor's white coat.

LA Business Report, next in the row on her bulletin board, went to sixty thousand local executives. It had a strong, no-nonsense appearance heralded by a sans-serif nameplate and headlines to match. Dark gray ink and neat blocks of copy made *LA Business Report* suitably spare and hard-edged.

At twenty pages, *Property Line* was the longest and chattiest of the four. PL circulated among fifty thousand members of an influential realtors' organization. Andrea liked its newsy tone, but not the endless mandatory photos of houses and the smiling realtors who finally sold them.

Garden Works, the last piece in her display, would be seen by about two thousand green-thumbed subscribers. It had black and green inks, with typewriter type. Folksy and sly, its how-to, using-what articles were certain to send more than a few readers straight to the garden store. Andrea made a note to tell Mark.

In all, the four newsletters represented more than a quarter of a million subscribers. Among them were reporters from bigger papers in Los Angeles, Ventura, and Orange counties who monitored the specialty newsletters and sometimes quoted their news. Like the time *Property Line* broke the plans for Glenwater Place. That story turned up in all the dailies the next morning, with attribution.

Already at work on their next issues, Andrea's four major clients counted on her to supervise the printing of their newsletters. Like most newsletter editors, the editors of these four ran their publications with skeletal staffs and would rather work on copy than on printing technicalities, desktop or otherwise. Andrea had proven she knew her way around an offset press, and the editors gave her full rein at press time. She had even gotten their permission to proof last-minute corrections on the bluelines.

Bluelines were the blue and gray paper proofs supplied by the printer for a final check before the presses ran. Corrections at that late stage were costly and rare, but they could and did occur. Normally in those cases, the printer prepared a second blueline that went back to the editor for another signoff. But Andrea saved her clients the trouble by carefully proofing and approving the revision herself. With her bosses' blessing, she personally ensured that eleventh-hour edits found their way seamlessly to the printed page.

Two of the four jobs that day showed edits on the bluelines. The front-page article in *Healthy Times* needed the word *billion* changed to *trillion*. An easy mistake to miss, Andrea thought as she studied the revised version pinned to the bulletin board. Who could envision annual U.S. health care costs swelling into the trillions?

The other, more extensive change appeared on the pages of *LA Business Report*. The editor had marked up a short profile of a company called Biovak, Inc., and its founder, Julian Shand. The article described Biovak as a rapidly growing biohazardous waste hauler that served hospitals, surgical centers, clinics, medical and dental offices, nursing homes, hospices, clinical and research laboratories, and veterinarians' offices at competitive rates.

The editor decided, somewhat tardily, to break up the long string of customer categories by listing them vertically next to bullets instead of in a sentence with commas. His notation on the blueline looked like this:

"Biovak's rapidly growing customer base includes:

• Hospitals

• Surgical centers

• Clinics

• Medical and dental offices

• Nursing homes

• Hospices

• Clinical and research laboratories

• Veterinarians' offices

The company's founder, Julian Shand, attributes Biovak's success to competitive pricing."

The editor was right, Andrea agreed. The alteration punched up the copy and made the whole article easier to read. But coming in as it did—the day before *LA Business Report* was due to print—the new configuration required some fancy footwork on her part.

Andrea fitted, specked, and faxed the revised copy to her typesetter, who prepared the new type and hand delivered a clean galley to Andrea's studio. Andrea quickly redid the paste-up, got in her car, and presented the press-ready revision to Pico Press. By early that morning the printer had produced a second blueline that Andrea proofed, found faultless, and approved for printing, right on schedule.

Every month the four newsletters posted above her desk went to press on the same day. It was a diabolically efficient schedule that sent Andrea, a typesetter, and the occasional freelance designer into paroxysms of activity as deadlines approached. Andrea and her contract employees raced from galleys, to mock-ups, to paste-ups to bluelines like batters rounding bases. At first, second, and third they stopped and waited impatiently for client approvals and the signal to advance. On days like today, when all four projects finally made it home, Andrea stood by her display and breathed a deep sigh of relief.

She looked at her watch. Six o'clock. Preoccupied by the demands of press day, she had hardly taken a moment to think about her husband, who by then had acquired a multimillion-dollar business and had no doubt worked up an appetite for the celebratory dinner she'd promised: grilled salmon, asparagus, strawberry shortcake, champagne—Mark's favorites, and fast. Did she have time for a shower? She did.

*   *   *   *

"Congratulations, darling." Andrea touched her glass to Mark's. "Hancock's is lucky to have you."

They sat in the dining room on opposite sides of a candle that sparkled in the crystal and deepened the tan on her husband's angular face. Mark was one of those men who grew better looking with age, like a tree. Now that Hancock's belonged to him he seemed to radiate energy. His new sense of purpose ran through him like sap.

Their workdays had been totally separate but similarly jam-packed, problematic, and satisfying. Morning, they agreed, dawned at least an eon ago. They related their respective stories over dinner, lingering, child-free, and dogless. It felt good, finally, to just sit.

Lindsey had gone to spend the night at a friend's house, a rare treat on a Thursday. Wiggles was in the doghouse, both literally and figuratively. From time to time, they could hear his leash rattle against the wooden dog abode outside. Andrea still found their pet's rampage hard to believe. She listened to the damp clang of metal on wood and wondered about it again. What had made him go nuts?

That afternoon the dog freed himself from the tether in the backyard, ran next door, dug up most of Mrs. Woodley's zucchini patch, and tore down two of the espaliered fuchsias she tended like a doting aunt. Their neighbor had just returned from a garden club beautification project when she witnessed the tail-end of the frenzy and chased Wiggles home. When Helen phoned, she was close to tears.

Mark pulled the Jeep into the driveway as Andrea took the call, still dripping from her bath. She realized guiltily that she had been too preoccupied to check on their pet when she got home from Pico Press, although by then the damage was done. She pulled on a long cotton skirt and sweater and went outside to break the news to Mark. They found their filthy dog curled in a corner by the back steps, too embarrassed to look either of them in the eye. Mark snapped a leash on the shame-faced animal and marched him to the scene of the crime.

"Bad dog," Mark intoned sternly, holding Wiggles's face near the ransacked soil in Mrs. Woodley's backyard. "Bad dog."

Both Mark and Andrea were graduates of puppy training school, though their pet had flunked. "Gentle but firm and consistent training over time is all he needs," the instructor told them. In the matter of Mrs. Woodley's garden, it wasn't difficult to be firm. The extent of the destruction shocked them both. Wiggles had always been an enthusiastic digger, but a digger with a short attention span. The scratches he made normally looked like the tracks of a big chicken. This was something else.

Andrea took one look at the mangled landscape and rushed to the door to apologize in person.

"Helen, this is terrible," she said when Mrs. Woodley answered the bell. "I can't tell you how sorry we are."

Mark joined the women at the step. Wiggles stood obediently to the rear, casting nervous glances at the three humans and the ruin around him. "I'm afraid we owe you more than an apology," Mark interjected, rubbing his head in disbelief. "Tomorrow I'll send over a crew from Hancock's to repair the damage. Andrea and I won't let this happen again."

Helen, who had regained some of her composure, softened with compassion for her neighbors. They were obviously mortified. She said she would appreciate the help from Hancock's, and told the Grants she didn't blame them. "You know I've always liked Wiggles," she said fretfully. "He's a dear dog, really. I can't imagine what made him do it."

By then the plundered garden had faded into darkness. Mark and Andrea took their leave with the dog in tow. The disgraced animal would spend the evening of their celebratory dinner securely attached to a lead next to his little shake house under the lemon trees.

Now, sitting over coffee and the remains of their dessert, they could hear Wiggles outside, rattling restlessly. The dog knew he was being punished and why. That was the point, of course. But it took a toll on the jailers too.

Andrea set her cup on the saucer and checked her watch. She looked at Mark. They were thinking the same thing.

"Let's go get him," they said almost in unison.

Wiggles, playing the humble ex-con, had the good sense to subdue his elation. He went straight for his cushion in the kitchen, trod a dent in the middle, curled up, and laid his head abruptly on his paws. He kept his eyes wide open, however, watching them.

Mark locked the back door and flicked off the yard light. Andrea closed the dishwasher and wiped a cloth across the counter.

"Semi-alone at last," he said, coming up behind her. Undaunted by the voyeur in the corner, he placed his hands on her waist and nuzzled her ear. Andrea dropped the cloth over a brass bar, turned toward him, and buried her face in his neck. He smelled like fresh air and split wood.

Pressing one hand into the small of her back, he slid the other down the curve that descended from her waist. She could feel his fingers gather her long cotton skirt like a slowly rising curtain. She tightened her arms around his neck and let the rest of her body relax. In her haste to dress when Helen phoned, she had skipped nonessential garments altogether, a fact Mark soon discovered with a little growl of pleasure.

Wiggles raised an ear in their direction. Mark lifted Andrea off the floor until her hips rested on the cool stone surface of the kitchen counter. He reached for the light switch and left their dog to listen curiously while they cooked up something new.

CHAPTER 12

▼

Mark woke before daybreak. The tangle of sheets that wound around his legs and across his sleeping wife bore little resemblance to the crisply outfitted bed he and Andrea had tumbled into the night before. Parts of her were visible in the semidarkness—a foot, an arm, and a smooth, round breast. Her glossy hair fanned out on the pillow like a sea palm caught in a current.

Resisting the temptation to rouse her, he eased off the bed, and went quietly to shower and shave. In the bathroom, he grinned at himself in the mirror and wondered if the buoyancy he felt had more to do with the night before or the day ahead. Both, he supposed. One thing became deliciously clear. What everyone said about the perfect job was true—you did wake up excited to go to work. The prospect of a day at the nursery felt utterly truant, vacation-like. He rubbed his chin. Maybe he would grow a beard.

Twenty minutes later, clean and shaven, he stood in his boxer shorts and considered the contents of his closet. Suits. Five feet of them lined up on wooden hangers like a queue of bankers who marched into a trash compactor. His wardrobe had not kept pace with his life. When would he wear a suit again? With the deliberation of a monk departing a monastery, he selected khaki slacks, a knit shirt, and a pair of rubber-soled deck shoes. Watch, wallet, pocketknife—he was ready.

With a parting glance at the vision in his bed, he tiptoed out the door and down the stairs. Wiggles lay conked out in the kitchen, exhausted by the crime and punishment of the previous day. Mark gathered up the clothing strewn across the floor and piled it on a chair. Wiggles raised one eyelid, then blinked it shut. Mark thought of Mrs. Woodley's wrecked garden and vowed to have repairs underway by noon.

He downed a glass of orange juice, found his keys, and headed for the garage. A dinged-up white van idled by the curb in front of the house, its rear door wide open. Next to the van, Mark saw a man and woman leaning over the open garbage cans grouped on the parkway, ready for collection. Scavengers? He supposed they were harmless, maybe even beneficial, reducing the volume of trash the way they did. By the time he got in the Jeep and backed down the driveway, the pair had vanished and the trash cans appeared as full as ever.

Twelve minutes later, Hancock's rookie owner unlocked the nursery gate with the round brass key on his key ring, feeling an unexpected chill of excitement. The simple act of opening his property for business seemed more momentous than the sober legal work that made his ownership official. Mark thought of Fred and Hancock Dunn standing on that very spot at daybreak. What did they think about on those early mornings?

He swung open the gates and moved a soaker hose off the path to the office. It would be easy to lose sight of the big picture, the prosperous sweep of foliage and future income that was his and his alone. Running a business like Hancock's meant keeping track of hundreds of details every day—clients to call, workers to assign, plants and materials to order and receive. No doubt the Dunn's kept the minutiae well on track.

But in Mark's opinion, the key to their success had been their belief in the importance of every customer who walked through the gate. A schoolgirl buying violets for her teacher felt as welcome and well-tended here as the master planner of a mega-mall. Actually, the schoolgirl probably became the master planner of the mega-mall. People on the West Side had long, fond memories of Hancock's Landscape Services, and Mark intended to keep it that way.

Rudy's Toyota was swinging into the lot when Mark unlocked the office door and turned on the lights. Rudy arrived early, Mark noticed. Good. The foreman had a busy day ahead.

Mark waylaid Rudy on the way to the greenhouse and quickly filled him in on Wiggles's misdeeds and the situation at Mrs. Woodley's. Then he noticed the man's pallor. Rudy looked like a vampire's latest meal. "Are you all right?" he asked the gray-faced foreman.

Rudy inhaled sharply. "I'm okay. Thursday night poker, you know."

Mark didn't know. He hoped a late night was all it was. He could hardly spare Rudy today. Mark informed the foreman that he planned to brief Carlos on his temporary assignment as Rudy's assistant, and send him with a truckload of camellias to Glenwater Place. Rudy could then pull a couple of workers off the project and deposit them at Mrs. Woodley's with a pair of espaliered fuchsias, five bags of mulch, two flats of zucchini seedlings, and instructions to cultivate, weed, lightly prune, and water Mrs. Woodley's entire garden. While they salvaged Helen's turf, Rudy could begin assembling his new crew, the olive trees, and the equipment needed to begin the job in Bel Air.

Rudy was well compensated for the demands of his job, and he looked it. His new, fully loaded Land Cruiser was the flashiest vehicle anybody at Hancock's drove, including Mark. The foreman liked flash. He wore more than one twinkling chain under his soft plaid shirt, and had recently added a diamond ring to the bulk beneath his deerskin work gloves. Mark noticed the color had returned to Rudy's face by the time he completed his business at the nursery and rushed off to Glenwater Place.

In the meantime, Carlos had arrived and was supervising the helpers in the morning chores. Maggie teetered in on toeless yellow heels that appeared to go with the stripe in her tank top and the plastic butterfly buried in her hair. The honeymoon hadn't ended yet.

"Good morning, Maggie," Mark greeted her cheerily.

"Morning, Mr. Grant." She offered him a blueberry muffin from the pink cardboard box she balanced on top of her handbag. "I usually bring these on Saturdays, but since this is your first morning...." Her voice trailed off uncertainly. "I'll have the coffee ready in a minute."

"Sorry," Mark apologized. "I got here first. I should have made the coffee." From her startled expression, he guessed Fred Dunn never undertook that chore. "Thanks for the muffins." He bit into one—fragrant, fresh, and loaded with berries. He could get used to this.

"Maggie, as soon as possible, I want you to begin a special project." He chewed and watched her face light up with interest. It occurred to him, not for the first time, that she had outgrown her job.

"I need an up-to-date list of Hancock's landscape clients for the past three years. Start with this year and work back. Name, address, phone number, a brief description of the work we did, what we charged, and anything else of importance you think I should know. I plan to contact all of those customers personally."

Maggie nodded. "Good idea. You want to reassure the customers, try to keep their business now that Fred is gone."

"Exactly right. I want the retail list updated too."

"I'll get started on it this morning." Her face shone as bright as the plastic insect above her ear.

Maggie reminded Mark of administrative assistants he had known at the bank, ace organizers who needed things to organize the way doctors needed patients. To them a mess was like a case of measles—something to cure. When Hancock's finally got a computer, there would be no stopping her.

He finished his muffin and stepped outside. Cool morning air hung damply over the nursery. At that early hour, only two customers occupied the lot, professional gardeners who came regularly, worked from purchase lists, and needed little help. Mark and Carlos exchanged a few words with them and set off on the tour they had postponed the previous day.

They started with the sun-loving plants arranged on risers near the front gate: geraniums, delphiniums, marguerites, a showy stand of purple hibiscus, salvia called "sizzler red." Carlos possessed intimate knowledge of every widget on the shelf. His understanding of Hancock's inventory came as no surprise. What impressed Mark was Carlos's range beyond the specimens on the lot. The horticulture whiz kid knew his stigmas from his stolons, his rhizomes from his roots. Annuals, biennials, perennials, ephemerals, hydrophytes, cosmopolites—Carlos, it seemed, could discuss them all, enthusiastically, in two languages.

They worked their way to the plants growing in filtered shade. Gardenia. Hydrangea. Periwinkle. Orchids in pale, exotic colors. The fuchsia aisle that reminded Mark of the mess at Mrs. Woodley's. He checked his watch. It was still early.

Carlos led Mark knowledgeably through the cactus display, the grocery-like stands of vegetable and herb sprouts, the section of pots, potting soil, and soil amendments. Mark halted near several pyramids of bagged earth.

"Carlos, do you know as much about soil amendments as you do about plants?"

Carlos grinned. "At school we also study dirt."

"Then tell me, are the commercial products pure? You know, carefully controlled. Or do they sometimes contain foreign material such as pieces of plastic or other debris?" Mark was still bothered by the bits of junk he found in the prepared soil at Glenwater Place.

Carlos looked back and forth between his boss and the bags as though he suspected a trick question. "I've never found foreigners in these," he ventured. "No, I'd be surprised to come across a piece of plastic." He pointed to a stack of plump sacks. "These potting mixes are steam sterilized—as consistent as cake mix. The soil amendments over here may be vegetable, animal, or mineral. See, they're all labeled. Some contain plant material like ground bark, peat moss, rice hulls, or wood shavings. The animal products include bone meal, right here, and cow manure, over there."

The pristine, professionally designed packages of cow dung always struck Mark as slightly ludicrous. But they sold by the truckload, especially around the end of February when gardeners spread the fertile mixture lavishly across tired landscapes. Near-black lawns and a familiar earthy scent were reliable harbingers of spring in Los Angeles.

Carlos continued. "Some of the inorganic amendments—the chunky materials that lighten the soil and hold water—look a little like Styrofoam or plastic. You know: perlite, pumice, vermiculite? They could fool someone."

Mark frowned. He was familiar with the mineral amendments. None resembled the refuse he found at Glenwater Place. Debris like that simply should not turn up in professionally cultivated planting beds, certainly not in soil prepared by Hancock's. Maybe the crews were getting careless.

He followed Carlos through the enclosed displays of houseplants and gardening equipment and back outside to the rear of the lot, where rows of extra inventory led to the greenhouse, the potting shed, and a paved loading area. As they neared the end of their walk, Mark raised the matter of Carlos assisting Rudy at Glenwater Place, an idea that clearly pleased Fred's protégé. So did Mark's suggestion that Carlos apply for his landscaper's license without delay. Like Maggie, Carlos appeared ready for new and greener acreage. Mark left the young man whistling happily while he loaded camellias into Hancock's flatbed truck. A few minutes later, the new assistant foreman gave two toots of the horn and drove away.

Mark spent the rest of the day assisting customers. Several who came merely to greet Hancock's new owner nonetheless departed with wagonloads of blooms. Inveterate gardeners like Mark himself had difficulty walking through a nursery without bundling an orphan home. There was the normal Friday surge of garden purchases for weekend projects, and a crew of event coordinators who bought Hancock's entire inventory of potted pink petunias for the tables at a sold-out charity ball. By closing time, Hancock's had grossed more than seven thousand dollars.

Mark was adding up the day's receipts when the phone in the office rang. Maggie stopped typing to pick it up. "Well hello there," he heard her say. "We're fine. Yes, he's right here." She eyed him and pressed a button. "It's San Francisco. Natalie Dunn."

Trying not to look too eager, Mark punched two more numbers into his HP12C, the trusty old calculator that had seen him through so many deals at the bank. He lifted the receiver.

"Natalie? This is a surprise."

"Hello, Mark," came the resonant voice. "I hope I'm not disturbing you."

"Not at all. In fact, we're just winding down from a very busy day."

"Good. That's one reason I called, to see how your first full day went. Everything as you expected?"

"Better. I appreciate the call." He leaned back in his chair and pictured her long white neck.

"I also have news. I'm going to be down there again next month to deliver a talk at my alma mater—the annual Silas K. Udahl Lecture. Maybe you've heard of it. It honors the memory of a former professor. Local luminaries are invited. There's a public reception."

"Congratulations," Mark said, impressed. He knew enough about academia to know the lecturer was honored too.

"Thanks. I just found out today. They want me to base the talk on an article I wrote last year about economic re-development via small business growth. I'll be in Los Angeles ahead of time to see Mother and update the research. Since you've had lending experience in the middle market, I'd appreciate your insights."

"Of course. I'd be happy to incite you."

She gave a throaty chuckle and promised to fax the article to him. A moment later Mark replaced the receiver, palpitating like a puppy.

He peered across the desk at Maggie and willed his pulse to slow. The bookkeeper concentrated on her typewriter, her two yellow shoes planted solidly on the floor. The sight of her, so reassuringly down to earth, calmed him.

What was it about Natalie Dunn that sent him into a spin? He had worked with and admired attractive women by the dozens. American Coastal was loaded with them. But he had never lost his equilibrium, or acted like an imbecile on some irresistible impulse. His attraction to Natalie felt different. Dangerous. And Mark suspected it wasn't entirely about her.

The butterfly in Maggie's hair darted and hovered, humming-bird-like, with the motion of her head. Mark watched it, wondering if forty-year-old men who lose their jobs come unglued, scoot off the beaten path like travelers who leave home without road maps. Did he miss an important outplacement lesson? The Webb, Watson, Latour and Meeks Tutorial on Post-Termination Testosterone Disorder? Maybe he should simply enjoy the malady while it lasted.

He totaled the day's receipts, cleared his desk, and advised Maggie not to work too late. He felt as juiced and risky as a man gripping a rip cord. He needed air.

On the way home, Mark stopped at the bank to deposit the day's receipts, then drove with the windows down and oldies blasting on the radio—The Doobie Brothers. Lyrics to old songs returned effortlessly from some deep wrinkle in his middle-aged brain. He steered and sang and bobbed his wind-blown head, nearly giddy with the novelty of his new existence. During the long freeway commutes of his former life he had listened, commando-like, in sealed-up isolation to the all-important traffic report.

Twelve minutes flat to Palm Street. Mark sailed past Mrs. Woodley's and turned into his own driveway, sobering at the thought of his neighbor's ransacked property. Andrea's car was gone. Mark decided to fetch Wiggles and go directly next door to inspect the repair job Hancock's had done at Helen's.

He leapt from the Jeep, set the security system, and pocketed the keys. Wiggles normally responded to the bleep of the car alarm with an excited squeal and a rush toward the driveway. Today Mark heard nothing.

"Wiggles. Here Wiggles." He walked toward the yard and spotted a length of chain curled in the grass. One end of the tether wound around the doghouse and out of sight.

"Wiggles?"

No response. Mark drew near the idle chain and followed its slack path to the shaded area behind the doghouse. It took him a moment to focus on the body stretched awkwardly in the shadow. Wiggles was dead.

CHAPTER 13

▼

Carlos stood, perplexed, with his hands on his hips. He and the crew Rudy assigned to Glenwater Place had put in a long afternoon planting nearly half the bushes specified in the plans for Camellia Court. The crew worked together efficiently, never questioning Carlos's authority in the absence of their usual foreman. Rudy had trained them well. So well that Carlos suspected their exemplary performance sprang from an earlier command of their boss's rather than anything he himself told them. Rudy's instructions apparently were to follow directions and work hard.

The sun hung low in the sky when Carlos dismissed the workers and returned to the deserted courtyard. He wanted a closer look at the contents of the fifteen-gallon drum sitting on the ground in front of him. He had never seen such unusual debris. Yet that day he personally unearthed enough of it to fill a large container.

He reached into the drum and rummaged through the odd assortment of items, brushing away soil that clung like lint. There were strange, rubber-like coils and rings. Bright blue shards. Strips of blotchy fabric. An amber bottle and a pea green saucer. Unusual cords, tubes, cylinders, bags. He fingered a clear container with sloping shoulders that looked like a water cooler for a dollhouse. *Que Diablo?* What were they? And what were they doing buried deep in the borders of Camellia Court?

Even more disturbing to Carlos were the reactions of the crew, when the four men bothered to show any interest at all. The most he got out of them was a grunt or a shrug, until one of the men said, "You never know what will turn up when you start digging. Once I found a fifty-dollar bill." At that the rest of the crew inexplicably burst into laughter.

Shadows were lengthening when a decrepit white van rolled past the orange cones that partially barricaded the entrance to Camellia Court. Carlos raised his eyes from the grubby loot, startled. The van sped noisily in his direction and clamored to a halt near the curb. A barrel-chested man wearing a dark jacket and reflector glasses rose from the driver's seat and walked toward him. Carlos swallowed. The man stopped a few feet away and took a long look at the jumble inside the fifteen-gallon drum. In a voice oiled with venom he said, "Well, *muchacho*. What have we here?" He tugged a pair of black leather gloves over ten porky fingers. Carlos edged backward.

Suddenly the intruder snatched Carlos by the collar and yanked his face within inches of his own. "I know you speak English, you little Mexican runt. So listen to me and pay close attention." He shook Carlos like a sack of beans. Carlos felt his teeth clack.

"Have you heard of the Federal Department of Waste Oversight? No, of course you haven't. Well I'm here to tell you the U.S. Government finds you in violation of Section 25678 of the Landfill Displacement Code. Do you know what that means? It means fines, Carlos, *muchos pesos*. It means jail. It means no more green cards for you and your wetback relatives."

Fear of the man's overpowering physical presence prevented Carlos from fully digesting the threats. The words "green card," however, hit him like a slap to the face. His eyes shone with fright. The man relaxed his grip.

"Since this is your first violation, Mr. Hernandez, I'm inclined to be lenient. But only if you say nothing about this, uh, landfill you disturbed. Do you understand?"

Carlos stared at him. How did he know his name?

"Do you understand?" The man shook Carlos again, hard. Carlos nodded.

"Fine. I could get in a lot of trouble for letting you off. So keep your mouth shut. And I'd advise you not to violate the code again."

Carlos could feel damp breath on his face.

"Go ahead and plant your little pansies." Hot spit hit Carlos's cheek. "But be a good citizen, Mr. Hernandez—oh, excuse me, a good resident alien—and make sure whatever you find stays buried nice and neat, way down deep."

He released Carlos with a shove that sent him staggering backward until his knees buckled and he fell hard on the dirt. The man hefted the drum from the ground and carried it and its contents to the back of the van. Carlos watched him open the back door and maneuver the pot into a large black plastic bag that he twisted into a fat knot. He slammed the door. Casting a final malignant look at Carlos, who hadn't moved from his spot on the ground, the man said, "Remember what I told you. Keep your yapper shut, or you and your family will be sorry."

The man got into the van and cranked the engine. A blast of dark exhaust fouled the evening air as the vehicle lurched forward and rattled loudly into the twilight. Camellia Court seemed deathly still.

Carlos sat for a moment, breathing hard, then heaved himself to his feet. He brushed dirt from his pants and climbed into Hancock's truck. His knees felt weak.

He drove to the nursery and parked in the loading area at the back of the lot. A bright light shone from the office, otherwise the property was dim. *Bueno.* He needed some time alone to think.

Using the key Fred Dunn had entrusted to him, Carlos quietly unlocked the door to the potting shed and slipped inside. The rich, damp odor of planting mix surrounded him like soothing vapor. He spent countless contented hours in that simple workroom while Fred Dunn had tended his seedlings and talked engagingly on many topics. Carlos owed much of what he knew about plants and landscaping to those instructive afternoons.

He found the ancient kerosene lamp stored by the door, and struck a match. The flame spread a comforting glow on the long wooden table piled high with clay pots, bagged soil, and an assortment of trowels, gloves, and shears. A pair of Fred's old denim overalls still hung from a peg on the wall. Carlos ran his hand along a softly frayed seam, wishing he could rub its owner's spirit from the thread. He never missed his father-like mentor more.

Bent with fatigue, Carlos picked up the lantern and walked dejectedly past the workbench. Fred not only hired, trained, and educated him but he also filled out endless forms, paid multiple fees, and dealt with legions of government bureaucrats who stood between Carlos and the coveted green card that pronounced him lawful, permanent, and employable. The process took nearly two years. The day Carlos received his U.S. Alien Residency Card, which wasn't even green, Fred gave him a surprise party in that very room.

Carlos's entire family came. His mother, father, seven brothers and sisters, two sisters-in-law, and one baby who was a bona fide U.S.-born American citizen. Carlos was the first of them to earn the laminated, rose-colored "green" card, an achievement matched later by two brothers, who had the good fortune to work for employers who recognized their potential, needed their skills, and were willing to act as their sponsors.

Carlos sat heavily on a large overturned garden pot Fred had used for a stool. He placed the lantern on the floor in front of him, and considered what had happened in Camellia Court.

Just remembering those fat lips flapping threats near his face made Carlos cringe. The bully's crudity did not mean he lied about who he was or his power to interfere with Carlos's credentials. As much as Carlos loved the United States, he was a realist when it came to the use and misuse of power. He knew, for example, that certain building codes were enforced as haphazardly as fruit falls from trees. Although most of the inspectors appeared to be decent, a bad apple never surprised him.

Carlos stared into the wavering flame. The idea of leaving debris buried in the planting beds, however, seemed ludicrous—contrary to everything Fred had taught him. Landfill? That was laughable. The stuff was garbage. Mr. Grant would throw a fit. But could Carlos risk the consequences of telling his new boss what he found?

He leaned dejectedly toward the lamp. From the darkness behind his foot a glint of light caught his eye. Then he saw it again, coming from where? Curious, he crouched down to investigate. A chip the size of a hoe head had broken off the rim of the pot that rested upside-down on the floor. Through the jagged opening he could see a flat, shiny surface that reflected the blaze from the lamp.

Wondering what Fred stored beneath his makeshift stool, Carlos tipped the weighty planter to one side and watched a spider scramble for cover. He moved the lantern closer and squinted in the darkness. Beneath Fred's stool rested an old steel box that shone like treasure in the warm light. Carlos slid the box from its dark hiding place and lowered the pot to the floor. A fine film of dust coated the top of the box. Carlos brushed some of the dirt away and noticed the lid was secured by a latch with a keyhole. Before he could examine the lock further, footsteps sounded on the gravel path outside. The door to the potting shed swung open and someone switched on the overhead light.

"Carlos? Is that you?"

Carlos blinked in the glare and stood. "Oh, hi Maggie."

The bookkeeper clicked toward him on precarious yellow heels. "I thought you must be in here when I saw the truck." She regarded the kerosene lamp. "Saving on the electric bill?"

Carlos shoved his hands into his pockets. He liked Maggie. But he wasn't ready to confide in her yet.

Her eyes fell on the metal case. "Where did you find this?" She dropped to her knees and fingered the latch. Locked.

"Carlos!" she exclaimed. "This must be the file that goes with the extra key on Fred's key ring. Mr. Grant will be so glad you found it."

CHAPTER 14

▼

Lindsey presided over the funeral, a somber affair that combined religion, sentimentality, and her favorite dog food commercial. "You were a lucky, lucky dog, Wiggles," she intoned, standing ramrod straight next to the doghouse that sheltered the lifeless, plaid-wrapped bundle.

She had never been to a funeral, but she had been a flower girl in her Aunt Ellen's wedding in Wisconsin. Andrea's younger sister was a leading-edge traditionalist who took symbolism seriously. Ellen had worn not only their mother's drop-waist satin wedding gown but also their Grandmother Blair's filigree locket, their Great Aunt Ellie's mother-of-pearl combs, and the lacy blue garter Andrea wore when she was a bride. Under her bouquet Ellen had carried an Irish linen handkerchief that belonged to their father.

Lindsey, the flower girl, had been done up in a pleated dress made from the same pink linen that skirted the twelve round tables at the outdoor reception. The petals she scattered in Ellen's path had been harvested that morning by four bridesmaids from the bougainvilleas that grew around the sorority house where they all had met. Ellen had even saved three empty Coors cans from the night Eddie proposed, and left them discreetly available to any groomsman who planned to rig up their getaway car.

Taking cues from her aunt's ceremonious march down the aisle, Lindsey planned Wiggles's Saturday morning memorial service in detail. Andrea and Mark watched their daughter's preparations with sorrow and relief.

The night before they nearly phoned for help when Lindsey's convulsive sobbing seemed likely to suck the air right out of her. She and Andrea got home just a minute or two after Mark discovered Wiggles's lifeless body lying in the grass. He tried to keep Lindsey away, but she was too smart and too quick. Wiggles's best friend sniffed trouble in the first molecules of air that rushed forth when she flung open the door of the Volvo. Lindsey leapt from the car and scooted around her father, who reached out to grab her too late. She had already seen the motionless tether, and she had seen the look on her father's face. When she broke free of his arms, tears were already forming in her eyes.

It was almost dark when Andrea lifted her grieving daughter from Wiggles's side and held her in her arms. Mark wrapped the small corpse in the sturdy plaid cushion cover he unzipped from the dog bed in the kitchen, and laid the bundle inside the doghouse. He had called Dr. Broder, the veterinarian, who said Mark could bring the body to her for cremation in the morning. In a voice shaking with emotion, Mark requested an autopsy.

Sometime during that fitful night Lindsey's distress turned to resolve, and she started to plan a ceremony in honor of her pet. When Andrea and Mark woke up in the morning, they found Lindsey already dressed in her favorite plaid shorts, organizing furniture on the lawn. Mark watched her cover a table with a white cloth, candles, and a vase of blooming jasmine. During breakfast she phoned her grandmother and Mrs. Woodley, who arrived soon thereafter and sat with Andrea and Mark under the lemon trees.

While a cassette player produced tunes from *Beauty and the Beast*, Lindsey made a solemn entrance from the rear carrying a shoe box in front of her like an offering. She placed the box carefully on the table, took from her pocket a piece of paper folded into a tiny square, and invited everyone to join her in a prayer. She unfolded the paper and read: "Now lay Wiggles down to sleep. We pray the Lord his soul to keep." With the deliberate, unhurried movements of a priest at the altar, she refolded the paper, replaced it in her pocket, and ceremoniously lifted the lid from the shoe box on the table.

"You were a lucky, lucky dog, Wiggles."

From the box she lifted a dingy yellow tennis ball. "Here's your ball." She placed the old Penn 3 reverently on the grass in front of the doghouse.

"Here's your bone from Mrs. Woodley's." *A bone?* Mark looked at Helen. She shook her head, surprised. Lindsey sat the bone on the ground next to the ball.

"Here are your other bones." The lineup of skeletal artifacts began to look like a display from the La Brea Tar Pits.

"Here's the new brush Grandma gave you. Here's your rubber glove. Here's the picture of all of us from last year's Christmas card."

Rubber glove? Mark met Andrea's quizzical glance.

"Yes, dear. A picture is worth a thousand words," Ginny sighed, blotting her eye with a handkerchief. "Wiggles was a lucky dog."

Mark looked at his mother sympathetically. Ginny received a load of bad news that week. His new business, now this.

"He certainly was," Mrs. Woodley agreed, sounding hopeful that the sad proceedings might be coming to an end.

Andrea dried her eyes, got up, and poured glasses of fresh lemonade. The funeral was more or less over. Helen approached Mark, who stood by the doghouse holding a bone gingerly between two fingers.

"Thank you for repairing my garden so beautifully," she said. "I'm very sorry about Wiggles. You don't think his death had anything to do with the trouble at my house, do you?"

Mark barely heard her. He looked up. "Did you give these bones to Wiggles?"

"No, of course not," Helen replied. "You know I wouldn't without asking you."

Frowning, Mark returned the bones to the shoe box. Lindsey watched tearfully while he knelt and lifted the rigid animal out of the doghouse. Together they carried the plaid-wrapped corpse and the box of bones to the Jeep.

*   *   *   *

It was mid-morning by the time Mark arrived at Hancock's to find the nursery doing a brisk Saturday business. Carlos was working at Glenwater Place, and the shorthanded sales staff looked glad to see their boss. Maggie and her exploding hair stood behind the counter at the open window ringing up sales as fast as a clerk in a grocery store.

Mark joined the fray. In short order, he sold twenty-one flats of summer annuals, a pair of yellow oleanders, eight dwarf poincianas, and a wagonload of river pebble landscape rock. One of his customers was Sam Folee of Folee's Nursery, a friendly enough chap with a cherubic face and a halo of yellow curls, who showed up to shake Mark's hand—and get a good look at the competition. Sam even bought a pair of garden clogs, just to be polite.

It felt good to be busy, although the pain of Wiggles's death lingered close to the surface. Now and then Mark felt it, like a cramp. Dr. Broder, the veterinarian, said she would phone as soon as she completed the pathology report. In the meantime, Mark found himself avoiding Hancock's redolent jasmine patch and the fuchsia aisle that nagged him uncomfortably.

"What a day!" Maggie dropped into the chair behind her desk. "I haven't been off my feet since seven this morning."

Mark poured each of them a glass of water, and sat down to work on the day's receipts. The bookkeeper leaned back and took a long drink. Her big hair had deflated a little, and there was a gray smudge on the ample front of her blouse. The honeymoon was settling into a comfortable marriage.

Mark unlocked the drawer that held his calculator. Maggie suddenly sat upright. "I almost forgot." A splash of water landed on her bosom. "You know that key we couldn't identify? The one on Fred's key ring?" Mark nodded.

"I think Carlos found the file it fits. In the potting shed. Locked."

Intrigued, Mark laid the calculator on the desk. "Let's go look."

They hurried through the nursery where the retail crew was ending the day by stacking empty pallets and raking the gravel pathways. Mark opened the door to the old wooden shed and turned on the light. The metal box sat at the back, next to the overturned pot under which Carlos had discovered it. Mark crouched down and went through his keys. The one labeled "Steel Case" slid easily into the lock.

"I knew it," Maggie said with satisfaction. "Fred wouldn't hang onto a useless key."

Mark snapped open the latch and slowly raised the lid. "What the—" Maggie's face wrinkled with disgust.

Mark lifted the box off the floor and placed it on the work bench where they could get a better look. Maggie stood next to him pinching her nose. "Something's rotten in there."

The contents of the box smelled bad, Mark agreed. He tried not to breathe. Amazingly, Fred's locked file appeared to contain rubbish. Crumpled newspapers. Ziploc bags. A length of dirt-streaked plastic tube. Mark gingerly lifted the tube between two fingers. It looked familiar. He placed the filthy strip of plastic on the table, puzzled.

"May I?" Maggie asked, donning a pair of garden gloves that were lying on the table. Mark nodded. She gripped one of the balled-up newspapers. "Something's in this," she said nervously. She sat the parcel on the table and slowly undid the paper. Inside was a small grubby jar topped with a metal stopper that had a hole in the middle. A metal band circled the bottom. Between the two metal parts was a label someone had already rubbed clean.

"Five percent dextrose," Maggie read. "Sterile. Single dose container. Mark, I think this is an IV bottle. Dextrose is an intravenous solution."

Mark decided gloves were a good idea. He found a pair and slipped them on. Maggie was already opening another crumpled newspaper. Four plastic syringes and three amber ampoules the size of AA batteries tumbled onto the table. Mark looked at them, speechless. Was Fred some kind of addict? He picked up one of the empty ampoules and read the printing on the side. "TRIDONEX. Nitroglycerin. Five milligrams-slash-milliliters." Wasn't that for heart attacks?

Maggie smoothed the newspaper on the table: *The Los Angeles Times.* "Mark, look at the date." She stared at the paper and whispered. "Two days before Fred died."

Mark fastened his eyes on the newsprint and a chill licked his skin. Two days before Fred died. Some related piece of information skirted his consciousness, but the thought eluded him. With growing apprehension, he turned back to the foul cache.

A smeared Ziploc bag sat on a piece of bent rubber that sprang open when Mark uncovered it. He jumped. Only a glove. He gaped at the dirty white rubber. The glove in the box looked exactly like the one Lindsey produced that morning at Wiggles's funeral.

A putrid odor rose like a swarm of gnats. Maggie pressed an arm over her nose and mouth. The Ziploc bag was tightly sealed, but seemed to reek nonetheless. Its contents were difficult to make out. The bag appeared to contain damp potting mix, a few grains of Sponge Rok, and something else. Bones? Mark held the bag up to the bright overhead light and squinted in disbelief. Through the plastic he saw the bony silhouette of a small, dirt-encrusted hand.

"There's something stuck to the back," Maggie said in a barely audible voice. Stunned, Mark turned the bag around. Taped on the outside was one of Hancock's distinctive yellow plant identification markers. In bold green letters the nameplate read, "Lot 449. Supermagic F1 Hybrid Grandiflora Pink Petunia."

CHAPTER 15

▼

"Are you busy?"

"That's a stupid question to ask LA's most desirable bachelor on a Saturday night," Rick replied. "I am at this moment placing a pizza in the oven. Wolfgang Puck."

"Take it out. And put on your dancing shoes. Cole Haan. We're going to a black-tie ball. I'll explain when I get there." Mark hung up.

When the two formally attired gate-crashers turned into the circular drive of the Beverly Hilton Hotel, Mark still hadn't told Rick what disease this sold-out charity event was all about. He had given an earful to his hastily dressed companion whose satin bow tie looked like the big hand and the little hand on a clock that read ten-thirty.

While the two of them careened up Wilshire Boulevard in Mark's Cherokee, Mark informed Rick about the locked file Fred Dunn had hidden shortly before his death, and the grisly contents of the Ziploc bag. The secret stash in Hancock's potting shed raised a dozen urgent questions, but Mark's immediate concern was the nineteen dozen potted petunias that adorned the dinner tables at tonight's high-profile gala in the Grand Ballroom of the Beverly Hilton Hotel. Mark himself sold the plants to the event coordinators who shopped at Hancock's on Friday afternoon. And all of the petunias came from Lot 449, the same batch of plants Fred apparently associated with the alarming stash locked in the metal box.

Was it possible that Fred found those bottles and bones buried in Hancock's own soil? What else could Mark conclude? He wasn't going to take a chance that a similar surprise awaited some mover or shaker who left this party with a Supermagic Grandiflora.

"Jeez," Rick said, once the unsavory implications of Mark's news had sunk in. "I almost forgot. Congratulations on your new business."

Mark was not amused. Clutched against the steering wheel in his right hand was a purchase slip he had retrieved from Hancock's files. Stapled to the paper was the not-for-profit statement that entitled the planners of that night's event to the discount Hancock's offered on supplies for charity fund-raisers. Mark glanced from the polished Jaguar in front of him to the creased papers in his hand.

"My god—a thousand dollars a plate." He couldn't afford to buy tickets to the event even if tickets were available. "Chairperson: Dottie DeLuca."

"The chairperson is the key," Rick agreed. "We've got to find her, charm her, and get her to make sure nobody leaves this party with a centerpiece."

Mark nodded, hoping Dottie DeLuca was susceptible to charm and, more importantly, that she could control several hundred strong-willed, rich people.

The Jeep reached the front of the line where valets rushed to open both front doors. Mark handed over his keys and led Rick through the shiny glass portals of the hotel. As they walked across the lobby several women stared in their direction. Handsome, possibly unattached men attracted attention at these events.

The party was in full swing. Only one elegantly clad committee member remained at the long, damask covered check-in table by the entrance to the ballroom. She had just jumped up to hug the similarly gowned anchorwoman from the six o'clock news. Mark knew the scene. He and Rick hadn't crashed a party in years, but the techniques were timeless.

Rick straightened his bow tie and glanced through the door to the noisy throng inside. Mark waited nervously, sucking Tic Tacs and checking his watch as if they expected to meet someone. He knew they had to act fast. The anchorwoman made her entrance to the party, leaving the committee member at the table to direct her smile at them.

Rick touched Mark's arm. "There's our ticket." He nodded in the direction of a tall, silver-haired gentleman who was talking to a group of people just inside the door. "Stay with me."

The greeter by the table called politely in their direction. At the same instant Rick exclaimed, "Gordon!" and bounded past her into the ballroom. "Great to see you," he said in a hearty voice, extending a hand to the distinguished personage. Mark stuck to his socially connected friend like an appendage, keeping watch on the gowned gatekeeper.

"Gordon, I'd like you to meet Mark Grant." Rick pulled Mark toward the safety of the crowd. "Mark, meet the new United Way chairman. Gordon and I worked together on last year's campaign."

The circle of people began to close around them, and another late arrival took the ticket taker's attention. They had made it.

Outside a nursery, Mark had never seen so many petunias in one place. Four fat pots of them and a thick tangle of gilded English ivy decked every table in the vast ballroom. He knew from experience on the charity circuit that some guests would claim a pot or two even before dinner was over. The appropriation of centerpieces hardly raised an eyebrow anymore. People walked away with armloads.

A waiter came by with glasses of champagne on a tray. Mark took two and handed one to Rick. "We're going to need this," he muttered.

Dottie DeLuca wasn't difficult to spot. Like any seasoned hostess, the chairwoman moved attentively among the party-goers, generating a flurry of excitement wherever she went. "Dottie!" her friends exclaimed. The bejeweled organizer had a little cap of red hair, wide-open eyes, and the flawless complexion of a woman who once saw too many wrinkles in the mirror. Mark took a long drink from his glass.

He eyed the petunias anxiously. People had begun to move toward the tables for dinner. The hand-lettered menu at the place closest to him proclaimed five elaborate courses, starting with a "crisp langoustine purse accompanied by mango-sunchoke chutney." Mark's stomach rumbled. A few couples remained on the dance floor while the orchestra belted out a medley of fox-trots. That was lucky. Among the dancers he and Rick would be less conspicuous during dinner.

"Mark Grant?" Startled, Mark jumped. A former colleague from American Coastal smiled toothily at him. Mark hadn't heard from Mel Beckman since the day he got his termination notice. The banker pumped Mark's hand.

"Hey, I hear you bought Hancock's. Congratulations. Doing any hiring? Heh, heh. You may be getting resumes from the rest of us any day now." Little beads of sweat dotted the vice president's forehead. He said he was co-hosting a table of American Coastal customers, among them the hot new entrepreneur, Julian Shand.

Mark had heard of Shand. The guy ran one of the fastest growing small companies in Los Angeles. Mark stared at the cigar-smoking chairman of Biovak, Inc., who sat with his blond date a few tables away. It took a lot of nerve to smoke at a disease ball, Mark thought with disgust, although he still didn't know what disease these well-heeled contributors were hoping to conquer.

Dottie DeLuca and her entourage were moving their way. Mel excused himself and went back to his seat. Mark sat his empty champagne glass on a table. "Here goes," he whispered to Rick. "This better be good."

When Dottie swiveled her sleek round head in his direction, Mark extended his hand, introduced himself, and congratulated the chairwoman on the brilliance of her planning. "Our companies could use a few executives with Dottie's organizational abilities. Don't you agree, Rick?"

"Without question," Rick smiled and shook the woman's hand. Dottie's pert nose twitched, smelling corporate contributions for whatever charity she worked.

"How nice of you to say so, uh, Mark? And what companies are those?"

"Why don't I tell you about it on the dance floor," Rick interjected smoothly. Getting Dottie to dance with Rick "Astaire" Edwards was key to their plan. "Would you do me the honor?"

Dottie demurred a moment, appraising the schmooze quotient in their immediate vicinity and, finding no bigger fish swimming by, said, "Yes, I would love a dance. I hope I'll see you later, Mark."

Mark smiled and nodded. *You will.*

After two stylish fox-trots and a high-energy jitterbug that attracted a small audience, Dottie and Rick looked like fast friends. They stood for a moment, deep in conversation. When Rick ushered the radiant fundraiser off the dance floor, she headed directly for Mark.

"Don't you worry another minute about those pots," she said, patting his hand. "I know just what to do."

Mark glanced at Rick, who wore a reassuring smile. Rick no doubt oiled the pathway by mentioning Burton-Abbey's broad philanthropic interests.

"Dottie's a great problem solver," Rick said, looking Mark straight in the eye. "And a perfectionist, like you."

"That's right," Dottie put in. "I don't want to risk a defective pot crumbling all over one of these people any more than you do. All hell would break loose. You were right to fire that supplier."

Mark nodded gravely and assumed the stern expression of a maître d' who found a slug in the salad.

"Now, here's the deal." Dottie leaned toward him, nose to nose. He could picture her wearing a green eyeshade.

"Reduce your bill for the petunias by two-thirds and call it a rental fee. After the party you can take them all back. I'll announce that the centerpieces are on loan and not for removal from the tables. But—and here you must go along with me—anyone present may bring a menu from the table to Hancock's within a week and receive a free, presumably repotted petunia. That's the deal."

Mark looked from Dottie to Rick. A smile crossed his lips. "Half."

Rick stared at him, incredulous. Dottie's eyes narrowed. She had not expected him to play hardball.

"I'll reduce my bill by half," he repeated. "The rest is fine." Mark sipped his second glass of champagne, hoping Dottie couldn't hear his stomach growl.

As he suspected, the chairwoman was not in the mood to haggle. Any reduction in her decorating expense would go straight to the bottom line. "Done," she said.

*   *   *   *

Four hours later, waiters helped Mark and Rick carry the nineteen dozen potted petunias to several large trolleys that would meet Hancock's truck on the loading dock at the back of the hotel. The orchestra was packing up and a few departing party-goers lingered by the door. In the entire unprecedented evening no guest had lifted a single blossom.

Mark watched Dottie DeLuca say goodnight to the United Way chairman. The man could take lessons from her, Mark thought admiringly. During dessert—a chocolate crème brûlée with ginger apricot sauce—Dottie delivered an engaging announcement about the "rented" petunias. Her clever speech elevated the pink flowers to emblems of the medical advances made possible by the generosity of each person present. To remove a centerpiece, and the dollars it represented, would be like snatching a lifesaving vial from a baby. Who would even think of it?

Plenty of people, however, could think of claiming a free potted petunia from Hancock's Landscape Services, judging by the numbers who slipped menus into evening bags. Mark couldn't wait to see all the new customers rushing through Hancock's gates.

Mel and the American Coastal crowd jostled boisterously out the door. Mark noticed that his former colleagues loosened up considerably after Julian Shand and his date left an hour or so earlier. A waiter hurried by jockeying four pots in his arms. Near the trolley, he lost his grip. Two plants fell to the floor with a crash. Mark held his breath while potting mix, petunia roots, and shards of clay spun across the polished floor. A narrow bottle rolled past his foot.

Dottie rushed in Mark's direction. "Thank goodness we didn't let those pots get away," she exclaimed, surveying the mess on the floor. Mark trapped the bottle under the toe of his shoe. Dottie got busy pointing out scattered dirt to two busboys with brooms. Mark kicked the bottle past a skirted table to Rick who scooped it up and put it in his pocket. Luckily, the small container appeared to be the only questionable item unleashed by the accident.

Mark watched until the rest of the plants safely reached the rolling carts and exited the ballroom in reliable hands. He loosened his collar, waved good-bye to Dottie, and headed for the door with Rick. Worry and starvation danced a rumba in his gut.

"Goodnight, gentlemen." They stopped and turned. It was the committeewoman whose checklist they had evaded on the way into the party. "We loved having you," she said with a tight little smile. "Next time, please buy tickets."

CHAPTER 16

▼

Sunday mornings were quiet at Hancock's, until around eleven-thirty when the gravel paths began to crunch with the footsteps of mellow customers full of post-worship goodwill and brunch. Maggie and Carlos had the morning off. The nursery was deserted when Mark arrived at dawn, balancing a cardboard cup of strong coffee while he unlocked the nursery gates.

He had slept little, knowing that two hundred twenty-six dubiously potted petunias awaited his inspection and, worse, that the reclaimed centerpieces could be the least of his troubles. All night long, dirt-caked junk crept across his mind like floats in a reclamation parade. Tubes. Gloves. Bottles. Bones. Grubby things he had seen more than once in places they should not be. Why? And from where had they come?

He spread a large tarp on the pavement next to Hancock's truck and began methodically unpotting the pink petunias a dozen at a time. With gloved hands, he carefully sifted through the packed dirt, searching among the white roots for—what? Another vial? Bones? Flesh? He shuddered.

All at once, the thought that had escaped him the previous day presented itself, intact. *George Alder.* The friend Fred phoned the day before he died. George worked for the Department of Environmental

Health. Did Fred believe the contamination was a serious environmental problem?

While his stomach churned, Mark replaced the first dozen plants and soil in their original pots, and repeated the procedure with another dozen. So far, he had found little more than a stray scrap of bark. He placed a pallet on a wagon and loaded it with twenty-four faultless petunias. Then he wheeled the colorful display to a spot near the checkout counter where guests from the gala could help themselves. He wondered how many plants Hancock's would give away.

A red Porsche Carrera hummed up the alley and swung into the small space behind Hancock's truck. Rick unfolded himself from the driver's seat and hung his Ray-Bans from the neck of his polo shirt. He lifted a box from the passenger seat and turned a sober face toward Mark.

"I thought you'd be here. I came to help." The beau of the ball reached into a pocket of his jeans and extracted the slender bottle he had fielded from the dance floor the night before. "Do you know what this is?"

"I'm afraid to ask."

"A fifty milligram ampoule of bretylium tosylate, a cardiac resuscitation drug. Empty. Brand name Bretosyl. It's ours."

"Burton-Abbeys'?"

"Right." Rick placed the ampoule on a corner of the tarp next to the piece of bark Mark had dug up. He extracted a pair of surgical gloves from the box he brought and pulled them on. Kneeling next to his friend, he reached for a pot of petunias and dumped the flowers on the tarp.

"You can imagine how thrilled I am to find one of my company's pharmaceutical products in a centerpiece at a black-tie ball." He picked up a trowel and hacked through crumbling dirt. "Have you seen Burton-Abbey's annual report?"

Mark placed a repotted plant on an empty pallet and shook his head.

"Slick, with three entire pages on the company's environmental programs: our review board, our emission standards, our enlightened product design, and recycling programs. There's even a four-color photograph of our chairman in a hard hat standing next to an ethylene oxide conversion chamber."

Mark looked at him blankly.

"Ethylene oxide gas is one of the most effective agents for sterilizing medical products. Naturally, the gas is toxic and its emission strictly controlled. Burton-Abbey's manufacturing plants went way beyond EPA compliance by installing equipment that converts used ethylene oxide into ethylene glycol, the main component of antifreeze. A hazardous gas becomes a recyclable liquid, get it?"

Mark nodded. Environmental issues were sore spots in Rick's industry.

Rick stabbed at a clot of potting soil. "Jeez, Mark. I'm making a presentation in a couple of weeks at a conference on sustainable development—*The Responsible Life Cycle of Products, from Discovery and Manufacture to Final Use and Disposal.* Very HTT."

"What's that?"

"Holier than thou. Then I, Mr. Clean himself, discover an environmentally correct Burton-Abbey vial, engineered at great expense to minimize its negative impact on the ecosystem, stuck, whole, in a pot of pink petunias in the center of someone's dinner table." He sliced through the dirt on the tarp. "So now what do I do?"

"FBRF."

"What?"

"Find the bastards responsible and fuck 'em."

By eleven fifteen they had searched and repotted all eighteen dozen and ten plants in the truck, wishing wearily that more than two pots had broken the night before. Mark stood and stretched his aching back. Rick brushed potting mix from the front of his shirt. In the previous two hours, they had spoken hardly a word. The implications of their task were too unnerving. And now they simply stood and looked.

Lined up on the tarp in front of them were five neat rows of earth-encrusted vials, syringes, cords, blades, strips, tubes, and fragments Mark couldn't identify.

"The first-aid kit from hell," Rick finally grunted, fingering a broken rectangular plate with dirty round markings. "This is a Bogner slide for diagnostic testing. Not Burton-Abbey's, if you're wondering." He replaced the slide on the tarp and picked up a gizmo with a metal ring on top. "This looks like the plunger from a Mita-pro control syringe. And this," he held up a bright orange section of plastic, "is what's left of a sharps container. Where the needles went is anybody's guess."

Mark walked grimly into the potting shed and returned a moment later carrying Fred's locked metal box and an old canvas bag. He sat the box on the tarp, turned the key in the lock, and opened the lid.

"That stinks," Rick observed needlessly.

While Rick unwrapped the contents of the box, Mark gathered the newly found objects from the tarp and dropped them inside the gunnysack.

"The dextrose is Burton-Abbey's," Rick said, holding the IV bottle he had just unwrapped up to the light. "So is the glove, a single-use disposable. Tridonex is from another company." He picked up the Ziploc bag. "The bones are someone else's too." He stared at the sealed plastic then carefully replaced it and the other items in the metal box. Mark laid the canvas bag containing the items from the pots on top, closed the lid, and turned the key.

Rick snapped off his surgical gloves so they turned inside out. "Want the bad news first?"

Mark's stomach clenched.

"This is medical waste. A serious case of medical waste." Rick stuffed one glove inside the other and tied the open wrist in a knot. "The really bad news is that it's biohazardous."

Mark felt his innards constrict like a snail under siege. "What's the good news?"

"There isn't any."

"Yoo-hoo. Oh, yoo-hoo." A grinning Dottie DeLuca flapped down the gravel path on a pair of gold-tone sandals, still buoyant from the success of her sold-out fundraiser. Predictably, the hands-on organizer wanted to make sure Hancock's pink petunias were plentiful, well potted, and free to all her menu-toting contributors.

"The display in front is divine," she cooed to Mark. "Oh, hello, Rick. Do you think you have enough? How nice to run into you." Dottie's neat red head turned back and forth between them. "I left a sample menu in your office. The clerk there said she saw the note you left about the petunias." Dottie looked at Rick. "Where did you learn to dance like that?"

Good, Maggie's here, Mark thought, glancing at his watch. He interrupted Dottie mid-sentence to thank her for helping him straighten out the problem with the centerpieces. He felt whipped.

Rick eyed his worn-out friend. "Don't worry about Mark," he said soothingly to Dottie. "He'll keep his end of the bargain. Now, why don't you and I waggle on over and pick out a really fabulous petunia. Talk to you later, Mark." He met Mark's grateful glance, took Dottie's arm, and led her away.

Mark folded the tarp and carried it and the locked box into the potting shed. He laid the tarp on a shelf and sat on the overturned clay pot Fred had used as a stool. Rubbing his eyes, he stared bleakly at the old metal file that held the seeds of something too awful to imagine. Nothing had prepared him for this.

CHAPTER 17

▼

Andrea rinsed Lindsey's Speedo under the faucet and watched a speckle of sand wash down the drain. Swimming had lifted her daughter's spirits, although returning to a lifeless, dogless house had been hard on all of them. They hadn't seen Mark since Wiggles's funeral. He left a hastily scrawled note about a charity event the night before, got home way past midnight, and departed for the nursery early that morning. Wringing the bright scrap of fabric like a neck, Andrea thought her absent husband could be more charitable toward his own bereaved family.

A car door slammed. Andrea listened expectantly for the footsteps on the pavement. Not Mark's. She sighed and dried her hands. Of course he had to work on Sundays now. His new business meant changes for the whole family; over time, they would adjust. Nevertheless, Wiggles's appalling death made the first weekend apart seem especially difficult.

Ginny walked into the kitchen wearing a faded blue hula hoop over her arm like a handbag. "Hello, dear. Look what I saved for a rainy day." A figure of speech. The day was soaked in sunshine.

Andrea felt a wave of warmth for her mother-in-law. In a page from her trusty book of platitudes, Ginny had received all the recent news with equanimity. "Nothing ventured, nothing gained," she responded bravely when Mark told her about his new career in the landscape business. Since Wiggles's death Ginny had been the most philosophical of all.

Andrea regarded the hula hoop. "You're going to demonstrate, I hope."

"Hi, Grandma." Fresh from an observant day at a beach teeming with teenagers, Lindsey had pinned her hair on top of her head with a red banana clip and tied her biggest T-shirt in a fat knot at the waist. Shiny red polish dotted the miniscule nails on her fingers and toes. Andrea smiled at her still emotionally frail seven-year-old and decided not to comment. Lindsey had taken her first tentative steps forward into life without Wiggles.

"What interesting hair," Ginny proclaimed, peering through her reading glasses at the double-pronged banana clip. "Did you do it that way on purpose?"

Lindsey giggled and lifted the hula hoop off her grandmother's arm. "It's supposed to be tussled. Can we go out and try this?"

"Tousled, I think," Ginny replied following Lindsey outside. "That hoop was your father's."

Andrea rolled the wet swimming suit in a towel and started toward the back door. She hadn't tried a hula hoop in years. When she passed her studio she heard the fax machine beep and hum and lurch from idle to busy. A fax on a Sunday?

She scrolled through the possibilities. Newsletter copy? Too early—the new deadline was Tuesday. Fan mail? Possible, but rare. Unsolicited junk? Probably.

She put the damp bundle on a chair and stepped into the office. The stack of paper in the fax tray was growing steadily. Andrea extracted a page. Puzzled, she lifted the sheaf of paper to find the cover sheet. *Economic Re-Development in Los Angeles Via Small Business Growth, by Professor Natalie H. Dunn.*

Andrea remembered Natalie Dunn from Fred's funeral, a striking young woman whose poise had touched them all. The mechanical song of the printer abruptly ceased. The final page of the long transmission was a facsimile of a handwritten note:

Dear Mark,

I hope this isn't too much trouble. Looking forward to seeing you.

Thanks, Natalie

When Mark's Jeep rolled into the driveway, Andrea and Ginny were sitting on lawn chairs sipping iced tea and watching Lindsey gyrate. The little girl's tousled hair crowned a face alight with pleasure. For the first time in two days Andrea felt her daughter's emotional wounds had truly begun to heal.

She took a drink and appraised her husband over the rim of her glass. Mark had set the car alarm and was walking across the lawn. In faded jeans and a white knit shirt he looked trim, broad-shouldered, collegiate. "A dish," her sister, Ellen, had said when Andrea first brought Mark home. Andrea still agreed. Even when she felt mildly miffed, as she did at that moment, she could appreciate the visual side of things. She also gave Mark ten points for coming home early.

"This acorn didn't fall far from the tree," Ginny called as he approached. "Remember when you used to hula like that?"

"Hi," Mark said dully, raising his chin in their direction. Andrea placed her glass on the ground. Minus five points for the charmless greeting. Mark leaned over and picked up the hoop Lindsey had just spun to the Earth.

"You try it, Daddy," she said.

Mark crouched low so that his eyes were level with Lindsey's. He laid the hoop aside and squeezed his daughter's narrow arms in his hands. "Lindsey, I want you to tell me something. It's very important."

Andrea watched from her chair as Lindsey's face darkened.

"What?" Since Wiggles's death, Lindsey had been far less talkative than usual.

"Remember the white rubber glove you brought to Wiggles's funeral?"

Lindsey nodded.

"Where did it come from?"

"I don't know. Wiggles found it." Her lower lip began to quiver.

"Yes, but where did he find it? Did he dig it up? Please think hard."

Under the intense questioning, Lindsey erupted in tears.

Andrea leapt out of her chair, furious. "That's enough!" She rushed to Lindsey's side, took her daughter in her arms, and aimed her anger at Mark. "What difference does it make where the glove came from? Couldn't you see she was enjoying herself?"

Mark stood and ran a hand through his hair. His face looked gray, but Andrea was in no mood to sympathize. She glared at him. How could he be so insensitive to his own heartbroken seven-year-old?

Ginny picked up the two empty glasses. "Well, I think I'll be going," she said, casting a worried glance in Lindsey's direction.

Indoors, the telephone rang.

"I'll get it," Ginny offered, hurrying toward the steps. In a moment her crispy white head poked back through the door. "Mark, it's for you."

Andrea watched until his back disappeared. She touched her daughter's scrambled hair and tried to swing her voice back into soothing ranges of pitch and volume. "Honey, it's okay to feel sad about Wiggles. Of course you miss him. We all do. Some day it won't hurt so much."

Lindsey sniffled and swung the hula hoop halfheartedly on her arm. The knot in her T-shirt had come undone and left a crinkled hemline hanging, sack-like, below her shorts. She began to fiddle with the clip in her hair, and her expression changed to self-absorbed concentration. The downpour had passed.

Andrea appropriated the hula hoop and slipped it over her own shoulders. "Watch, Tunafish. This should be good for a laugh."

When Andrea succeeded in eliciting a smile from her daughter by failing strenuously, she picked up the vintage plastic hoop and led Lindsey inside. They found Mark sitting, stone-faced, opposite Ginny at the kitchen table. Ginny abruptly stopped talking. Mark looked at Lindsey.

"I'm sorry I upset you, sweetie. I hope you'll forgive me."

Lindsey had, in fact, nearly forgotten all about her father's unnerving questions. She placed a munificent hand upon his knee. He cupped the tiny red fingernails in his palm and bent toward her conspiratorially.

"Grandma has a surprise for you. She wants you to spend a few days at her house. Isn't that right, Ginny?"

Startled, Andrea looked at her mother-in-law, who met her eye and nodded. "Now that school is out, a change of scenery will do her good," Ginny said reasonably. "And my swimming pool could use some action."

Under the banana clip, Lindsey's streaked face brightened. Ginny had said the magic words. "Can I, Mom?" she asked eagerly.

Andrea looked from her daughter to Ginny to Mark, torn between the merits of the idea and the irritation she felt at Mark and Ginny's failure to consult her.

"*May* I," she corrected Lindsey, stalling. "Yes, I suppose you may."

"Good decision!" Lindsey replied, raising a forefinger in the air. "I'll go pack." She bounded out of the room to assemble her collection of swimsuits, goggles, flippers, and floats.

Ginny rose and patted Andrea on the arm. "I'll help her." She left.

Andrea stood with her hands on her hips, glowering at Mark. "What was that all about?"

"You'd better sit down."

"Why?"

"Dr. Broder called."

"The vet?"

"When I delivered Wiggles's body, I requested an autopsy."

"You didn't tell me."

"I know. I'm sorry." He paused. "Wiggles was poisoned."

Andrea stared at him, stupefied.

"In his stomach they found strychnine. Meat laced with strychnine." He looked at her. "It wasn't an accident."

Andrea lowered herself into a chair. "Poisoned? Here? In our own backyard?"

"Dr. Broder is going to file a police report. She said an officer will come around in a day or so to complete the paperwork. I knew you wouldn't want Lindsey here."

Andrea nodded while her thoughts raced. Who would poison Wiggles?

"There's no news yet about the bones."

"Bones?" she parroted stupidly. Her voice sounded shrill inside her skull.

"I also asked Dr. Broder to identify the bones Lindsey brought out on Saturday. The ones she said Wiggles found. Apparently the identification is taking longer than expected."

Andrea frowned. She hadn't looked closely at Lindsey's memorial display. She assumed the bones were, well, dog bones. Bones for dogs. Beef. None of this sounded reassuring, and her husband looked like a man who had sampled strychnine himself.

He reached across the table and placed his hand on hers. Taut with a calcifying mix of shock and anger, she could not respond. Beneath his warm fingers, her fist felt like chalk.

"There is more that I need to tell you," Mark began. Before he could elaborate, Lindsey clamored into the kitchen with Ginny. Between them they carried a small blue suitcase, two stuffed duffel bags, and Lindsey's new neon pink backpack. The expedition appeared to be a budding success.

Andrea withdrew her hand from Mark's, got up, and hugged her daughter protectively. She felt like the besieged who send their children out of bomb zones. Ginny's house was only a few miles away, up on Mulholland, but suddenly her mother-in-law's home seemed a remote, safe, poison-free haven.

She grasped Lindsey's brightly manicured fingers and held them in a little bundle all the way to Ginny's car. Mark loaded the luggage and Lindsey's bicycle into the trunk. Everyone kissed and said numerous goodbyes. They all waved until the big sedan turned the corner at the end of the block. Andrea watched the car vanish and felt a wave of deep fatigue.

CHAPTER 18

▼

"You call this food?" Maggie snorted, scrutinizing the calligraphy on a stack of dinner menus from Saturday's gala. "A langoustine purse?"

"That's seafood pastry, I believe," Mark answered, punching another number into his calculator. "I didn't actually eat one."

He regarded her across their tiny office. Recklessly coiffed as always, Maggie provided the only ray of light on that bleak Monday morning. She told him that more than eighty people from the benefit showed up on Sunday to claim free petunias.

As Mark predicted, nearly all of them purchased additional plants and garden supplies as well. Maggie herself sold a dozen pairs of pigskin garden gloves, ten polyethylene kneeler cushions, several ratchet anvil pruners, a couple of Earthquencher soaker hoses, two galvanized watering cans, and a seven-foot tubular steel rose arch. Meanwhile, she said, the nursery crew could barely keep up with the demand for pallets on wagons to haul hand-picked greenery around the gravel paths.

"That charity crowd eats funny. And they like to be waited on," she added disapprovingly, slipping the menus into a drawer. Bright strings of beads cascaded down her bosom, clacking on the desk. "We did everything but park their cars. No, I think we did that too."

"We'll wash their cars if we have to. Look at these totals." Mark jotted down a number and handed her his tally—the bottom-line results of his deal with Dottie DeLuca. If he had gotten that kind of return on his transactions at American Coastal, he would be chairman of the board.

Maggie looked at the number and her eyebrows shot up like a pair of hotwired minks.

Mark glanced at the clock on the wall. Sunday's gross could be their last good news for a long, long time. That morning, as soon as he arrived at the nursery, he called George Alder, Fred Dunn's old friend at the Department of Environmental Health. George wanted to know why Fred phoned him the day before he died, and Mark was pretty sure he knew the answer.

Fred had been looking for trustworthy advice about the stash he found in Hancock's potted pink petunias. That had to be it. The careful wraps and labels, the locked and hidden box, the call to a knowledgeable friend Fred hadn't seen in months all pointed to the same conclusion. Unfortunately Fred didn't live long enough to reach his former classmate. But advice from George was clearly what Fred sought, and Mark intended to get it. Fast.

Not surprisingly, the answer machine in George's office said to expect no human beings before eight-thirty.

Mark tapped his pen on a yellow legal pad. He hadn't been able to explain the whole mess to Andrea. The night before, after Lindsey left with Ginny, Andrea seemed so quiet and withdrawn, he felt he had to ration the bad news. On top of Wiggles's poisoning, the specter of biohazardous medical waste tainting the business on which he'd spent their last dime was simply too potent, like dumping malathion on top of Orthene. He decided to say nothing until he had spoken with George Alder. Maybe he wouldn't have to tell Andrea at all.

Mark was banking on the fact that the found objects were concentrated in a single batch of petunias, the well traveled and now cleaned up Lot 449. Perhaps that would be the end of it as far as Hancock's was concerned. He hoped so.

But the odd bits of plastic that showed up elsewhere, at Glenwater Place and his own dog's funeral, were beginning to fester in his mind like wounds. Was the contamination more widespread? And if the items he and Rick locked in the steel case were indeed biohazardous, as Rick believed, wouldn't their random occurrence constitute a serious risk to public health?

Foul play that tainted Hancock's was bad enough. But if the hazard to people and property went beyond Mark's own investment, what would his responsibility be then?

He got up from his chair and stood in the open doorway. The warm outdoor air smelled garden sweet, a heady combination of stephanotis, citrus, and freshly pruned greens. Essence of Southern California, a land where earnest lawmakers labored mightily to protect obscure living things, and regulations by the bushel governed what people threw away. Mark had seen workers handling hazardous waste. They walked around sealed up in space suits.

George Alder would probably confiscate Hancock's entire inventory. Order some kind of quarantine. Close him down. Mark pictured the nursery gates rusting under police tape, and felt a leaden weight press on his chest.

He leaned against the doorjamb. Behind him Maggie's typewriter clattered at eighty words a minute. She had nearly finished the client lists he requested. He looked out across a sea of blooms and reminded himself that Fred Dunn virtually gave his life to this business. Yet Fred trusted his friend George enough to phone him the very day he unearthed those first questionable items. Then and now, consulting George seemed the only responsible thing to do.

The typewriter fell silent. "Are you going to tell Mr. Alder the whole gruesome story on the phone or wait until you see him?" Maggie wanted to know. The words had barely passed her lips when the telephone rang. They looked at the clock: eight twenty-five.

"Hancock's," Maggie answered. "Yes, Mr. Alder. I'll put him on." She pressed a button and looked at Mark. "He didn't waste any time, did he?"

Mark picked up the receiver. "George? Thanks for returning my call. I think I know why Fred Dunn phoned you the day before he died."

*   *   *   *

The moment Mark laid his eyes on George Alder he felt better. A sturdy, rounded man with a no-nonsense stride and gentle brown eyes, Fred's old friend walked into the nursery exuding warmth and competence. George arrived from downtown less than an hour after he and Mark had spoken. Mark kept their conversation brief, disclosing few details over the phone. The way George dropped everything and came so quickly revealed a great deal about his regard for Fred, Mark realized. He would be touched if he weren't so worried.

George gripped Mark's hand and patted him on the shoulder at the same time, a fatherly gesture that nearly unglued him. "Golly, it's good to meet you," George said.

Maggie greeted their visitor, fluffed her hair, and offered coffee. The two men carried their cups outside.

On the way to the potting shed, Mark told George everything. Once he got started, the words tumbled out. The steel case. The vials. The dated newspaper. The petunia identification marker taped on the Ziploc bag that contained the little hand. George took it all in without a sign of shock or horror, like a psychiatrist listening to the nightmares of a patient. Two furrows formed between his warm brown eyes.

Mark opened the door to the shed and led George to the metal box. He knelt and fumbled with the silver key. George sat his cup on the workbench, and slipped a pair of gloves over his hands. Mark lifted the box to the bench and opened the lid.

"It's all yours."

George methodically unwrapped, examined, and rewrapped each item in the collection, seemingly impervious to the smell and implications of his task. When he got to the Ziploc bag he held the plastic to the light for a moment and laid it aside without comment. Mark sat on the overturned clay pot in the corner listening to his innards rumble.

Once the older man had seen every piece in the box, he replaced them one by one, arranged the canvas sack on top the way Mark had packed it before, closed the lid, removed his gloves, and spoke.

"I can see why Fred called me. And why you must be worried too." George picked up Mark's key ring from the bench. "May I?" Without waiting for an answer he turned the small silver key in the lock.

"As you suspected, Mark, these items would be classified as medical waste. What we call biohazardous medical waste."

Mark's stomach did a double back flip and presumably ended up where it belonged.

"You should know, however, that nearly all biohazards deteriorate quickly when exposed to air and elements, as these clearly have been."

Really? Mark pictured water treatment plants he had seen, and reservoirs. Acres of water shimmering in the sun. He felt a glimmer of hope.

"The question is: Where did this medical waste come from?" George leaned against the bench and worked the small key around its metal loop. "Several different sources, I'd say." Mark was listening with rapt attention.

"The drug ampoules and syringes suggest a clinical setting, a doctor's office or hospital. The slide is probably from a diagnostic lab. Could be independent or part of a large medical center. The remains in the plastic bag..." He looked at Mark, who was barely breathing. "...are likely those of a Rhesus macaque monkey."

Mark gasped. "A monkey? That little hand?"

"Right. Five fingers, five fingernails, an opposable thumb. Looks a lot like a human hand, doesn't it?" George freed the silver key from the ring and put it in his pocket.

"The animal remains are almost certainly from a research lab. A university, perhaps. Rhesus macs are widely used in AIDS research, although they only contract the simian immunodeficiency virus—a cousin to the human immunodeficiency virus that causes AIDS."

George shook his head and paced a few steps beyond the bench. "Not very efficient, when you think about it. Infected monkeys take six months to a year to develop AIDS. The time lag makes testing very slow."

Mark stared at the steel case, stricken. Had he, Maggie, Rick, and who knew how many others been exposed to HIV?

George read his mind. "Don't worry, Son. You can't get HIV by looking. Besides, the chance that the virus is still alive within that bag of bones is slim to nil."

Mark nodded and tried to swallow.

"What concerns me far more is the complete absence of sharps. We found syringes, syringe plungers, and part of a sharps container, but no needles. Where do you suppose the needles went?"

If George expected an answer, he was looking at the wrong guy. Mark's mouth had dried up. He felt like he had lockjaw.

"Sorry. I like to think out loud," George said, noticing the look on Mark's face. He handed back the ring of keys. "The people in my department are paid to answer these questions, and we will. You've done your job by calling me." George picked up the locked file and started to leave.

Mark sprang to his feet. That was it? He hurried ahead of George to open the door. "How are you going to find out where the stuff came from?"

"Tracking documents. Medical waste in California is the most over-documented trash on earth. Generators are required to keep records of the waste they generate. Haulers are required to keep records of the waste they haul. Treatment facilities keep records of the waste they treat, grind, compact, incinerate, and bury. Guess who gets to see, compare, and reconcile those records on demand—me."

Mark held the door of the potting shed, impressed.

"We'll find the hole and plug it," George said. "Someone probably got careless and threw biowaste into the wrong sack. Or a sack into the wrong bin. Or a bin into the wrong truck. Probably some of each. It happens. We'll find out who did it. In the process I see no reason to bring public attention to Hancock's."

His words washed through Mark like a dose of Maalox.

"I would, however, appreciate your cooperation in the investigation."

Mark would do handsprings for George. "Of course."

"It is possible you will find more of these items before we sew up the leak. Perhaps the residue of one stray load. If something does turn up, bag it and call me as you did before."

"Right." Mark tried to subdue his elation. He should have known there would be a rational, fixable cause of the stray items. The two men walked through the nursery, past the office, and out the front gates to George's Buick.

"One more thing," George added, opening the trunk of his car. "In an investigation of this nature, it's important to be discreet. We don't want to tip off the negligent parties before we find them, nor do we wish to alarm the public unnecessarily. Do you understand?"

"Oh, I do, yes." Mark suppressed a grin. He couldn't have asked for a better outcome to this dreaded conference.

George lowered the metal box into a space between several official-looking binders. "These are some of the tracking documents I told you about," he said, holding one of the binders open so that Mark could take a look. "Notice the detail: name and signature of the generator, type and quantity of waste generated." George flipped a page. "Name and signature of hauler; type and quantity of waste hauled, sterilized, incinerated, stored, or dumped, with corresponding dates and signatures. Every medical waste hauler has to maintain these records. It's the law." George closed the binder and slammed the trunk.

"I'm only sorry Fred passed away with this problem on his mind," Alder said, shaking his head. He looked skyward. "If he's watching, he's probably relieved to know we can contain the problem, don't you think?"

"I'm sure of it," Mark nodded, pumping George's hand warmly. "And he's not the only one."

*   *   *   *

Two miles away, on the south border of Camellia Court, Carlos slipped another syringe into his pocket. No one noticed. He glanced at the four crew members who were busy digging holes for the last dozen camellias. When he had a chance, he would empty his pockets again into the garbage bag he had hidden behind the seat in the truck. A large bag that was now at least half full.

Carlos didn't know where all this trash was coming from, or why it was buried at Glenwater Place. He did know that letting it stay there was wrong.

CHAPTER 19

▼

Natalie Dunn placed a picnic basket on Mark's desk and handed over a bottle of wine. "If you won't come to lunch, lunch will come to you," she said in the voice that reminded him of vintage cognac. She was early.

Wednesdays were normally uneventful at Hancock's, and Mark agreed to meet the professor in his office to discuss her upcoming lecture. Both Maggie and Carlos had the day off. Two retail assistants puttered in the nursery outside. Mark had just finished reading the essay Natalie faxed him, when she walked through the door. He hadn't expected the food.

"You look like you've done this before," he said, watching her smooth a checkered cloth over his desk and cover it with plates, glasses and platters, ripe cheese, fresh fruit, dark olives, and crusty bread.

"Yes, a time or two," she said, handing him a corkscrew. "Only Dad preferred submarine sandwiches." She smiled across the mouth-watering bounty, and his juices jumped. Mutinous thoughts stirred pleasantly in his brain.

Mark dragged his eyes from hers and focused on the wine bottle. She had chosen well—a deep red Beaujolais that needed to breathe. He unfolded the pocketknife that had belonged to her father and grandfather, and applied it to the foil around the cork. Natalie noticed the knife, and their eyes met briefly again.

"I read your paper," Mark said, breaking the silence. "Economic re-development is a timely subject in LA. I wouldn't be surprised if your lecture makes the local news." He picked up the corkscrew she had unpacked and eased the cork out of the bottle.

"Thanks. My case studies are dated, though—nearly two years old. I was hoping you could suggest some more current examples."

"Small companies that are revitalizing the city? That shouldn't be too difficult." He poured the wine, picked up his glass, and sniffed the jammy bouquet. "Is it too soon to drink this?"

She lifted her glass. "Let's toast." In the mote-specked light her blue eyes danced. "To risk. Because the time is never exactly right for anything."

He looked at her and thought of his sudden plunge into the landscape business. The small fortune he had gambled to buy Hancock's. The rush of excitement his new career still gave him. The minefield he saw in Natalie herself.

"To risk."

They touched glasses. The taste of laser-guided fruit flooded his mouth, with an edgy overlay that would soften in a minute or two. Mark turned his glass in his hand and regarded her.

"Have you considered Folee's?"

"A case study on Folee's Nursery?" She made a face. "No way. Maybe years ago, when Great-grandfather Folee started the business from nothing in a shack on a vacant lot. But today all that company does is force smaller operations to sell out. Folee's doesn't raise the standard of competition. It crushes the competition."

Mark chewed on a mouthful of bread and Brie. He wondered about the professor's understanding of market forces. She probably held a bias against her father's chief competitor. But she was correct on one score. Folee's could no longer be considered small. He watched her bite into a slice of pear.

"How about Biovak, Inc.?"

"Biovak? That sounds familiar."

He nodded. "It's one of the fastest growing small businesses in southern California. Waste management. Privately held by a whiz named Julian Shand who's currently at the top of every loan officer's prospect list."

She opened a notebook and jotted the information. "Where is Biovak located?"

"Downtown. The warehouse district, I think. Not the greatest location." He pictured her long, silken legs emerging from a car in that rat's nest.

"Perfect. You read my paper. The whole premise is that leading-edge businesses—leading edge in the geographic sense—can revitalize decaying neighborhoods. Create jobs. Attract other businesses. Raise the standard of living for the entire community."

Mark nodded. "I read it. I don't know if Biovak is revitalizing the neighborhood, but I do know the company's only a couple of years old and it is minting money. I could probably get you an introduction through American Coastal."

He wouldn't mind an excuse to phone Mel Beckman. Mark wanted to maintain his contacts at the bank. And he knew Mel would be delighted to have an excuse to phone Julian Shand.

"Relationship management," they called it. Beckman was supposed to build a relationship with Shand. Invite him to thousand-dollar-a-plate dinners, call him up and chat. Sometimes it worked. What began as a loan could develop into a multitude of services that mated bank to customer in a lucrative, long-term marriage. Beckman had worked hard to become Biovak's number one suitor.

"How long are you going to be in Los Angeles?" Mark asked Natalie.

"Just over two weeks. The lecture is on Thursday, June fourteenth. Then I have to go back to San Francisco to prepare for summer session."

"Fine. I'll call Beckman today." He glanced at his calendar. Glenwater Place was scheduled to open on the sixteenth, two days after her talk. The mayor was going to cut a ribbon. There would be music, food, and the public's first look at Hancock's heralded landscaping.

"Why don't you stay through Saturday for the opening of Glenwater Place?" Mark asked, inspired. "Bring your mother. That project meant a lot to your dad, and I'd like both of you to see what Hancock's has done."

Natalie looked at him with shining eyes. "I'd like that. We both would." She dropped her moist gaze to scribble a note in the margin of her book. "Which reminds me, before I leave here today I want to find an orchid for Mother."

Afternoon sun poured through the open window. A bee landed on the sill. Mark and Natalie finished the Beaujolais and made impressive inroads on three wedges of cheese. They talked easily, relaxed. Bread crumbs littered the checkered tablecloth. Mark popped a grape into his mouth and watched a customer walk past the office door. He knew he should return to work, but his body seemed to have melted like syrup into the contours of his maple chair.

Natalie dropped a wad of plastic wrap into the waste basket and surveyed the mess on the desk. Mark reached out impulsively and covered her hand with his. She sat unmoving and looked at him. Slowly her palm turned upward, like a caress.

Mark's fingers closed around hers. Her skin felt as fine as the petals on a poppy. He ached to tell her how worried he had been about Hancock's. That Wiggles had been poisoned and the police had no leads. That Lindsey went to Ginny's and Andrea seemed withdrawn and unapproachable. He wanted to tell Natalie she attracted him like a polestar, and have her beam those understanding eyes on him all day. But he couldn't get started, so he simply sat and looked at her.

"Mr. Grant?" Rudy Vale stood in the doorway holding a sheaf of receipts. The foreman's appraisal swept the tablecloth, the wine glasses, the hands. Mark quickly let go and sat back in his chair.

"Uh, I wanted you to know we've finished the job in Bel Air. I'll be going back to Glenwater Place to relieve Carlos tomorrow."

"That's fine, Rudy. Thanks," Mark croaked and cleared his throat. He rose like a recovering hypnotic and accepted the papers from Rudy.

The foreman drummed his fingers against the door frame and took another look at Natalie. "Hello, Miss Dunn."

"Hi, Rudy."

Rudy backed out the door and crunched down the path.

Mark opened a drawer in the file cabinet and took longer than necessary to stow the receipts. Behind him he could hear Natalie packing the remains of the picnic. When he turned around she was fastening the buckles on the basket.

"Did you want to say something?" she asked softly.

He cleared his throat again. "No." His voice seemed fully functional again. "Thanks for lunch."

She looked at him a moment, walked around the desk, leaned into his chest, and touched her lips to his mouth. The bee on the sill buzzed noisily and flew smack against the glass.

When Mark was a senior at Northwestern, he pressed two hundred pounds on a dare at the gym. The effort nearly split his gut. He remembered it at that moment, when every fiber in him strained to grab this woman and return her kiss.

It was a risk he wasn't prepared to take.

Natalie abruptly stepped back, unused to tepid kisses applied like paint. Without another word she picked up her notebook and the picnic basket and walked out the door. Mark felt a drop of sweat roll down his neck.

CHAPTER 20

▼

Mel Beckman was glad to phone Julian Shand about the celebrated young female professor who wanted to interview him. Mark's former colleague called the very next morning to say Natalie's meeting was all arranged.

"Shand will give her a tour of the plant, allow an hour or so for the interview, and—depending on how it goes—invite her to lunch," Mel reported.

Mark pictured the cocky, cigar-smoking chairman of Biovak he had seen at the Beverly Hilton, and wondered whether he and Mel had done Natalie a favor. Maybe she should hire a bodyguard. Given Shand's eye for the ladies and the ugly neighborhood in which his business was located, maybe she should hire two.

He thanked Mel and hung up, deciding Natalie could take care of herself. The professor was no slouch when it came to men. And the paper she had written about economic re-development was slick with urban savvy. If anyone could handle a foray into the warehouse district, it was Professor Natalie H. Dunn.

Mark considered the paperwork piled in front of him, and wondered if a checkered cloth would ever brighten his desktop again. Probably not, based on Natalie's hasty departure the previous afternoon. It was just as well. Her lunches made him sweat. Like Fred, he would be better off sticking to submarine sandwiches.

Although it was Thursday, Mark felt energized, Monday-morning-ish, as if the week were just beginning. It was, in a way. His second week at Hancock's, and now he could settle into the work he enjoyed instead of worrying incessantly about someone else's wayward trash. Rick had sounded relieved too when Mark explained George Alder's no-nonsense attitude to the items they had found in the petunia pots. Fred's old friend had lifted a landfill off both their shoulders.

Mark intended to spend the morning refining his marketing strategy for Hancock's landscape business. When Maggie finished her client list he would possess a complete picture of the company's off-site projects for the past three years. He planned to prioritize those customers and move quickly to contact all of them with an interesting offer—a deal, an open house, a bonus for referrals—he wasn't sure yet exactly what.

He eyed the bookkeeper's star-spangled shoulder blades. Her wardrobe defied description.

Carlos hurried past the office door carrying the *California License Law and Reference Book*, the study guide for the state contractor's licensing exam. Carlos and the guide had been inseparable for days. The bright young man already understood more about nurseries and landscaping than most of the contractors Mark knew. Business management and construction law made up the other half of the exam, and Mark was sure Carlos would absorb that information like vermiculite.

Hancock's new owner grinned out the door to no one in particular. After a rocky start, his little venture seemed to be humming along nicely. For a brief, shining moment, he felt the euphoria he had anticipated when he dared to dream about owning a business. He placed a fresh legal pad on his desk, picked up a pen, and started to work.

*   *   *   *

Helen Woodley planned to spend her Thursday morning tending the planter boxes on her patio. The geraniums and lobelia she had selected the previous season had billowed and trailed so abundantly, they nearly concealed their containers. The flourishing plants needed pinching, trimming, deadheading—lots of fuss, and a beautiful day for it too. Helen adjusted her straw hat and regarded the planters with relish.

She intended to dig up and repot the geranium nearest the kitchen door for the garden club plant sale. Herbs would grow well in that location, and Helen had already coaxed eager shoots of basil, parsley, chives, and dill from seeds in her kitchen window.

With a large clay pot and a package of potting soil at the ready, she gently dug out the lavender lobelia and its long, pale roots. Setting the trailing plant aside, she turned her attention and her drop-shank trowel to the geranium in the center of the container—a show-stopping *Pelargonium hortorum.* It had big, healthy red flower clusters and thick, shrubby leaves. A plant she could contribute with pride.

She eased her trowel into the soil and probed gingerly around the geranium roots. The metal tool cut through the rich planting mix like a knife through bread. Midway around the root ball the blade struck something hard. Helen frowned and poked again. Rock hard. Digging more aggressively, she used her free hand to hold back the loosened soil. In a moment she held the foreign object in her hand—a cracked petri dish.

"How odd," she said aloud. When she finally uprooted the entire geranium, she decided the situation was worse than odd. In the soil around the *pelargonium,* she had unearthed a dirt-caked angioplasty ring, part of a venous reservoir, a tiny hemostasis valve, and what looked like two fragments from blood filters.

Helen removed her garden gloves and stood, stupefied. A former nurse, she knew surgical supplies when she saw them. But here? Dumfounded, she went into the house to phone Mark Grant at Hancock's.

*   *   *   *

About the same time that morning, Beth Dunn waved goodbye to Natalie, who was driving downtown for a meeting, and turned her attention to the orchid her daughter had given her. Orchids were

Beth's specialty. Fred used to supply her with the finest raw materials—specimen bulbs, exotic potting blends, gourmet fertilizers—which she turned into prize-winning orchid plants, indoors and out. Over the years, garden club juries had awarded her more than a few accolades for her home-grown blooms. In her capable hands and the moist coastal air of Pacific Palisades, the orchids thrived.

Natalie's gift was a large-flowered *Cymbidium* with striking bronze petals. Beth intended to install the plant near the front door of the house, in a cast stone urn at the focal point of her collection. She knew just the spot.

But Beth would not repot the orchid that day. She nearly fainted when her third scoop of rich, specially blended orchid mix turned up a dirt-encrusted skeleton about the size of a premature baby, minus legs. Beth dropped her spade and gaped at the delicate remains.

*   *   *   *

Up on Mulholland Drive, Ginny Grant hummed tunelessly while she selected sun-ripened tomatoes for her jalapeño salsa. Like Mark, Lindsey loved salsa. Beyond the vegetable garden Ginny could see her granddaughter splashing contentedly in the swimming pool.

Lindsey was an unusually self-sufficient child, Ginny had come to realize during the little girl's extended visit. Solitude seemed a solace to her in the wake of Wiggles's death. For four whole days the busy seven-year-old hadn't once asked to entertain a friend, or even chatted on the phone with another child, although she had spoken with Andrea and Mark. The life of a semi-recluse, with swimming pool, bicycle, and a long, winding driveway, seemed to suit Lindsey just fine for the time being. Ginny was happy to indulge her.

She yanked a tomato from its plant. "Vine," some people called it, although the sprawling tomato plant is incapable of climbing. Ginny inspected the stakes that supported her tied-up crop. One of them wobbled precariously in the dirt. She moved it back and forth and discovered it was broken at the base.

Glancing at Lindsey, who had arranged her towel and herself on a lawn chair, Ginny hurried to the garage to find a new stake. She returned a few moments later with the item she needed and a basket containing a mallet, assorted gloves, a small trowel, scissors, and twine.

Ginny was accustomed to finding bits of plastic in her garden, even small bottles like the ones she cleaned and used for storing fresh herbs. In the rocky, unpredictable soil where she lived, junk turned up all the time. But she wasn't prepared for the blade that nearly sliced through her glove when she tried to loosen the soil around the stub of the old tomato stake.

She stared in amazement at the slashed fabric. What in her garden could slice canvas like that? She pulled off the neatly incised glove. Luckily her skin wasn't cut.

Worry creased Ginny's forehead as she changed into a pair of heavy duty, thorn-proof gloves, wondering if even those could withstand the sharp object in the soil. Using her trowel she probed the dirt until she struck metal, then carefully eased out the treacherous blade. She had no idea what the thing was. Part of a tool, maybe. She placed the object in her basket, frowning. Lindsey liked to run around barefoot, and Ginny herself enjoyed digging in the dirt with her bare hands. She decided to investigate further, just in case.

She dug cautiously around the tomato plants, occasionally lifting a trowel full of dirt into the air. As she watched the soil sift slowly back to earth she made her next disturbing discovery. What she found in the ensuing twenty minutes chased all thoughts of salsa from her mind.

*   *   *   *

Mark had nearly finished composing a friendly letter of introduction to Hancock's landscape clients when the first telephone call shattered the calm of his morning. It was Helen. *This can't be happening,* he thought, listening to her reel off the medical names of the objects she had found in her planter boxes. More junk on her property.

Maggie heard enough of the conversation to stop typing and swivel around in her chair. The second phone line rang and she spun back again.

"Oh, hello, Beth. He's on another call, but I'll tell him it's you." Maggie put Beth on hold.

Mark informed Helen that the bizarre medical waste in her soil could be explained, and said he would hurry over to tell her about it and collect the objects himself. He rang off hoping he hadn't sounded like a complete fool, trying hard not to worry. George Alder had said, after all, that a few more items could appear.

Maggie pointed to the flashing light on his telephone. "Beth Dunn."

Mark thought of Natalie and pushed a button. "Hi, Beth." He listened to her frightened report, stunned. His stomach began to roil.

"It's an animal, Beth, not a baby," he said hoping this was true. "I'll try to explain when I get there." The day was turning as sour as the taste in his mouth. Mark reached for a box of Tic Tacs and wondered whether a full moon was rising.

"Maggie, get me some garbage bags, gloves, ID markers, a felt pen, and a trowel, please."

"Sure. Your mother's on hold. Shall I ask her to call back?"

This time he hadn't even heard the phone ring. "Yes."

He got up and searched for his keys under the papers on his desk. Through the window he saw Carlos escorting a customer with a wagonload of wisteria.

"Mark," Maggie said urgently, holding her hand over the mouthpiece. "Ginny says she found a blade of some sort in her garden. Sharp, like a knife or razor. That's not all. She wants you to get up there as soon as you can."

Like the tempest in his gut, his garbage route grew: Little Holmby, Pacific Palisades, and now his mother's, up on Mulholland Drive.

Affluent areas that dotted the West Side from deep inland to the edge of the ocean to the crest of the Santa Monica Mountains. He ran his hand through his hair. How widespread could this contamination be?

Before the phone could ring again, Mark punched the free line. "Tell my mother I'll be there as soon as I can. I'm calling George Alder."

Maggie spoke to Ginny, then hurried outside to gather the supplies Mark requested.

When George answered, Mark quickly outlined the news. He said he was on his way to collect waste from three locations, beginning at his mother's up on Mulholland.

"My daughter is staying there, George. Our dog died. It's a long story. But now I'm worried that Ginny's property isn't safe."

Undaunted, George asked measured questions and listened carefully to Mark's responses. He was taking notes. A professional at work. Mark admired the man's unflappability. But then, George's livelihood wasn't on the line.

"I'm sorry your mother and your friends had to become involved," George said. "This actually makes my job simpler. A large quantity of stray waste is always easier to track than a single bag or two. The leak should stand out like a tidal wave. We'll change the parameters of our search, and get on it right away."

Mark leaned back in his chair. George was cool in a crisis. But his methodical approach didn't cancel the immediate problem of the trash that was turning up in the gardens of Hancock's customers all over the West Side. Now three more people needed to be discreet.

George was thinking the same thing. "It won't help if these women panic, Mark. You know them. Tell them they did the right thing by calling you. Urge them to cooperate further by keeping our investigation confidential. It will all blow over in a few days."

Mark said he would do as George instructed.

"And Mark," George added. "Your daughter will be fine at her grandmother's. Just tell her to wear shoes for now."

Mark hung up as Carlos appeared at the checkout window with his wisteria-toting customer.

"Is the truck here, Carlos?"

"Yes, Mr. Grant."

"I'm going to take it for a couple of hours. May I use your keys?"

Carlos fished in his pocket and extracted a key ring. A muddy plastic syringe clattered to the pavement. Both men stared as if they expected it to explode.

CHAPTER 21

▼ ———————

The doghouse weighed more than she expected. Andrea dragged the abandoned structure to the curb and left it beside the grocery bag that held the rest of Wiggles's possessions. Leash, tether, bowl, brush, ball, and rawhide bone—real estate and residue, the tangible legacy of a dearly departed pet.

She stood for a moment next to the curbside offerings, catching her breath and saying good-bye. If luck were in her favor, a scavenger would take everything before garbage collection the next day and spare her the sight of Wiggles's meager estate being hoisted into a dump truck. A tear spilled down her cheek.

She could have donated the doggy paraphernalia. Every six months or so she took a box of used toys, books, and clothing to the hospital thrift shop. Big items, such as the doghouse, the shop would pick up on a monthly schedule. But Andrea couldn't bear to wait. Since Wiggles died, the sight of his empty shelter choked her with emotion. She wanted it out of there, now.

With a sigh she turned and climbed the grassy slope to the house. The police had come, completed their report, and gone. The items by the curb, like the trash in the cans, would disappear by early the next day one way or another. That weekend she and Mark would go get Lindsey from Ginny's and try to carve out some time for each other.

They might never know who killed their dog, or why. It was time to try to return to normal.

Work would take her mind off Wiggles's death, if nothing else would. In a burst of bravado, she had moved that month's production schedule up one week to bring the four newsletters she produced in line with a mid-month distribution cycle. In the two years since she had started her graphics business, she had argued that newsletters should be in readers' hands well before the first of the month to maximize their usefulness as planning tools. Otherwise why bother with the calendar listings, deadline reminders, and time-specific information the editors seemed to relish?

Alphaprint and Pico Press were willing. And to Andrea's simultaneous gratification and dismay, all four newsletter chiefs agreed at virtually the same time. *Healthy Times, LA Business Report, Property Line,* and *Garden Works* would come out seven days earlier, beginning with the next issue. Two weeks remained until publication day. Copy was dropping on her desk like eucalyptus bark. The typesetter would arrive any moment to help spec manuscripts. For the next fourteen days Andrea was going to have her hands full.

*   *   *   *

Natalie accelerated up the on-ramp and lowered her visor against the afternoon sun. Rush hour on the Santa Monica Freeway: ten lanes of cars twelve feet apart going seventy miles an hour. Like the running of the bulls, freeway traffic was a thrill she normally avoided. Today, however, she gunned her mother's silver Taurus into the crush as eagerly as a Pamplonan *adolescente.* She couldn't wait to put pavement between herself and the appalling neighborhood she had just visited.

The warehouse district: two square miles of commerce and chaos east of downtown, between San Pedro Street and the Los Angeles River. More than three billion dollars worth of trucked-in goods passed through the area's steel-gated loading docks each year, while a round-the-clock parade of prostitutes, drug dealers, and petty thieves did a brisk trade along restless, trash-strewn streets. Even on a scholarly mission in broad daylight Natalie found the area chilling. She darted into the fast lane and glanced at the bleak skyline in her rearview mirror.

Deep inside that labyrinth of sheet metal and razor wire stood the darling of the local business community, Biovak, Inc., one of the fastest growing enterprises in the region. Mel Beckman called the company a money machine. After meeting its owner, Julian Shand, Natalie could see why.

In the mirror she caught a glimpse of the bright red security badge still attached to her lapel. Shand told her red was the color code for Thursday. She unclipped the visitor's pass and tossed it in her purse. Biovak's tight security did not surprise her, considering the underbelly it called home. She glanced at her speakerphone and quickly pressed the number for Hancock's. Maggie's breathless hello filled the car.

"Hi, Maggie. Is Mark there?"

"He's out in the truck. I don't think he's back yet. Uh, let me look."

The bookkeeper sounded more flustered than usual. Natalie pictured Maggie's copious hair standing on end.

"Natalie? He just drove in. I'll put you on hold."

The Harbor Freeway interchange held Natalie's attention until Mark answered. She passed a Chevy pick-up flapping with gardeners in loose T-shirts, and heard him say hello.

"Thanks for arranging the interview with Julian Shand," she chatted into space. "Biovak is pretty amazing. I'm on the way home now."

"At four-thirty? That was a long lunch."

He was in a snit about something, she could tell. "I preferred yesterday's lunch," she cooed.

He didn't respond. The man was exasperatingly unteasable. She decided to play it straight.

"Mark, have you met Julian Shand?"

"No."

"An interesting and repugnant man. He's a highly original thinker with some lousy habits. Like resting his hot, entrepreneurial hand on the nearest female thigh."

"I hope you decked him."

"He got the message. Like I did yesterday."

Naturally, Mark ignored that remark. "Did you get what you needed for your lecture?" he asked politely.

"That and more. Listen to this. Shand recruits and employs homeless transients who prowl the streets in the warehouse district. Pays by the hour, minimum wage. Gives everyone a shower, a meal, and clean protective clothing. Most of them work in the consolidation warehouse, also known as the transfer station."

"What's that?"

"I only saw part of it. It's the warehouse where they unload, sort, and repackage medical waste and reroute it to a final destination—incinerator, recycling facility, landfill, whatever. It's a fascinating operation."

"Medical waste?"

"Right. Guess how many tons of regulated medical waste an average hospital generates each month."

He didn't answer.

"Eighty-four hundred. Tons. Per month. Add to that six hundred tons a month per laboratory. Four hundred tons per blood bank. Three hundred ninety tons per nursing home—you get the picture. Shand is sitting on a gold mine."

She heard Mark suck in his breath. "Are you with me?" she asked.

"Yeah. A gold mine. Where do the rest of the Biovak employees work, the ones who aren't in the warehouse?"

"Wait until you hear this," she enthused, warming to her subject and her listener. "Shand operates two fleets of vehicles: calls them inbound and outbound. The inbound fleet picks up and hauls medical waste from generators to the consolidation warehouse. Generators are hospitals, doctor's offices, et cetera. Places that generate waste. They're his customers, right? So naturally he wants the inbound vehicles to be presentable. They are. Big, gleaming white trucks labeled Biovak under a brilliant red cross. You would think Florence Nightingale herself drove one. Biovak employees who perform well in the warehouse and stay clean and sober get promoted to the inbound fleet."

"I see," he said thoughtfully. "Who drives the outbound fleet?"

"That's the best part." Natalie gripped the wheel and stepped on the brake. Traffic was slowing near the San Diego Freeway.

"The outbound fleet has to impress no one. It hauls the sorted waste from Biovak's consolidation warehouse to treatment plants, landfills, the dump. Places he pays to take the stuff. There's no point in using expensive trucks for that."

"So?"

"So the vans in this outbound fleet are piles of junk. Rolling scrap metal, engines tuned." Natalie chuckled. "You've never seen so many ramshackle white vans lined up in a parking lot in your life. All unmarked, of course. Shand paints them himself. Saves a fortune.

"And get this," she continued. "Driving those lemons is the best job at Biovak. Shand promotes the top inbound drivers and gives them a big raise to jockey those decrepit heaps around town. Otherwise, he says, even the homeless wouldn't go near them."

She quelled a chuckle. Mark apparently was not amused.

"Mark, are you there?"

"Uh, yeah."

"Is something the matter?"

"Are you seeing Shand again?"

"I don't think so. Why?"

"I'd rather not explain on the phone. I'll be in touch." He hung up.

Mark placed the receiver in the cradle, stunned by Natalie's news. He raked his fingers through his hair, aghast at the picture forming in his mind. A medical waste hauler who minted money? Why would that be? Everything seemed to fit. The ubiquitous trash. The junky white vans he had seen on his own street. The dependent drivers who wouldn't talk. Biovak's phenomenal revenues. Shand must be dumping cargo in places where dumping was free. Half-empty garbage cans awaiting collection, for example. The dug-up property of unsuspecting landscape customers. So what if he putrefied the environment, endangered public health, and violated every code in the book? He was minting money.

Which explained why Julian Shand was that year's corporate calendar boy. He changed the paradigm. Pushed the edge of the envelope. Swam with the sharks. And ran a colossal con.

Anger rose in Mark like the mercury in an old thermometer. On that day alone he had collected a sack of surgical supplies, a box of bones, and enough hypodermic needles to shoot up all the addicts in East LA. His mother's vegetable patch was riddled with them. What decrepit white van visited her garden? And when?

Carlos stepped through the door like a man on the threshold of doom. In his arms he carried a fat, knotted Hefty Bag. Mark didn't have to ask what was inside. The syringe that tumbled out of Carlos's pocket earlier told the whole story.

"Have a seat," he said to his frightened young employee.

Carlos sat.

"Now start at the beginning and tell me everything."

"Okey-dok—er—yes, Mr. Grant."

CHAPTER 22

▼

Lindsey tied her shoelaces and tiptoed out of the house. Her grandmother would sleep another hour or so, then get up and make a special breakfast. They had already enjoyed Pigs in a Blanket, Eggs in a Nest, and a poppy seed turnover Ginny called "Ants in the Pants." Lindsey had permission to ride her bike before breakfast if she stayed on Ginny's property.

Cool, fresh air swept her face and made the blue tassels on her handlebars stand straight out as she coasted down the long, winding driveway. Near the end of the pavement she pressed on the brakes, got off, and leaned the bike against a tree. She took a box of raisins from her backpack and hung the bag over a handlebar. Climbing a short path up a rise, she located her favorite spot and gazed out over the San Fernando Valley.

The view from that secluded knoll still held her spellbound, three days after she had discovered it. For miles in every direction stretched streets, buildings, and trees as clear and tiny as the details on a dollhouse. In the distance were mountains, and above them sky the color of the bluest Crayola. She settled on a boulder, placed two raisins on her tongue, and imagined herself flying an airplane.

When all the raisins were eaten, she got up, and left her jet on cruise control. She could hear earthbound vehicles rattle past, and knew her grandmother would be expecting her.

She made her way down the path and found her bike right where she left it. But something was different about her backpack. It had moved a little, toward the end of the handlebar. The center looked plump, as though someone had stuffed a picnic inside. Breakfast?

Smelling a treat, Lindsey darted sparkling eyes from tree to bush. Her grandmother came up with the best surprises. Where could Ginny be hiding?

Lindsey opened the sack and peered inside. Puzzled, she reached in and removed the anonymous gifts one by one. A smile formed on her lips. She knew who must have played this trick, and it wasn't her grandmother.

"Rick?" she called, looking right and left. "Uncle Rick, where are you?"

*   *   *   *

Mark tried with mixed success to simultaneously shave and keep a watch out the window on the trash by the curb. Until he decided on a plan of action, he was relying on routine to keep himself glued. The rasp of the razor against his beard was the only thing that seemed normal on that fatigue-ridden Friday morning.

Bona fide scavengers had already removed the doghouse and accoutrements Andrea left near the garbage cans. Mark saw the scavengers, a man and a boy in an old pick-up truck brimming with furniture, tires, scrap metal, and wood. The boy gestured broadly over Wiggles's belongings, which obviously pleased him far more than the junk he and the older man usually found. Mark watched the unknown youth skip with delight as he resurrected leash, ball, and rawhide bone. The sight of Wiggles's toys clutched in small, excited hands struck a bittersweet chord deep within him.

In the glow of the rising sun, four half-empty barrels remained like bait in front of the house. If Mark's theory were correct, someone in a dinged-up white van would come along any moment to hoist a bag or two into the void. He had seen those so-called scavengers before, right there on his own property. He cringed at the recollection. What a sap.

The story Carlos told him about the debris he found in Camellia Court also featured an old white van and, worse, a goon who threatened Carlos and his entire family. The involvement of Glenwater Place, Mark's ghastly suspicions about Biovak, and the increasingly ominous overtones of the whole shabby mess had kept Mark awake most of the night. He would have to tell George Alder. The Department of Environmental Health would probably have to go public with its investigation. And then what would happen to Hancock's? What would happen to Mark's family? He hadn't even told Andrea yet.

Mark scraped a band of shave cream from his neck, wondering if he should simply slit his throat and be done with it. Two weeks after becoming the owner of Hancock's Landscape Services, he yearned for the simple terror of losing his job. The nightmare that had unfolded at the nursery since he signed on the bottom line threatened far more than his livelihood. He held the razor under the tap and watched his whiskers swirl into the vortex. Now it threatened the people he loved.

The sound of a vehicle rounding the corner chugged through the damp morning air. An engine hummed directly below and outside the bathroom window. Mark dropped his razor into the sink and sidled up to the louvered glass. A large sedan rolled past the garbage cans.

Mark blinked and looked again. "What the...?"

It was Ginny. Her car made a slow, wide turn, and eased into the driveway. The front passenger door sprang open and released Lindsey, who ran to the house grasping her neon pink backpack. What were those two doing here at this hour? Mark wiped the remaining shave cream from his face and hurried downstairs.

Andrea, who had worked late and gotten up early, walked out of her studio to join Mark in the kitchen. "Well this is a surprise," she said, slipping a blue pencil behind her ear. "Hi, honey."

"I thought it best to come right over," Ginny explained, gulping air. "Look what Lindsey found."

The three adults watched while Lindsey upended her backpack on the table. Mark gaped, appalled. Like a scene in a recurring dream, out spilled three intravenous bottles, four amber ampoules, two precision vacutainers, and a very large syringe. From her purse Ginny removed an object wrapped in tissue and handed it directly to Mark. A vial. Curled inside the container was a piece of paper.

"Keep that to yourself," she said in a low whisper.

"What's going on?" Andrea wanted to know. "Are these from Rick?"

"I thought so too, Mommy," Lindsey said excitedly. "See the siren squirt gun? Grandma doesn't think Rick put them in my backpack. They're too dirty. Anyway, how could he? He lives so far away it's not realipstick."

"Realistic," Mark said reflexively, extracting the curled paper from the vial. Andrea picked up the syringe and turned it over in her hand.

"Uh, you probably shouldn't handle that," he said, looking at her hard.

A quizzical expression crossed her face. She started to speak, then changed her mind and replaced the syringe on the table.

Mark unrolled the typed message and felt the color flee from his partially-shaven face.

Stop running to the DEH. Keep your mouth shut or you and *your daughter will be sorry.*

"What does it say, Daddy?"

Mark looked at Ginny, who stood behind Lindsey with her hands on her granddaughter's shoulders. Ginny knew the gist of things since the day before when Mark had tried to explain the needles in her garden. And obviously she had read the note.

"It says the surprises in your backpack are not from Rick, honey. That's all. They're from someone we don't know." She patted Lindsey reassuringly. "Now why don't you wash your hands? Then we'll go to the car and bring in your bags. I brought along our breakfast. Something new: Granny's Granola."

Andrea plucked the paper from Mark's fingers. She read the message and her mouth went slack. Her wide eyes fell on Lindsey who was chattering to Ginny as she dried her hands on a towel. The monologue continued as the two of them walked out the door. Mark followed Andrea's gaze, heartsick. Lindsey sounded like her old, voluble self. Now this.

Andrea turned abruptly to face him. The blue pencil fell to the floor. "What on earth is the DEH?"

"Department of Environmental Health."

She sucked in her breath. "You know what this is about, don't you?" Her dark eyes drilled into him, accusatory and afraid.

He nodded. "Things have happened very fast. Let's go into the study."

He preceded her, carrying coffee paraphernalia on a tray. At his desk he made room for the mugs like an orderly preparing a sick room. He wasn't sure yet who the patient would be, but the prospect of sharing his heavy burden gave him a small, anxious lift. He watched Andrea close the door behind her.

She stood next to the sofa with her back as straight as a column of copy, eyes wide with worry. The headline across her face read *Prepared for the Worst*.

Mark handed her a cup of coffee, sat down next to her, and started talking. He had unloaded most of the story before, on George Alder. Now there were ugly new chapters to add, and Mark spared his wife no detail. The waste turning up all over the West Side. Carlos's chilling encounter at Glenwater Place. Natalie's description of the outbound Biovak fleet. The picture of big-time foul play forming in his own besieged mind.

When he finished Andrea sat very still. Hardly a muscle had moved the entire time he talked, but the skin across her fine cheekbones faded from creamy to cretaceous.

"Those people killed Wiggles," she finally said, looking away. She picked up a needlepoint pillow Ginny had given them that read "Don't Get Mad, Get Even."

"Wiggles must have unearthed something illicit over at Helen's," she continued, processing the story. "And now the people who dump the stuff are threatening Lindsey because of the discoveries you've made at Hancock's." She fixed her eyes on Mark. "You can't talk to George Alder again. It's too dangerous."

Mark got up and poured himself another jolt of caffeine. She was right. The person who put the note in Lindsey's backpack had some way of knowing about his conversation with George. Maybe Hancock's phone was tapped. The ease with which they'd reached his daughter frightened him.

Andrea rose and stood. "Mark, they killed our dog and threatened Lindsey. We're talking about our child." Her voice cracked.

He looked at her anguished expression and felt a constriction in his chest. "We're also talking about an enterprise that threatens people far beyond our own family." His voice fell to a near whisper. "Don't you see? Hancock's—the business I now own—appears to be a conduit for the criminal distribution of biohazardous medical waste. City trash collection may be another. The scheme works because the people who know are either paid off or too scared to speak or...."

"Or what?"

"Or dead."

Andrea stood as blank and staring as a starlet in the waxworks. A chill rushed through Mark. He forced his eyes away from hers. Fred Dunn's death had never been explained to his complete satisfaction. A scoop of rubble dropped by accident precisely where Hancock's owner stood? Mark looked back at Andrea.

"They've already contaminated Glenwater Place, where hundreds of people will soon live, work, shop, and eat. The development opens in two weeks."

He raked his fingers through his hair. "And think of Hancock's retail customers. Helen. Beth. Ginny. Countless more we've never met. The hazards reach far beyond our own family, and way beyond Hancock's. I can't sit back and do nothing."

Andrea lifted a cup of cold coffee to her lips and put it down again. "Let's send Lindsey to Ellen's," she said suddenly. "Today. We won't tell anybody."

Of course, Mark thought. Ginny's house clearly wasn't safe. Lindsey adored her Aunt Ellen and Uncle Eddie. Their restored Victorian house in rural Wisconsin would be the perfect hideout. As long as all of them—Mark, Andrea, and Ginny—kept Lindsey's whereabouts unknown. A shard of alarm cut through him as Ginny walked into the room.

"Lindsey's upstairs," Ginny said.

Andrea poured her mother-in-law a cup of coffee from the thermos on the tray. Mark stared at the two women while ice water trickled through his veins. "Did either of you tell anyone that Lindsey was staying at Ginny's?"

The women looked at each other and shook their heads.

"I know I didn't," Andrea said with conviction. "All I've talked about morning, noon, and night is newsletters."

"Lindsey and I were regular hermits," Ginny offered. "I even skipped my garden club."

Mark slammed his coffee mug on the table, splashing brown liquid across the polished surface. He and he alone had revealed his daughter's location.

"I'll be back later."

"Where are you going?"

He was already out the door. He backed the Cherokee around Ginny's car and beyond the half-empty trash cans sitting next to the curb. No battered white van would come near Palm Street that day. Not a single bootlegged baggie. And Mark knew why.

*   *   *   *

At Hancock's, Mark hurried into his office and went directly to the file cabinet. The drawer he jerked open held Maggie's immaculately ordered expense receipts for the current year. He pulled the telephone bills.

Fanning the phone receipts on his desk, he selected the bill for April and spread the itemized charges on top of the other papers. Then he flipped through his Rolodex and jotted down two telephone numbers. Home and office for George Alder.

Hand trembling, he ran his finger down the date column on the bill to April twenty-third, the day before Fred Dunn was killed. Twelve calls were made out of Hancock's immediate zone that day. He glanced at the numbers he had written down. Not one of those twelve calls went to Fred's old friend at the Department of Environmental Health.

Was George mistaken about the day he said Fred phoned? Mark searched backward through the bill. April twenty-second, twenty-first, twentieth—back a whole week, then two.

The truth stared up at Mark in painful clarity. George Alder, the kindly man he trusted like a father, was part of it too.

CHAPTER 23

▼

Ellen and Eddie were out of town. They had gone to celebrate their first wedding anniversary at the same inn in Vermont where they had spent their honeymoon. La Petite Armoire, it was called, in the vicinity of the Green Mountains. Andrea found out from Ellen's house sitter, who gave her the phone number of the rustic establishment.

"We even have the same room," her sister burbled to Andrea over the long-distance line. "With the same calico comforter, the same ruffled pillows, and the same dried flower arrangement where I stuck some baby's breath from my bridal bouquet. It's still there!"

Ellen said she and Eddie would return to Wisconsin on Wednesday night, and Lindsey would be welcome to arrive Thursday and stay as long as necessary. "You know we'll love having her," Ellen said.

Andrea hadn't explained the details of the emergency, only that she and Mark faced serious problems in his new business and felt Lindsey would be better off away from the stress—far away, especially if she could visit her favorite aunt and uncle.

"I'll overlook the fact that we're her only aunt and uncle," Ellen said with a chuckle.

"There's one more thing," Andrea added. "Don't tell anyone she's coming."

Ellen had inherited more than their Great Aunt Sarah's crystal punch bowl and their Grandfather Blair's ivory-handled walking sticks. She also got the family gene for grit, a gift as dazzlingly hard-edged as the glass in her cupboard and as smartly brandished as the canes by her front door. Ellen's courage in a crisis had been legend since the day she outran a swarm of angry bees while the rest of the family watched in horror from the front porch. Rather than lead the revved-up stingers toward the open mouths and bare, waving arms on the porch, Ellen ran zigzag across the lawn, back and forth to the road and out of sight like a crazed Pied Piper. The bees never found her, but Andrea did, twenty minutes later, swinging high on the big swing set in the playground of the school where Ellen attended fourth grade.

Andrea hung up the phone on her desk knowing Lindsey would be as safe with Ellen as anywhere on Earth, but not until Thursday. For five more days, she and Mark would have to act as though they acquiesced to the hoods who threatened their daughter's life. Do nothing. Say nothing. Simply succumb. And then what? She swiveled in her chair.

It was the first of June. The landscape outside her windows looked radiant. Across the green expanse of lawn bloomed masses of flowers: jasmine, agapanthus, lavish masses of pure white roses. Andrea picked up the receiver and rang Hancock's.

"Hi, darling," she said, trying to sound nonchalant. "The swim meet has been postponed until Thursday. The coach had to go out of town."

"Uh, I see." Mark responded. "Just a second."

Andrea heard him say something to Rudy about a shipment of red twig dogwood. In a moment he was back.

"Thanks for letting me know. By the way, my phone isn't tapped. It's worse. I'll tell you later."

Worse? What could be worse? Andrea's heart ached. Her husband sounded like a man at the bottom of a deep, dark hole.

Mark spoke again. "I'll order Lindsey's plane ticket as soon as we hang up. Thursday morning, right?"

"Right," she answered, keeping her voice steady. The next few days were going to be difficult for all of them. "Would you mind stopping on the way home to rent some movies for her?"

"Sure."

"Thanks. It's going to be a long weekend." She didn't want to hang up.

"I know."

She heard him disconnect, and her eyes glistened. She fumbled the receiver back into its cradle, sunk by the weight of the gross unfairness of things. How could a man's dream, so clean and straightforward and so joyfully pursued, turn into such a quagmire?

Through the puddles in her eyes the roses outside her window wavered on their stems like water lilies. She blinked and stared at the blossoms until they shivered into focus. Nine prize-winning rose bushes—Mark's surprise to her on their ninth anniversary. French Lace Floribundas. From Hancock's.

The tears that had lined up to gush forth flowed instead to some furious hot core within her. She sat upright in her chair. Clear-eyed and steaming, she turned her fury on the criminals who killed her dog, threatened her daughter, and threw her husband into the crisis of his life.

"If you think we're giving up, you're sadly mistaken," she announced in the direction of the flower-laden bushes. She spun her chair away from the desk and hurried outside.

*   *   *   *

Mark rented *Babes in Toyland*, *Black Beauty*, and *The Brave Little Toaster*—movies he grabbed quickly off the alphabetical shelves. He hoped the films would keep Lindsey occupied while he and Andrea planned their next move. Once Lindsey was out of harm's way, they wouldn't have time to waste. He tossed the bag into the Cherokee and headed home.

The garbage cans were gone from the curb. Good, he thought with a surge of gratitude for Andrea, who undertook can-hauling duty. Both of them would have to carry on as normally as possible for the time being, at least until Lindsey departed. Then they would have more room to maneuver. But maneuver how?

As he drove up the driveway the strain squeezed his head like a helmet. If Biovak was in cahoots with the Department of Environmental Health, who else might be involved? He locked the Jeep and crossed the lawn, eyeing the four empty trash barrels that rested by the side of the house, trying not to imagine what gory, illegal rubbish they had harbored. The sheer audacity of this scam still astounded him.

He spotted Lindsey in the backyard twirling the old blue hula hoop around her neck. The trick rendered her speechless but she managed a bobbing, lopsided grin when she noticed him walking across the lawn. Beyond Lindsey he saw Andrea wearing a pair of filthy jeans, leaning on a shovel. She raised her head.

"Oh, hello, honey."

He gaped at the scene in front of him.

"I never was much good at gardening. But I think you'll find the rose bed well cultivated."

The six blooming rose bushes sat side by side on their root balls, upright, leaning into each other, or tipped out flat like a row of elaborately hatted church women who drank too much punch. Past the bushes the recently vacated soil in the rose bed looked beaten up and lumpless. The bushes hadn't been cultivated, they'd been evacuated.

Mark crept closer. Sweat glowed on Andrea's fine-boned face and wicked into her hairline like gel. Her streaked T-shirt stuck becomingly against her chest. She placed a hand on her hip and smiled.

"You were right about one thing."

"What's that?"

"You said we'd both be sweating bullets pretty soon."

He touched her sleek, damp hair. Placing his wife and child in mortal danger was not what he intended when he purchased Hancock's.

"What did you find?" he asked.

"Enough to know it's been going on at least two years." She delved into the pocket of her jeans and extracted what looked like part of a slide for diagnostic testing.

"That's all?"

"That's all. In a thirty by four-foot planting bed for nine large rose bushes. Believe me, I've covered every millimeter."

"They were cautious in those days."

"Yes."

"Helen's new planter box is a tenth the size and it yielded eight fragments."

"They're getting careless."

"Or confident," Mark said. "Mel Beckman told me Shand is planning to expand into Texas and Florida. Biovak needs capital to grow." He sat the bag of videos on the grass and scooped up a handful of loose soil from the rose bed. "Hazardous waste disposal generates a lot of cash. Especially when the hauler figures out how to circumvent enough treatment and disposal fees. People can be bought. I found out today Shand has at least one ally at the DEH."

Andrea looked at him sharply.

"George Alder."

She gasped.

"He knew Lindsey was staying with Ginny. What's more, Hancock's phone records show Fred never called him. Alder contacted Beth and me to find out what, if anything, Fred told us before he died."

"And to make sure you would go straight to George with your own discoveries," Andrea said, the sense of the plan dawning on her.

Mark nodded. "The quantities of new trash we've found indicate a certain reckless assurance. Clearly they've bought or threatened an army of local gardeners—immigrants, probably, like Carlos. Fortunately Carlos withstood the pressure—so far. I wouldn't be surprised if public officials other than George are in on it, or at least persuaded to look the other way. Building inspectors, a council member or two, some fuzz."

Andrea let the shovel fall to the ground. "So where do we turn?"

"Look at me! Daddy, look!" Lindsey shouted, spinning the hula hoop around her knees.

Mark stood close to Andrea watching their seven-year-old play. "That's what we have to figure out."

CHAPTER 24

▼

"Natalie, I'd like you to meet my friend Rick Edwards. Rick, this is Natalie Dunn."

Rick held Natalie's hand a shade longer than necessary, Mark noted with interest. She wore a short denim skirt and the radiant smile of a person who thought this hastily arranged Sunday lunch was a party instead of an emergency. Rick thought the same thing. He sparkled brightly in Natalie's direction, then beamed his charm on Andrea, who accepted a kiss and a large bunch of lilies.

Mark and Andrea wanted the lunch to look like a party. Their daughter was safely installed inside the house with a playmate, a sitter, and an eagerly anticipated movie. Mark had placed a table on the lawn in the back yard on which Andrea laid pale yellow linens, polished silver, gleaming crystal. Zydeco music played softly through outdoor speakers, Buckwheat Zydeco, just loud enough to shield their conversation from any passerby who might be interested. Andrea wore a crisp white sundress. Mark served Pimm's Cup. They did not look like a couple whose world was falling apart.

"I understand you're a graphic designer," Natalie said to Andrea as the four of them strolled across the grass.

"Yes, newsletters, mostly. *Healthy Times, LA Business Report—*"

"*LA Business Report* is yours? I subscribe to that. And I recommend it to my students."

"Natalie's in town to prepare for a guest lecture," Mark explained. "*Economic Re-development…*," he looked at Natalie.

"*…in Los Angeles via Small Business Growth*," she finished. "Mark helped me update the research by introducing me to a new company called Biovak. *LA Business Report* did a piece on it recently."

Mark and Andrea exchanged glances. Andrea removed the lid from a ceramic tureen shaped like a cabbage and began to ladle cucumber soup into bowls.

"I'd like to hear that lecture," Rick said, snapping out of the trance that Natalie's velvety voice had thrown over him. "Is it open to the public?"

"I'll send you an invitation," she replied, smiling.

Rick handed Natalie a business card. She swept her violet eyes across the logo.

"Burton-Abbey. You've got quite a reputation."

"You can say that again," Mark said. Rick shot him a look.

"A positive image in the business community, I should say," Natalie rejoined. "What did I read recently? Something about cartons?"

Rick lit up like a Labrador who just sighted a duck. "Uh-huh. In the *Journal.* We're converting to unbleached packaging materials. White cartons look better but they give off chlorine vapors when they're burned. The environmental impact of materials has become a factor in Burton-Abbey's purchasing. I'm giving a talk myself this month. *The Responsible Life-cycle of Products.*"

Andrea dropped the ladle loudly into the tureen. Mark looked at her. Neither of them could continue the charade much longer.

"If you will pull your chairs to the table we can start," Andrea said briskly.

Rick leapt up to scoot Natalie's chair across the grass. Mark beat him to Andrea's and took the opportunity to place a steady hand on her shoulder. The four of them jostled into place around the table and unfurled their napkins.

Andrea picked up her spoon and dipped into the chilled soup. Natalie and Rick did the same, murmuring compliments. Mark watched his friends ruefully, knowing he was about to ruin the false perfection of that Sunday afternoon. He cleared his throat.

"Uh, Natalie, Rick. We have something to discuss."

Rick patted his napkin against his lips. "Right. The real reason you called this meeting, har, har." He winked at Natalie.

"He's not joking." Andrea put down her spoon. "We invited both of you here for a reason."

Natalie drilled perceptive blue eyes into Andrea, then Mark, and a furrow creased her brow. "Tell us," she said softly.

✳   ✳   ✳   ✳

Next to gardening, the pastime Helen Woodley enjoyed most was walking, especially on a fine Sunday afternoon when she could inspect hedges and borders and colorful plantings all over the neighborhood. The Moores' gap garden was doing well, she noticed. In the narrow spaces between the pavers on their driveway, the couple had installed an inspired combination of deep red oxalis and bright green Irish moss. The Owens down the street had done the same with their sidewalk, using hardy Corsican mint. Whenever a crowd came or went, the Owens' trampled walkway smelled like juleps on Derby Day.

Helen strolled past the Whitmans' drought-resistant perennial garden, the Harris's hanging baskets of begonias, and the Browns' six-foot Matilija poppy, a fantastic bush with big white and yellow flowers that resembled fried eggs. She closed her eyes and inhaled the warm, sweetly scented air. Palm Street in June was paradise.

As she neared her own property, Helen heard music and voices. The Grants were having a garden party, she surmised, spotting a red sports car and a silver coupe of some sort parked in her neighbors' driveway. She cast sidelong glances toward the noise until she reached the short stretch of pavement with a direct line of vision into the Grants' backyard.

Helen prided herself on her consideration as a neighbor. She was exceedingly fond of Andrea and Mark, and knew their mutual affection rested, in part, on each homeowner's ability to turn eyes and ears the other direction. But on that balmy afternoon the sheer beauty of the scene in the Grants' carefully tended garden stopped Helen in her tracks.

Against a backdrop of deep green ivy and profusely blooming jasmine sat Andrea and Mark and another attractive couple around a yellow-skirted table laden with china. Helen touched her sunglasses. Andrea looked ethereal in white. Mark looked like a movie star warming up for an Oscar nomination. He was leaning forward, speaking in a low voice that had apparently enthralled his listeners.

The guests, an uncommonly handsome pair who looked familiar, sat with their eyes fixed on Mark. Helen believed she could have a myocardial infarction right there on the sidewalk and no one would notice.

While she watched, the male guest exclaimed something she couldn't hear and sprang from his chair. His yellow napkin fluttered to the grass. The young woman next to him retrieved the napkin and spoke. A gentle wind ruffled the tablecloth and music floated across the fragrant air. Andrea stood, placed bowls on a tray, passed a platter, and sat down. No one seemed to be eating much, Helen observed, lost in the richness of the pantomime.

Through her narrow field of vision she saw the standing young man reach for his wine glass and drain it in a single, dramatic tilt of his head. Andrea pointed to something in the yard beyond Helen's view. Everyone looked. Mark ran his fingers through his hair, a gesture Helen had seen him make before when he was agitated. Was he agitated?

She squinted in his direction. She thought Mark had seemed unnaturally calm on Thursday when he collected the surgical debris buried in her planter boxes. Now his hair stuck out where he had rumpled it and he was motioning with both hands. Suddenly the woman guest began to speak, like a person with a bright idea. Her companion sat down heavily and interjected a few words. Andrea spilled red wine on her sundress. Everyone started talking at once.

At that very moment an old white van, a real jalopy, rounded the corner to Palm Street and rattled past Helen, smothering the music with engine noise and the garden scents with noxious fumes. The vehicle banged down the block and disappeared. Helen wrinkled her nose in disgust and decided to hurry home before anything else happened to upset the loveliness of the afternoon.

✳   ✳   ✳   ✳

"I still say we need proof. Irrefutable proof," Rick declared above the other three voices. "We can't take on Biovak and the DEH based on some old white vans people have seen."

"Shhh!" Andrea cautioned, dabbing water on her dress. She glanced toward a noise in the street. Mark followed her gaze and glimpsed a person disappearing behind the hedge. It was only Helen.

"Keep your voice down, Edwards."

"Rick is correct," Natalie said calmly. "All we have now is circumstantial evidence that a criminal network exists."

Mark pushed a piece of marinated roast beef around his plate. He wasn't surprised that Rick and Natalie viewed the crisis as their problem too. Natalie still felt a strong attachment to the landscape business her grandfather had founded. And Rick built his entire career on the lifesaving products that were now fouling the environment. Safe disposal had become a hot button in his industry, and Rick himself held a finger on the switch.

Nonetheless, Mark felt touched by the depth of his friends' concern. As he had hoped, both of them assumed they would be a part of the solution—in spite of the obvious risks. He regarded Natalie and Rick gratefully and took a deep breath. He had thought through the next step already.

"We have to get the tracking documents."

Silence struck as the implications of Mark's statement became clear. Tracking documents. The records waste haulers keep of the cargo they pick up, transport, treat, and dump. Unless the crooks at Biovak went to the trouble of expertly doctoring every invoice that accompanied every truckload—and why should they, with no fear of an audit by the DEH?—the company's own records could supply the evidence Mark needed.

Mark looked at Rick, Natalie, and Andrea. Music fell over the table, unappreciated, like a soft blanket over a corpse. They would have to raid Biovak's files.

Lindsey and her playmate burst out of the kitchen and ran across the lawn. Their sitter appeared in the doorway.

"Wintermission!" Lindsey shouted, stopping next to Andrea. "Hi, Uncle Rick." She looked shyly from Rick to Natalie.

"Natalie, I'd like you to meet our daughter, Lindsey, and Paula, her friend from school," Andrea said automatically, trained from birth in these rituals. The introductions gave them all a breather. Andrea got up and cleared plates while Lindsey related the entire plot of *Babes in Toyland.* Mark went to make espresso and came back. Natalie watched Rick morph from a calculating counterterrorist to a jolly uncle who attracted seven-year-olds the way peas attract perch. In a little while the sitter reeled in her charges along with a plate of walnut bars, and the girls went back inside.

Andrea and Mark sat down. The four adults resumed their planning in low, urgent tones, ignoring the remains of their dessert and the lengthening shadows, until the sun dropped well below the peak of the house and evening chilled the yard. When Rick and Natalie rose to leave, they embraced Andrea and Mark and each other like old friends who wouldn't meet again for years. Or at least until the following Thursday.

CHAPTER 25

▼

On Thursday morning Lindsey grinned good-bye and boarded the plane with one hand gripping her new purple knapsack and the other holding on to an instantly adored flight attendant who promised to give her a tour of the cockpit.

Andrea watched her daughter disappear down the gangway with a mixture of sadness and relief. The preceding few days had put a strain on all of them, while Lindsey chafed at her restricted schedule and Mark tiptoed around Hancock's like a man walking on a wire. It galled Andrea, too, to behave as though they had caved in to the men who threatened Lindsey, yet fear for their daughter's safety gave them few options.

Andrea slipped on her sunglasses and hurried toward the main terminal, hoping no one had followed her and her daughter to the airport. She had read enough spy thrillers to know that amateurs stood out like dopes. Nevertheless, she had done her best. She had driven Lindsey to Pico Press, where they parked and walked in the front door, through the building, and out the back door to neighboring Alpha Print, where Andrea called a taxi. She planned to follow a similarly circuitous route in reverse on the way home.

If Mark's suspicions concerning the death of Fred Dunn were correct, the precaution made sense, and also seemed pathetically inadequate. The more information they pieced together about Biovak's ruthless methods, the more the multimillion dollar operation resembled a reign of terror. Mounting evidence pointed to the illegal distribution of medical waste as the growth industry of the decade. Mark, unfortunately, had gotten in on the ground floor.

Andrea stepped through the automatic doors of the passenger terminal and scanned the crowd on the sidewalk. A limousine the length of a rail car, license plate *TALENT1,* sat by the curb generating a froth of activity by a dozen traffic cops and baggage handlers. She picked her way around the throng to the taxi line, and in no time was wedged into the sprung back seat of a decrepit vehicle shimmying up La Tijera. The driver, a hirsute young man with limited verbal skills, compensated for his meager vocabulary by playing talk radio at high volume. He seemed engrossed in a discussion about the relative merits of commercial paper and government securities.

Andrea stared out the window as her mind turned to Mark and Natalie and Rick. Were they as nervous as she? Probably, though Natalie seemed like a cool customer. Fred's daughter could easily have said good-bye and walked away from the whole shabby mess. She chose instead to help Mark defend the company that bore her grandfather's name. Andrea gave both Natalie and Rick high marks and depthless gratitude for their loyalty.

The truth was, Mark's intricately calibrated scheme would never work without all four of them—if it were going to work at all. Teamwork, Mark always said, could accomplish the impossible. The taxi ripped around a corner, and Andrea grabbed the back of the cracked leather seat. Lindsey's departure marked the beginning of a bold plan that put all of them at risk, professionally and personally. Like some of the passes Mark threw in college, it was a long, long shot. Yet none of them could come up with a better idea, so they had little choice but to get set, listen to the audibles, and run.

Somewhere near the Santa Monica interchange the words *Glenwater Place* yanked Andrea out of her reverie.

...the West Side's newest gathering place, with movie theaters, cafés, fine dining, beautiful gardens, and shops galore opens one week from this Saturday, the radio announcer declared. *Join me and a host of celebrities from noon to six for the gala celebration in this spectacular landmark setting...*

The driver abruptly lowered the volume. "We take the Santa Monica?"

"Uh, yes. West."

When he raised the sound again, the commercial had ended. Andrea had heard enough to make her shudder. Ten days until the opening of Glenwater Place. After that, Hancock's showcase project would buzz with people day and night, exposing them to what hidden risks?

She eyed the Algerian ivy that grew profusely on both sides of the freeway. Was there any real danger in sipping cappuccino at a table two feet from waste-contaminated landscaping? Or walking on a sidewalk across buried biohazards? Maybe not in the short term. But the long-term prospects for planting hazardous trash in gardens were dire. Tainted soil, plants, food. A compromised water supply. The inevitable spread of disease. The death of gardens and their hope, patience, and quiet joy. Hancock's unwitting involvement in the foul play made Andrea's head throb.

The driver exited on Bundy and worked his way through heavy traffic to Pico Boulevard. Andrea paid him off in front of Alpha Print and walked quickly through the building, nodding to a press operator she recognized. She hurried out the back door and across the sidewalk to Pico Press where her Volvo sat inconspicuously in a lot filled with vehicles. Nobody appeared to skulk nearby.

Wondering whether she had foiled a pack of pursuers or merely entertained her daughter, Andrea exited the benign, stalker-free parking lot, and drove unmolested to an art supply store to pick up the items she had ordered. After a quick stop for strong coffee, she returned home, locked the door behind her, and went directly to her studio.

As she had anticipated, the cerise poster board, color 2106, matched almost exactly the cherry red security pass Natalie received during her visit to Biovak. Red, the color for Thursday. Shand handed that information to Natalie gift wrapped.

Andrea held the badge next to the poster board and decided the infinitesimal color difference would disappear once the card rested inside its cheap plastic badge holder. Shand was a tightwad, no doubt about it.

She cut three neat rectangles, two-and-a-quarter by three–and-a-half inches, and lined them up like boxcars on her drawing board. One each for Mark, Natalie, and Rick, just in case. Andrea had argued vociferously to be included, but lost to Mark's calm voice of reason.

Natalie, he explained, must go along because she had toured Biovak and knew the layout. Mark was familiar with the tracking documents they needed. And Rick would be far safer than Andrea in the role of undercover lookout on the dicey streets of the warehouse district. Besides, the three of them needed someone out of harm's way who knew they were inside Biovak and could send help if anything went wrong. Andrea would stay at home.

She stared at Biovak's security pass and shivered. Enough could go wrong at that place without someone noticing the fake credentials. Fortunately, Shand's cheap badges were easy to duplicate.

One of his cost-containment measures, she discovered, was to create a corporate logo out of readily available commercial templates instead of commissioning a designer to draw something original. Or maybe he did hire a designer who gave him the hack job he deserved. It would serve him right.

Biovak's logo combined the Y junction symbol from a traffic control template with a quarter-inch circle centered inside the Y like an olive in a martini. Like scum in a funnel, she thought with disgust. She positioned the template over the lower left corner of one of the blank badges and carefully inked in the junction symbol. When the funnel was dry she would add the scum.

Biovak's real badges were printed rather than hand lettered, but the difference would be imperceptible to a casual observer. At least she hoped so. She laid her pen down and flexed her fingers.

She planned to duplicate the lettering on the badges with dry transfer sheets, a process she used routinely on paste-ups. It required choosing a matching typeface and rubbing the letters off a commercial transfer sheet onto the poster board. Nothing complicated. She would do the word *VISITOR* in three-eighths-inch Futura and, next to the logo, *Biovak, Inc.* in quarter-inch Modern Bold, just like the sample. One pass each for Mark, Natalie, and Rick. She picked up a burnishing tool and went to work. In little more than twenty-four hours, all of them would know—one way or another—how convincing the badges were.

Shadows were lengthening in the garden outside her studio windows and she had nearly completed the third badge when the telephone rang. Rather than interrupt the delicate transfer of scum into funnel, she let her answering machine click into motion. The steely voice identified itself as an official from the Los Angeles International Airport. "Mrs. Grant, please return this call as soon as possible." He began to recite his beeper number.

Ignoring the work on her table, Andrea snatched up the receiver. "Hello? Hello? This is Andrea Grant."

CHAPTER 26

▼

Mark spent Thursday at Hancock's trying to act normal, a feat under Maggie's perceptive surveillance. Since the morning she had fielded distraught phone calls from Helen, Beth, and Ginny, Maggie knew Hancock's and her boss were in deep trouble, no matter what George Alder had said. To Mark's intense relief, his bookkeeper remained as cool and efficient as a nurse in an emergency room, never pressing for details of the miraculous cure he planned. Maggie seemed to understand that—for now, at least—to assist him meant simply to wait and watch.

Carlos was worried too. Mark tried to reassure Fred's young protégé that the man who accosted him in Camellia Court didn't have a credential to stand on. Carlos nevertheless walked around like a person expecting bad news. He reined in his restless energy by nearly memorizing the *License Law and Reference Book*, and by taking the day off to appear, at long last, for the contractor's licensing exam. Mark hoped he wasn't too over-prepared to pass. Carlos had mastered a symphony when the simple tune of the computer-assisted multiple choice test required only a space bar and four arrow keys.

The absence of his top assistant gave Mark plenty to do in the nursery, a welcome distraction from the worry that gurgled in his gut.

Around noon he checked his watch. Nine hours until he, Natalie, and Rick slipped into the rat hole Shand called a business.

"Excuse me," a customer said, tapping the pavement with the toe of her black cowboy boot. "I've got spittlebugs."

By the time Mark fixed her up with a spray bottle, gloves, and an ample supply of Sevin, several more anxious amateurs awaited his ministrations. The last of them trundled his purchases away just as a new shipment of perennials arrived, and Mark spent the next hour directing the placement of daylilies, dianthus, ivy geraniums, and Shasta daisies. Then more customers, a round of paperwork, and it was time to go home.

As he rose to leave the office, Maggie answered the phone. Frowning, she switched the call to him. "It's for you."

At the other end of the line a gravel-voiced individual delivered a message that made Mark's heart stop. "Mr. Grant, we have your daughter."

Mark stared, sightless, at the grain in the old maple desk. He sank into a chair. "What...who are you?"

"Insurance agents," the voice sneered. "Your daughter, Lindsey, is our little insurance policy. We weren't too pleased when you tried to send her away. If you're thinking of blabbing to the DEH you'd better think again."

Mark held the receiver close to his lips and returned the threat. "If you harm a hair on her head I'll make it my life's work to see you fry," he spit into the mouthpiece, trembling.

"Don't worry, your daughter's fine, and we plan to take excellent care of her," the voice continued, undaunted. "She's quite the little swimmer. We will return her, undrowned, when you have had a few hours to reflect on your options." The voice had paused to let the word "undrowned" sink in.

Mark swallowed and said nothing.

"Don't underestimate us, Mr. Grant. We can grab your daughter, your wife, your mother, or you anytime we please. I would advise you to get with the program. Are you listening?"

"I'm listening," Mark managed.

"First, call your airline and say Lindsey is all right; she went to the bathroom, missed her plane and was smart enough to take a cab home. If you want to see her before bedtime you will do this."

Mark said nothing.

"Then, I strongly recommend that you act like the businessman you always wanted to be. Follow through on your contracts. Open Glenwater Place. Look the other way when you have to. Keep your mouth shut and you'll be a big success."

The phone went dead.

Mark drove home in a blind sweat. Andrea met him at the door, having called Maggie and heard he was on the way. They held each other wordlessly for a long moment, then went inside to compare what they knew.

According to the official who phoned Andrea, Lindsey's flight out of Los Angeles had been delayed at the gate due to a problem with the air-conditioning. He told Andrea that because of the heat the crew invited the passengers to disembark. A flight attendant escorted Lindsey to a chair in the waiting area and left her there while she returned to assist other passengers. When the flight attendant returned, Lindsey was gone.

"Apparently another passenger disappeared too," Andrea informed Mark. "A man who paid cash for his ticket two days ago." She paused to blow her nose. "How could they have known Lindsey was leaving on that flight?"

He paced the room, looked at his watch. "I have no idea. Clearly they're still worried I'll go to the DEH. The smug son of a bitch who called me said nothing about our plans for tonight." He ran his fingers through his hair. "They're trying to scare us, but they don't know as much as they think."

Andrea looked at him and swallowed. Both of them understood what was coming next.

"We've got to risk it," Mark said, taking her hands in his. "Our red security badges are only good today, Thursday. We don't know the colors for the other days, and next week will be too late." He spoke as persuasively as he could while the specter of their kidnapped child held him by the throat.

"Shand wouldn't dream we'd pilfer documents from Biovak while they're holding our daughter. They'll be off their guard. I'm willing to bet he and his cronies don't even know we've connected Biovak to the dumping. We'll stay away from the DEH, the police, and every other outsider who might threaten their operation until Lindsey is free. Our only hope of stopping them is to gather enough evidence ourselves to blow the operation sky high."

White-faced, Andrea stared at him. The arguments seemed logical, but she swallowed them like a dose of caustic chemicals. As she rose from her chair she looked older, defeated. "I'll call the airline," she said. "And Ellen."

He watched her go, hating their situation, filled with a volatile mix of anger and anxiety. What he needed was poise, he told himself. Poise. The prissy little word his football coach used when rabid, raging players stood around frothing at the mouth, butting heads. "Stay poised and crush 'em."

Mark checked the time again and forced himself to focus on the contents of his briefcase. Flashlight, cameras, extra film, batteries. A measly arsenal. He tucked in two black plastic bags and arranged several file folders on top.

Andrea returned, slumped by the weight of her lies to the airline and her sister. She hovered near Mark, wanting to help. "Promise you'll be careful. That man was right. We must not underestimate Shand."

Mark closed his briefcase. In the waning light of evening her skin looked translucent, a pale sea around the dark shoreline of each eye. He touched her cheek, glad to the bone that her role that night was to stay home, out of harm's way.

"I promise," he said softly, wrapping her in his arms.

No, he was not going to underestimate Julian Shand. He was counting on Shand to be nowhere near Biovak. The company's founder had boasted to Natalie that the consolidation warehouse ran like a clock, twenty-four hours a day, although he himself rarely went near the place after dark. "I'm usually out generating new business, raising capital for expansion, and so forth," the great schmoozer had said. He also told Natalie that Biovak's night shift operated under the supervision of a rising star named Amp, whom Shand had rescued from a life of petty crime. *Sure.*

Fortunately for them, Amp never laid eyes on Natalie, a pleasure Mark hoped to deny the gangster/supervisor once again. If Amp got in their way…. Mark gulped. He hoped Amp wouldn't.

He released Andrea gently and looked at the clock. Almost nine.

"Call from the Jeep when you're out of there," she said, handing him his briefcase. "Be safe."

✳   ✳   ✳   ✳

Natalie and Rick were waiting at a bus stop near Rick's condominium on Wilshire. Like Mark, Natalie wore tailored slacks and a blazer and carried a briefcase. Rick had on a gray hooded sweatshirt and a black leather fanny pack. All three of them wore running shoes.

Rick climbed into the back seat. Natalie sat in front. The news about Lindsey's kidnapping drew a gasp from Natalie. Rick let out a low whistle.

"Our little crap game has entered the big leagues," Rick said, taking in the implications. "Are you sure you want to go ahead with this?"

"I'm sure," Mark answered. "And so is Andrea."

They sat in the Jeep while Mark repeated the arguments he had made at home. The badges. The urgency. The surprise. The likelihood that the kidnappers were trying to scare them, and would return Lindsey that evening, unharmed. And the undeniable fact that exposing Biovak was the only way to end Shand's threats. He looked from Rick to Natalie. "Are you two still with me?"

An unspoken current ran between the passengers. Natalie reached out and touched Mark's arm. "We're with you."

Night had blackened the sky by the time Mark eased the Cherokee off the freeway, up Central Avenue, and into the chilling maze of steel-shuttered buildings that was the warehouse district. He and his co-conspirators eyed the neighborhood and fell silent.

Hulking, graffiti-covered walls gave way to a smattering of dingy hotels and low-rent cantinas where drinkers, addicts, and prostitutes lined up ghoulishly under flashing strings of colored lights. A hundred pairs of bloodshot eyes followed the Cherokee's progress down the shuddering cement of Seventh Street. Even inside the tightly closed, air-conditioned vehicle there rose a pungent smell of overripe vegetables, sawdust, diesel fuel, and urine.

"Eau de rue," Natalie commented, observing a cardboard encampment. A truck thundered past and the Jeep shook.

Suddenly a wild-haired wraith darted across their headlights with a crowbar in his hand. Mark stomped on the brake and the apparition disappeared in the darkness. Against the steering wheel Mark's white knuckles stood out like bones in a bag.

"Are we there yet?" Rick whined from the back seat. Mark heard him screw a lens into a camera.

Natalie ignored Rick's comment. "Three more blocks, then turn right," she said tersely.

Near Biovak they passed a fire burning in a bathtub. Mark slowed and approached Shand's fenced-in property with caution. *Biovak, Inc.*, a small sign read. The name alone gave Mark the willies. Through new chain-link on the east side of the property he could see a large paved area, four dimly lit loading docks and a closed garage door. In the back seat Rick began to snap pictures.

"That's where the inbound fleet unloads the waste it collects from customers," Natalie said, leaning toward the window. "The garage contains areas for painting and washing vehicles."

Mark nodded, recalling her description of the flawless inbound flotilla. Twenty or so impeccable white trucks bearing shiny red crosses sat idle near the inbound docks. About a dozen assorted other vehicles were parked nearby. There wasn't a soul in sight.

Mark drove to the corner and turned. The south side of the property offered a different scene entirely. At the far end of the warehouse they could see another bank of loading docks where people and vans converged busily in a cold, incandescent glare. Light shone brightly from each of five bays onto a queue of old white vehicles lined up and running like cars waiting at a gas pump. Mark checked his rearview mirror and continued cautiously forward.

"This wasn't happening the day I was here," Natalie said, peering at the activity on the docks. "Those old vans are the outbound fleet."

"They're receiving cargo," Rick observed.

Mark watched with narrowed eyes. Right. Cargo to dump all over West Los Angeles before trash collection in the morning. One of those vans would probably rattle up Palm Street before the sun rose. The muscles in his jaw began to jump.

Silhouetted against the light in each loading bay stood a man in a white suit handing bundles from a cart down to a van, one by one. The five loading docks served five queues of vehicles with drivers who maneuvered to the front of their line, leapt out, and ran around to fling open rear doors and receive their illicit payloads. Enough banged-up white vans were parked in the lot to keep the process going most of the night.

A beefy man with a clipboard appeared to be keeping track of the shipments. Mark guessed he was the supervisor, Amp. Rapid camera clicks from the back seat indicated Rick had spotted him too. Mark squinted at the T-shirted muscle man in the loading dock and hoped they wouldn't lay eyes on that formidable individual again.

He cracked his window. The dock workers were talking to the drivers and each other. Mark heard laughter. The men seemed unconcerned about the contents of those dark sacks, though most of them wore gloves. Mark counted twelve bags hefted into one vehicle before its driver slammed the door, swaggered to the driver's seat, climbed in, and drove off. The unmarked van sped across the lot and through an open gate where it became another anonymous rattletrap on the seething streets of LA.

"Oh, oh. Here comes one," Natalie warned, sinking into her seat.

Mark pulled his head low in his collar and tried to keep his eyes on the road straight ahead. He heard Rick dive from the back seat onto the floor. The driver who careened toward them seemed equally intent on anonymity, and clanked past without turning his head. Mark exhaled.

He drove quickly past the open gate and around the corner. Biovak occupied an entire city block. The west side of the plant appeared deserted and dim. A windowless cinderblock wall stretched bleakly from end to end, unrelieved by a single shrub or blade of growing grass. Around the next right turn they found a similar expanse of fence, dirt, and concrete interrupted halfway down the block by a rude gash that was Biovak's main entrance. Under a floodlight stood a glass-walled guard station and, in it, a guard. Farther down, on the opposite side of the street, the fire they had seen earlier still glowed eerily in the bathtub. Otherwise, the north side of the block was empty.

Rick poked his head between the seats. "At least we'll have no trouble finding a place to park."

Mark quickly passed the guard, turned right, and circled the block again, past the empty inbound docks on the east and the busy outbound operation on the south, with its open exit spewing chewed-up white vans driven by men who far surpassed Mark in scrunching down behind the wheel.

He turned the corner to the deserted west side of the property, extinguished the headlights, and pulled to the curb halfway up the block. Parked midway between the main gate on the north and the outbound gate on the south, the Jeep would be equally accessible— and inaccessible—from whichever exit they chose. It was the best he could do.

He handed the keys to Rick, who hung his camera on its neck strap under his sweatshirt. Natalie clipped her visitor's pass to her lapel. Mark did the same, and noticed his hand was shaking. He reached into the back seat for his briefcase. They checked their watches. It was nine twenty-eight.

CHAPTER 27

▼

Mark walked with Natalie up the deserted sidewalk to the northwest corner of Biovak's fenced-in property. A balmy wind against his skin was the only clue that this barren landscape belonged to southern California. Instead of palm trees rooted in soil there were steel shafts sunk in cement. Drainpipes climbed walls that begged for bougainvillea. Cinderblock stood where boxwood belonged. There was not an inkling of ocean or a glimmer of glamour. Under invasive pools of security lights the defoliated moonscape resembled a sound stage for someone's nightmare. But this bleak scene was real.

Mark and Natalie turned the gray corner and walked into view of the guardhouse halfway up the block. Mark touched the red visitor's badge attached to his jacket. He glanced sideways at Natalie, who was buttoning her navy blue blazer, shoulders squared, like a candidate at a job interview.

"Let me do the talking," he said in an undertone. "This guard may not like uppity broads."

Fortunately for him Natalie's attention was focused on the road-block ahead. Inside the glass-walled guard station the night watchman spotted them and rose to his feet. He had a neck like a sycamore. Mark plastered a pleasant expression on his face and lengthened his stride.

"Good evening," he said, extending his hand to the startled guard. "I'm Thurgood Churchill with American Coastal Bank. This is my colleague, Violet Beamer. Did Mr. Shand tell you we might stop by?"

Natalie glared at Mark, unimpressed by the aliases, then flashed her warmest smile at the watchman whose name tag read *Jefferson.* He looked about twenty years old. Jefferson studied the unexpected visitors with a frown.

Mark shifted his briefcase to his right hand and fished in a pocket for one of the American Coastal business cards Andrea had doctored up. Jefferson visibly tensed. His hand moved toward the holster on his hip. Mark extracted the card with what he hoped was a nonthreatening flourish and wondered whether he was about to be shot.

Jefferson held the card under his flashlight and said nothing.

"Mr. Jefferson," Natalie declared authoritatively. "The American Coastal loan review committee requires periodic unscheduled visits to customers' premises. The rule, you know, is spelled out in the Federal Banking Act." She paused. "Of 1983."

Would he fall for it? A similar strategy almost, but not quite, fooled Carlos. Mark watched the guard intently.

"Julian always cooperates," Natalie continued, velvet-voiced, changing tactics. "We go into the office, do some paperwork, and leave as unobtrusively as possible."

Mark glanced pointedly at the timepiece on his wrist. "It's a formality that doesn't take long. We know our way." He stepped forward.

An arm shot up like a gate on the Metrolink.

"Where'd you get those passes?"

Jefferson aimed a flashlight in the direction of Mark's pounding heart and peered at the plastic covered poster board. Mark hoped the badge wasn't bouncing against his chest.

"From Julian—red for Thursday. We have the complete set."

Was Natalie mistaken about the daily color code? Mark met Jefferson's slitty eyes and held them, thinking of linebackers he had stared down on the field.

"Okay," Jefferson finally said, handing back Mark's business card. "Sign in."

The guard handed a clipboard to Natalie and turned toward the electronic console inside the booth. Natalie glanced triumphantly at Mark and jotted *Violet I. Beamer* on the visitor roster. Mark noticed a pair of illegible names above hers. He was scrawling *Thurgood Churchill* on the line below *Violet I. Beamer* when Jefferson picked up the telephone and pressed two buttons. "I'll let Mr. Shand know you're here."

Before Mark could grab the receiver, Rick shot out of the darkness behind him and into Jefferson like a goat charging a rhino.

"What the—?" Jefferson managed to say before Rick deftly plunged a hypodermic needle deep into his tree trunk of a neck. In seconds, the mighty sycamore collapsed like a sack of leaves. Natalie reached across Jefferson's limp body and hung up the receiver. Mark removed the pistol from its holster, emptied the bullets into his own pocket, and over-handed the unloaded weapon into the black void beyond Biovak's security fence.

From the leather pouch on his belt, Rick produced a pint of whiskey and dumped most of it on Jefferson's dark cotton shirt. The rest he emptied into a pitiful patch of weeds next to the guardhouse.

"That little nightcap should hold him for a couple of hours," Rick said, helping Mark wrestle the unconscious form into the guard booth. He laid the empty bottle on Jefferson's wide chest. "He'll have a hell of a hangover, but no lasting effects."

"Thanks," Mark said.

"Burton-Abbey and Early Times are pleased to be of service." Rick picked up the syringe, pulled out the used needle, and inserted it into a small plastic container he retrieved from the stash on his belt. Mark noticed he was wearing surgical gloves.

"Am I to understand that Mr. Shand is in there?" asked Rick, tilting his head toward the building.

"Either he's on the premises or he has a two-digit phone number," Mark said, looking at the double doors. He couldn't believe their bad luck. Shand was the one person at Biovak he knew they couldn't con.

"We can go in anyway," Natalie urged. "The file room is near the front, not far from these doors. Shand is probably in back by the loading docks."

Mark had to agree. It seemed unlikely that Biovak's CEO would be hanging out in the file room at that hour, especially when all the action appeared to be on the south side of the building. With a jolt, Mark realized something else. Lindsey could be in there too.

"Yeah, okay," Rick said, agreeing with Natalie. "But if that cannibal comes sniffing around the file room, you two make like trees and leave, understand? This time I won't be right behind you to save your fancy asses."

Natalie looked at Mark, reading his mind. "You don't think they brought Lindsey here, do you?"

Mark both wished and worried they would find his daughter inside. How could he and Natalie pluck a seven-year-old from that pit without throwing the whole place into a panic? It seemed unlikely, however, that Shand would want Lindsey near his center of operations. He shuddered. The voice on the phone had mentioned swimming.

"No, I don't think she's here. If we do see her...." He didn't know how to finish. "Let's worry about that when the time comes."

Natalie nodded, turned to Rick, and kissed him on the cheek. "Thanks for coming to our rescue. Now watch your own hind end, okay?"

Their affection startled Mark. Natalie and Rick? He realized they must have seen each other—perhaps more than once—since the brunch on the previous Sunday.

Rick pressed a button on Jefferson's neatly labeled console, and the double doors to Biovak buzzed. Natalie started walking. Mark picked up his briefcase and followed her up the circular drive.

Inside the front doors stood an unmanned switchboard. The countertop above the switchboard was empty except for a critically ill chrysanthemum, a recent issue of *Sports Today,* and a black microphone. The console sat in the middle of a broad carpeted space from which corridors opened left and right. Natalie nodded toward the right, and Mark silently led the way.

The hall was dimly lit and very cold. Above the chill Mark smelled an odor that reminded him simultaneously of a hospital and a dump. The shiny linoleum corridor passed a cloakroom, a Coke machine, and men's and women's lavatories, then turned abruptly to the left. Mark peered around the corner and saw a row of closed, frosted glass doors that looked like offices. All were dark. They had guessed correctly; everyone—including Shand—was at the other end.

From the far reaches of the warehouse came the clang of metal, the hum of machinery, the shouts of men and women engaged in heavy labor. In the immediate vicinity, a person could hear a hypodermic needle drop.

Natalie pointed to the second door on the right. Mark stepped forward, tried the knob, and nodded. They went inside and closed the door. Light shone weakly through the frosted glass, otherwise the room was black. They groped for flashlights. Mark found his, switched it on, and gasped.

He blinked two or three times. Eyes? Yes, eyes stared directly at him, unblinking—and sightless.

Natalie sucked in her breath. She fumbled for her flashlight, and directed it on the vacant stare.

"My god."

Suspended in liquid at various depths inside a large glass container were dozens of eyeballs—blue, brown, green, gray—round, unflinching, and unquestionably dead. The grotesque collection sat on top of a file cabinet as nonchalantly as a jar of jelly beans. It took Mark and Natalie a moment to recover.

"I didn't see that before," she whispered.

"It probably isn't on the official tour," he said, sweeping his light around the room. File cabinets, table, computer—no additional pickled parts.

"Eyes are a nice touch in an office, don't you think?" He directed his light toward the labels on the file drawers, thankful that Biovak and its paper trail were only two years old. The ocular shrine did not inspire confidence. Fortunately, the first documents they needed weren't hard to find.

"*TD Generator,*" he read and pulled open a drawer. "Arranged by month." He closed the drawer and opened the one just below it. "They go back two years."

Mark handed the flashlight to Natalie and riffed quickly through the manila folders. "These are just like the tracking documents George Alder showed me," he said excitedly. "They're the forms Biovak gives to each medical waste generator and the DEH." He pulled a page and scanned the typed information. The paper clearly named Biovak as the hauler who made a regular collection on March 23 from a private hospital on the West Side, Saint Marks. Under *Type of Medical Waste* appeared a list that made Mark's hair prickle.

Fluid blood products, containers, and equipment

Laboratory waste, including human cultures, discarded live and attenuated vaccines, culture dishes, and devices used to transfer, inoculate, and mix cultures

Human surgery specimens and body tissues including amputations

Morgue, pathology, and autopsy waste including specimen containers, slides, body tissue, organs, and bones—

Mark swallowed and skipped to the next section.

Quantity: 324 biohazard bags

63 sharps containers

175 nonhazardous waste bags

120 mixed waste bags

Total: 13.43 tons

He shone the light behind the paper and squinted at the typeface. As he expected, the numbers were unaltered. Haulers like Biovak charge customers by the pound. Shand had nothing to gain by shaving quantities on the collection documents, except, perhaps, safety from snoops like Mark and Natalie. With George Alder in his pocket, Shand didn't have to worry about an audit by the DEH.

"Here's half the picture," Mark whispered. "Start with this month and work back."

While Natalie photographed the contents of the file, Mark searched the drawers for Biovak's paid receipts. With the incoming poundage in hand, they needed evidence to show how many pounds of medical waste made it from the consolidation warehouse to legitimate dumps, incinerators, and treatment facilities. Documenting Biovak's legal distribution activities required receipts from a number of different vendors. If Mark's suspicions were correct, those receipts would be few in number.

He ran his light down the cabinet, opening and closing drawers, occasionally stopping to flip through a folder.

"Computers were supposed to eliminate paper, weren't they?"

Natalie snapped the shutter on her camera and the light popped. She was kneeling on the floor over an open file, turning the forms from one side to the other like pages in a book. "We're lucky Biovak isn't fully automated," she said in a low voice, firing the camera again. "Breaking into a computer might require more than a visitor's badge."

"They didn't bother to lock these files," Mark noted, peering into a drawer labeled *Human Resources*. "They're probably careless about computer access too."

He walked his fingers over a row of tabs arranged alphabetically. *Acker, Louie. Albonini, R. Amora, Eve.* Were they warehouse workers? Drivers? Mark pulled a handful of files marked *Human Resources* and spread them on the floor. Most contained only a job application form, a sheet of sketchy personal information, and a Polaroid photo of a weathered, dusty face. Under their names, some of the applicants had scrawled interesting addresses. *Holy Sisters Shelter, Second Floor. Santa Ana Underpass (Rain Only).* Under *Affiliations* the profiles listed various twelve-step programs, detox centers, halfway houses, and parole boards.

Mark took a flash camera from his briefcase and started quickly through the pile. He was going to need witnesses to supplement his pilfered and possibly inadmissible evidence. Personnel files were a bonus he hadn't counted on.

He photographed the contents of several, kneeling next to Natalie, turning pages as fast as he could. *Cramer. Crippen. Deets.* Then he saw it. *Dunn, F.*

CHAPTER 28

▼

Mark stared at the typed letters in disbelief. Fred? In Biovak's personnel files? There had to be an explanation, and Mark knew he wasn't going to like it. He glanced at Natalie, decided to say nothing, and gingerly opened the fat manila folder.

Instead of a job application and mug shot the file contained a sheaf of papers and documents stuffed together in no apparent order. Newspaper clippings, correspondence, blank stationery and forms. Mark leafed quickly through them. A cover story from *Los Tiempos Espanoles* pictured Fred and his smiling protégé, Carlos Hernandez. There were copies of several letters Fred wrote to government departments of labor and immigration on Carlos's behalf. Lists of Spanish names Mark didn't recognize. A graduation day photo of Fred and George Alder wearing caps and gowns. Blank Hancock's letterhead, checks, and contract forms. Even a few plant identification tags in Hancock's trademark shades of green and yellow.

How did Shand obtain those things? And what use was he planning to make of them? Mark slid the papers back into the file while an unpleasant theory took shape in his mind.

"What did you find?" Natalie asked, straightening up from her task on the floor. Through the dim light Mark saw her rub the back of her neck.

"A personnel file on your dad."

She stared at him.

"We both know Fred wasn't moonlighting at Biovak. Shand must be dreaming up a way to incriminate your dad and Hancock's in case Biovak's dumping scheme comes to light. Fake letters and checks with Fred's forged signature could do a lot of damage. Make your father look like a player—the boss of the alien employees, perhaps. Or at least a crony of George Alder, who's in this up to his eyeballs, excuse the expression. Blackmail comes to mind. By now there's probably a file on me, too."

With less nonchalance than he projected, Mark aimed his light on the tabs in the drawer. *Goebel. Gonzales. Grant.* Seeing his own name in the lineup, he caught his breath. "Voilà," he croaked.

Natalie stood by his side while he opened the folder. The file was mercifully slim, but what it held made him cringe. A copy of the entire purchase proposal he had prepared for Beth Dunn when he bid on Hancock's Landscape Services. Financials. Projections. Everything. Someone must have gone through Maggie's records.

Even more alarming to Mark was the idea that Shand might try to implicate him too. Just how—beyond extorting compliance through threats to his family—Mark didn't know. Maybe he could fabricate evidence showing Mark had been aware of the dumping business when he purchased Hancock's. Beth offered Mark unusually favorable financing. Shand could make Fred's wife out to be part of it too. Such a scheme seemed possible, even likely. Julian Shand was way too cagey not to cover his tracks.

Mark was tempted to take the file but decided against adding to the burden—and the risk—of his and Natalie's retreat from the file room. He stuffed the papers back in order, wishing he could simply incinerate the whole place. Clearly Biovak's founder envisioned more for Hancock's than a passive role as a dumping ground. Could Shand shift blame entirely? Mark was certain he would try.

Already George Alder had gotten Mark to keep his mouth shut about the illegal dumping, and Mark had willingly urged others to do the same. Maggie, Carlos, Rick, Helen, Beth, Ginny—no reason to "alarm the public unnecessarily," Alder had said. What a crock.

"Let's concentrate on nailing Julian Shand," Natalie said, kneeling next to the files on the floor. "I believe the stakes just went up again."

"They have my daughter," Mark reminded her, and felt his heart constrict. "The stakes couldn't go any higher."

He closed the *Human Resources* drawer and opened several others in quick succession, working to tamp down his emotions. He still hadn't found what he was looking for—receipts from Biovak's legal distribution business. Without those, Natalie's photos of the collection documents would be worthless.

A distant clamor echoed down the hall outside the door. Work in the warehouse seemed to have reached fever pitch. Mark squinted into the circle of light on the files and wondered how long the solitude at the front of the building would last. What if Julian Shand himself decided to walk in their direction?

A folder marked *Reg/MWI* in a near-empty drawer caught his attention. He trained his light on the top page. "I think we found them."

Reg/MWI stood for *Regional Medical Waste Incinerator,* according to the dozen or so waste unloading documents inside. Twelve trips to permitted medical waste incinerators spanned Biovak's entire two years of business. The next file in the drawer contained paid invoices from a number of landfill operators, and a third held receipts for steam sterilization from a medical waste treatment facility. A metal brace held the folders upright; the rest of the drawer was empty.

Like haulers, waste handlers charge by weight, and they clearly itemized billable poundage. It didn't take Louis Pasteur to figure out that the total weight accounted for in those three slender files fell far short of the quantities listed in the generator tracking documents Natalie was working through. The difference in weight between the waste Biovak collected and the waste it disposed of legally would be the approximate tonnage of the illicit dumps in and around Los Angeles.

"Let's race," Mark said, grabbing his flash camera. In the privacy of the closed office he wouldn't be needing the miniature Minox camera he had brought, after all.

Natalie snapped the lid on another film cartridge and dropped a new roll into her camera. "When I'm down to three files I might consider it."

For the next fifteen minutes they worked side by side in the semi-darkness, popping flash bulbs like fireworks. Mark glanced at the window in the door and hoped no one would enter the corridor and notice their pyrotechnics. From the top of the cabinet the dislocated eyes stared unflinchingly into the bursts of light.

"They're going to need Visine," he commented, daring to realize their hazardous mission was almost complete. In a few minutes he and Natalie would be out of there.

He finished photographing the three outbound files, returned the folders to their drawer, and photographed a slim collection of Biovak's financial statements. When he finished he replaced that file and took a handful of papers from Natalie's stack. She had worked her way back eighteen months.

Down the corridor a door slammed. Footsteps sounded in the hall. Mark heard voices and the squeak of rubber soles on linoleum.

He and Natalie quickly extinguished their flashlights. In the dim light from the hall they managed to refile the open folders in approximate order and quietly close the drawers. Mark's mind raced. What if someone entered the room? Natalie stuffed their cameras into her briefcase. He looked around for a place to hide. There was none.

The voices came closer, two men, their footsteps swift and deliberate. Did a Biovak employee discover the guard, Jefferson, conked out on the job? Or worse, catch Rick?

Mark grabbed Natalie by the arm and pulled her to the wall next to the door. They couldn't hide in that barren file room, but Natalie might be able to run if he could keep both men busy.

"Hang on to that film, and get ready to bolt," he whispered.

The men were only a few feet away. Through the frosted glass Mark saw two blurred figures, one dressed from head down in white. The man in white brushed against the glass in the door as he walked by. Natalie recoiled. The men continued up the hall toward the reception area. Mark squeezed Natalie's arm and breathed a small sigh of relief.

They heard a door close and the sound of coins dropping into the Coke machine. A toilet flushed. Then, unbelievably, Muzak wafted through the corridor, a saccharine tune piped from where? By whom? Mark looked at Natalie's shadowy form and fought a hysterical urge to laugh.

The music abruptly stopped and a voice sounded through a loud-speaker. "Attention Mr. Green. Call on line one. Please pick up line one, Mr. Green." The loudspeaker crackled and the Muzak resumed.

Mark stared at the translucent glass, as still and unseeing as the eyeballs in the jar. One of those men had been on his way to the switchboard. And now—Mark swallowed—that man was stationed behind the microphone at the front desk.

A door banged. Footsteps sounded. The second person was on his way back, walking fast. Natalie shrank into the shadows. Mark moved to the other side of the door, willing the man to go by without stopping. Suddenly the white silhouette appeared outside the glass. The door to the file room swung open.

Against the glare from the hall stood a stocky figure who groped for the light switch. Mark reached above the file cabinet, grasped the nearest heavy object, and heaved. The jar hit the man squarely in the forehead and fell to the floor, shattering in a torrent of broken glass, greasy fluid, and eyeballs rolling across the doorway a second before the man himself crumpled face down on the linoleum.

Mark and Natalie listened for the sound of someone running toward them, but they heard only the lilting strains of "Chattanooga Choo Choo." Mark stared at the inert body, shocked at the violence of his own action. He had come to Biovak prepared to burgle; this was something else.

Wordlessly Natalie helped Mark drag the dead weight all the way into the room. Mark closed the door. She switched on a flashlight. The unconscious man wore white overalls with a hood that hung down his back. Mark simultaneously feared and wished the man were dead. What would happen when he woke up? A foul odor rose around them, formaldehyde and more. Mark suppressed a wave of nausea, rolled the man over, and raked in his breath.

"It's Rudy."

Rudy Vale's glassy eyes stared up at them like candidates for the next jar full. Under the open neck of the jumpsuit were a plaid flannel collar and two gold chains. A heavy key ring hung from Rudy's white canvas belt. Mark recognized several keys from Hancock's, and the implications of the foreman's duplicity hit him hard. No wonder Hancock's customers became unwitting proprietors of toxic waste dumps. Or that documents from Hancock's turned up in this file room. Rudy worked for Shand.

"Thursday night poker, my eye," Mark said, unhooking Rudy's key ring. He put the keys in his pocket along with the bullets from Jefferson's gun.

"Help me get him out of this suit."

They wrestled Rudy's dead weight from the jumpsuit, brushing away stray glass and one errant eyeball. When they had wriggled both feet out of the legs, Mark stood and shook the garment. *RUDY* was embroidered in red block letters on the pocket.

"Put this on," he said to Natalie.

"Me? I'll drown in there. You wear it."

"Don't argue, just put it on."

She wrinkled her nose and did as he said. In a moment she was zipping the suit to her neck. It fit like a parachute. Mark helped her roll up the sleeves and legs. She tucked her hair into the hood. In a pocket she found gloves and protective glasses and put those on too.

"We'll never get past the front desk with that disc jockey sitting there. Our best bet now is through the back where they might be too busy to notice that Rudy just dropped about sixty pounds."

"Ninety," Natalie shot back.

"Act as though you're escorting me, a visitor, to the parking lot. If Shand is around he won't recognize me. I've only seen him once, and at the time he was more interested in a blond."

"There's a locker room at the end of this corridor," Natalie said. "Let's try to find you one of these suits."

Mark quickly moved the contents of Natalie's briefcase to his own and slid her empty case deep into a narrow space between the file cabinet and the wall. He brushed off his jacket, hoping neither of them reeked like the mess in the room, and adjusted his visitor's pass. On the floor Rudy groaned.

"Let's get out of here."

CHAPTER 29

▼

Andrea leaned into the warm pool of light over her drawing board and tried to concentrate on the paste-up for *Property Line.* Lindsey had been abducted five hours earlier. Her captors implied they would return her that evening. *Where was she?* Mark departed for Biovak exactly one hour, nine minutes ago. Did she really expect to work while her daughter was missing and her husband out risking life, limb, and the fate of their child in that sinkhole called Biovak? Of course not. But there was comfort in her studio, and she couldn't think where else to be.

She forced herself to focus on the grid in front of her. One week remained until her four biggest clients went to press. She hadn't begun to crop and size the photos for PL's jam-packed twenty pages. Fortunately the other three newsletters were in better shape, thanks to the typesetter's overtime and a surge of her own nervous energy. *Healthy Times* needed captions. *Garden Works* was missing an ad. *LA Business Report* still had too much copy in its second-page article about the opening of Glenwater Place. But those were normal last-minute adjustments, easily fixed.

Andrea looked at her watch. Ten fifteen. Six minutes had passed since the last time she looked. She stared at a dark rectangle of glass in the window and thought about the last time she saw Lindsey, hand-in-hand with a flight attendant, disappearing into a plane.

Blinking back tears, she willed herself not to crumble. Too many people, including her daughter, depended on her that night. She tried to envision Mark and Natalie creeping through Biovak's consolidation warehouse, but all she saw was her own pale reflection. Other images that came to mind, such as Dante's circles of hell, quickly vanished in a dark synapse of fear and ignorance. What did a medical waste transfer station look like?

Natalie had assured Andrea that she and Mark only needed to enter Biovak's business offices, a separate suite of rooms some distance apart from the consolidation warehouse. A business office Andrea could picture. She picked up a photograph and tried to concentrate on her work.

At ten seventeen the phone rang, and she jumped, sprung by the noise from a tight coil of tension. She dropped the photo she was cropping and snatched the receiver off the cradle.

"Blair Graphics."

Silence.

"Hello? Is anyone there?"

On the other end she heard a click. Wrong number? Her heart dropped like a stone in her chest. She replaced the receiver. Ten seventeen was too early for Mark to phone. She looked at her watch. Ten eighteen.

She ordered herself to compute proportion ratios for six photos before checking the time again. She had actually finished four of the calculations when a glint of light in the window caught her eye. She looked up. A headlight? Not possible. Even reflected light from Palm Street wouldn't shine at the back of the house.

Telling herself to calm down, she methodically measured another photo. Something, a noise, distracted her again and she swiveled around in her chair. In the glass on the three sides of the former porch, she saw only her desk, her drawing board, and herself. She regarded her reflection in the black windows and touched her shiny hair, suddenly self-conscious in that bright fishbowl of a room. Was someone watching her?

A chill gripped her scalp and skittered down her arms. Cozy no more, she felt utterly exposed and vulnerable, a bulb in a shadeless lamp. She lowered her eyes, fixed them on the photograph before her, and wrestled her fear. Surely she was being unreasonable, sucked in by the power of suggestion. Half-crazed with worry over Lindsey and Mark, naturally she felt off balance and edgy. That didn't mean there were ghouls in the garden.

On an impulse, she reached above her head and switched off the lamp over her drawing board, plunging herself and the hard reflections around her into comforting blackness. Evening had fallen while she tried to work, and the rooms in the house behind her were dark too. She stared into the night, waiting for her pupils to adjust.

Then she saw it, in the yard outside her window. A light. Her breathing stopped. The narrow beam zig-zagged across the grass, in and out of view as though someone carried a flashlight on the far side of his body. As abruptly as it appeared, the light went out. Andrea exhaled. Keeping her eyes on the blackness where the light had been, she slipped off her chair, torn between the urge to watch and the compulsion to check locks throughout the house. Did she remember to bolt the front door? The kitchen? She backed away from her work area, shifting her sight across the ebony expanse of French windows that in daylight provided a wide-angle view of the garden. On her right, near the lemon trees, she saw it again, a beam of light. And then, another light, to the left, behind the replanted rose bushes. There were two people out there.

Frantic now, she fled from the studio into the kitchen where the illuminated clock on the oven read ten forty-one. She tested the kitchen door—locked—and ran through the hall to the front of the house, willing herself to regain calm. If Mark and the others had been discovered at Biovak, they would need her help. But she couldn't call the police, not yet. Not until Lindsey was safe. Mark had made her promise not to intervene at all before midnight unless she knew for certain they were in trouble. Sending help prematurely could force them to abort the entire plan, wreck their chances of saving Hancock's, and get all four of them thrown in jail. It was possible the trespassers on her property had nothing to do with the raid on Biovak, she reasoned. Maybe, she told herself, they were simple psychopaths bent on rape and mayhem.

She turned the dead bolt on the front door and heard it click into place. Through the open shutters in the living room she saw a shadowy figure, a man, round the corner from the back and stop in the driveway. In the light from the street she could tell he carried a gun.

Two options came instantly to mind. She could monitor the intruders' actions through uncovered windows from the darkness of the house. That way she would know where they were and could mount her defense accordingly. Or, she could quickly draw the blinds, turn on all the lights, make a lot of noise, and hope they would think a houseful of people just woke up. Emerged from a dark screening room—something. The ruse might scare the trespassers away, but Andrea wouldn't know for certain when or if they departed.

She decided on the latter, brighter course of action. If she were going to be frightened, she would rather not be in the dark.

Propelled by a plan, she conquered her ragged breathing and hurried from window to window, snapping down shutters, closing curtains, and, as soon as all the windows were covered, turning on every lamp and overhead light. First the living room. Then the dining room. In the study she tuned in talk radio at low volume. In the back bedroom she turned on the television. In the kitchen she selected a knife.

When the downstairs was lit and humming, she bounded up the stairs, two by two, to the other bedrooms, wondering if she would throw a circuit breaker. Adrenaline pumped through her. She quickly switched on lights, activated a dozen electrical circuits, and accidentally knocked over a pile of audio tapes in Lindsey's room. She grabbed the old recording of Wiggles barking at a squirrel, ran to the master bedroom, and locked the door behind her.

Panting with exertion, she laid the knife on the bedside table and inserted the recording into the tape player on the bookcase. Wiggles's excited yip filled the room. Andrea turned up the volume and tried to take charge of her pulse. She sank into a chair in bright light beside the telephone and listened to her deceased dog bark.

Seconds later the telephone rang. She sat motionless until it rang again, and then she slowly lifted the receiver.

CHAPTER 30

▼

Mark poked his head into the dimly lit corridor and looked both ways. Empty. Natalie followed him out of the file room, swishing inside Rudy's capacious overalls. She quietly closed the door on the foreman's formalin-drenched body. The air smelled better out there, Mark noticed, remembering how foul it had seemed when they first entered the building.

He gripped the handle on the briefcase that contained twenty-nine precious rolls of film—the dynamite they needed to demolish Shand's little house of horrors. With his free hand he patted the visitor's pass still attached to the lapel of his blazer. It had survived the messy confrontation with Rudy, dry and intact. If he couldn't find another pair of coveralls, the poster board badge would be his only shield on their perilous walk through the warehouse.

Side by side, he and Natalie quickly distanced themselves from the man at the front desk. They hurried down the corridor, deep into the building toward a metal door marked *Locker Room No Unauthorized Admittance.* Natalie rustled inside her spacious suit. Mark glanced at her. Even wearing the puffy hood and graceless plastic eyewear she looked lovely, her refreshingly animated eyes sparkling and clear. He had been a dope not to guess Rick would fall for her.

As they approached the end of the corridor, Muzak launched a cheerful rendition of *I Left My Heart in San Francisco*.

"Organ music," Mark whispered. "How apropos." He stopped next to the forbidding metal door and waited for his own heart to stop hammering. It didn't. "Are you ready?"

"Violet I. Beamer at your service," Natalie muttered, tightening the drawstring under her chin.

"Sorry, Violet. You're Rudy now."

"Oh right. That worm."

They pushed past the weighty door and entered a small antechamber that opened onto a spotless white room lined with lockers. Someone was there.

A tall, thin man with unruly red hair stood at the intersection of two rows of lockers, zipping himself into a jumpsuit. He appeared to be the only person in the room. Mark gripped his briefcase and steeled himself for a confrontation.

Natalie nodded her hooded head in the man's direction. His face looked as bland and blank as a peeled egg. Feet planted in the corner, he hardly seemed to notice the newcomers, but appeared intent on zipping, then unzipping, and zipping again the long closure down his front.

Mark studied the man's vacant face. Zip. Unzip. Zip. Unzip. Pixilated for sure.

"Not a candidate for the outbound fleet," Mark murmured, glancing around the room for a pair of overalls. What looked like a laundry bin on wheels was parked near the mentally challenged redhead. Mark sidled over and lifted a soiled garment gingerly between forefinger and thumb, keeping a lookout on the tall man and the door through which they had entered.

The man followed Mark's movements, but remained passive and zipping while Mark selected an only moderately disgusting used jumpsuit and put it on. The thin man watched him zip it up and broke into a wide, toothless grin.

Covered like Natalie from head to toe in white, Mark breathed a lit-tle easier. The embroidery on his chest read *LOU.* He opened his brief-case and unloaded the rolls of film and the small camera into the deep pockets on each thigh of his suit. Then he extracted a folded black gar-bage bag and closed the leather case. The toothless man watched him slide the briefcase inside the bag and tie the black plastic in a knot.

Mark would ditch the bag if necessary. Like Natalie he had made sure his briefcase and its contents held no identification of any kind. No monogram, label, business cards—nothing, he hoped, that could connect him to this foray. Even so, common sense told him the fewer of their own possessions they left on the premises, the better.

Remembering one more thing, Mark unzipped his jumpsuit again, located the silver pocketknife in his blazer, and transferred the mea-ger weapon to the top pocket of the overalls. Rezipping the jumpsuit, he smiled sheepishly at his mute and grinning observer, grabbed glasses and gloves from a basket, and turned to lead Natalie out of the locker room.

She followed him around a corner and through a maze of mottled sinks and showers, more lockers, a door marked *Cafeteria* and an exit labeled *Consolidation Warehouse.* Beneath the sign on the warehouse door hung a stern reminder from the Occupational Safety and Health Administration about the proper attire for persons passing that way.

Mark scanned the list. Once he put on plastic glasses and gloves he and Natalie would be dressed impeccably—as if Shand and his min-ions really cared about such things. Biovak's CEO was no fool. Shand obviously maintained appearances for the benefit of government regu-lators, lenders, and other interested observers who would be satisfied by a quick tour of a meticulously tricked-out facility. The meals, showers, and clothing, however, were probably genuine. A hard-up, rootless, and possibly addicted warehouse crew was key to Biovak's success. Shand preyed upon his workers' dependencies and no doubt expected loyalty, or at least silence, in return.

Mark slipped on the protective eyewear and wondered if Shand himself lurked behind the warehouse door. Dressed in undercover attire, he and Natalie had more room to maneuver, but not much. Natalie looked shrunken inside Rudy's overalls. And Mark was beginning to think his Nikes had been a mistake. Too flashy for this crowd? He tugged on his pant legs, swallowed hard, and reached for the door.

"Where do you think you're going?" came a shrill voice behind them.

Under his breath Mark cursed. He turned to see a small, gnarly man emerge from the showers with a nasty expression on his face. The little man wore purple shorts and rubber flip flops, and had calves like clinging hairy animals. Against his bare chest he carried a stack of folded towels.

"How many times do I have to tell you imbeciles? You can't go in there without a shower. Get back here and strip."

Mark had assumed showers took place on the way out, after work, but in this pit anything was possible. "Uh, we showered earlier, thanks," he mumbled, ushering Natalie past him toward the door.

"Hey! Stop right where you are." The officious little creep craned his neck toward Natalie. "And just who do you think you're kidding, *Rudy*?" He dropped the towels and scuttled toward them, snapping his flip flops importantly against the soles of his feet.

Mark reached out and grabbed him, simultaneously lifting the man's flailing body off the floor and clamping a hand over his wet, indignant mouth. "Go get a jumpsuit," he said to Natalie. "Hurry."

While she rushed back to the locker area, Mark wrestled his squirming prisoner into the shower room. The gray concrete stalls were damp and dim, complete—Mark was sure—with raging tides of warty pathogens. Large, cracked bars of soap and a few mangled sponges hung from hooks on ropes.

The pint-sized man, all muscle and kick, weighed more than his appearance had suggested. Mark hefted him through the aisles to an isolated corner at the rear of the stalls near several sweating water pipes.

The room felt subtropical; inside his blazer and canvas overalls Mark was steaming. Then he felt a searing pain in his left hand. "Shit!"

The man had sunk his teeth in Mark's palm and wasn't letting go. Mark tugged and felt his skin tear, chewed like a piece of bony chicken. Swiftly he swung one leg around his captive's shins and dropped him forward, face down on the floor, his own left hand still immobilized between sharp, tenacious incisors. Every movement hurt like hell. Pinning the man under his knee, he reached around and achieved a firm grip on the pug nose just above his own injured hand. He pinched without mercy. His opponent's face turned several hues of red before the man succumbed to pain and oxygen deprivation, and unclenched his jaw. Mark extracted his throbbing hand and quickly stuffed a sponge between the man's weapons-grade choppers. At that moment Natalie rustled through the door in her billowing suit carrying a white coverall.

"It's the first one I grabbed and it's a mess," she said, holding up a grossly smeared and dripping expanse of canvas. "What happened to your hand?"

The filth on the jumpsuit seemed to have a calming effect on their prisoner, or perhaps he went into shock. Pale-faced and whimpering he ceased his struggle, apparently preferring a smooth passage into the relatively clean interior of the jumpsuit to a fight that would bring his bare skin in contact with the mire caked on the outside. It occurred to Mark that dirt-averse individuals probably made excellent shower attendants.

Together he and Natalie maneuvered the frightened man into the suit, zipped the zipper, and tied the long grungy arms in knots at the rear, like a straightjacket. The legs Mark tied securely around a water pipe fixed to the wall. Using towels and several lengths of rope attached to soap and sponges, he gagged their prisoner, and tightly reinforced the body wrap.

"Aren't you glad you use Dial?" asked Mark, wincing as he pulled a glove over his tattered hand. He took Natalie by the elbow, and they hurried from the shower room.

CHAPTER 31

▼

The door to the warehouse swung onto a broad metal landing that overlooked a bustling plant the size of a soccer field. Stairs led down from the landing to the left and right, and a third, narrower staircase rose sharply to a catwalk that appeared to encircle the warehouse about fifteen feet above the floor.

Directly ahead, in the bowels of the place, stood an efficiently engineered network of conveyers, turntables, benches, and chutes that resembled prosperous industrial facilities the world over. Mark knew the look. Concrete and stainless steel; metal racks and rolling carts. Except for the noxious odor this could be a distribution center for parcels. It was, in a way.

"Shand's probably up there," Natalie whispered, pointing directly above them. "The catwalk leads to a control room and observation booth."

Mark eyed the low white ceiling above them. Anyone in the control room commanded a clear view of the entire operation, from the closed and silent inbound docks on the far side of the building to the brightly lit and buzzing outbound operation below them on the right. In the middle of the plant, two assembly lines of workers sealed in white were filling garbage bags at the ends of grinders and chutes, and placing the bags on conveyers that ran through gauntlets of knot-tiers. The landing on which Mark and Natalie stood appeared to be the only safe haven. For the moment at least, Shand couldn't see them.

Mark darted his eyes from corner to corner, quickly assessing the deployment of thirty or so white-suited personnel, the possibilities for concealment en route to the outbound loading bays, and the likely location of the foreman called Amp. He lifted his hand to touch the smooth outline of the knife in his pocket.

The stairs on the right side of the landing afforded the most direct route to the open air beyond the outbound docks. But those stairs were clearly marked *Do Not Enter.* They were one-way only, up. The one-way down arrow guided traffic across the empty landing to the stairs on the left. Shift changes in that hellhole must be as orderly as a Nazi dress parade, Mark thought, wondering whether he and Natalie dared violate the directions in the total absence of traffic on the stairs. Although the two of them were not visible to the control room above, the landing on which they stood was as good as center stage to any warehouse worker who cared to look in their direction. Mark decided against a flagrant violation, and motioned to Natalie to go left.

Speed or finesse? Mark descended the steps in front of Natalie, acutely aware that the path they had chosen led directly away from the outbound exit, their only avenue of escape. If they turned and bolted too soon, they would never make it across the warehouse, past the loading docks, and through the phalanx of drivers outside who would have plenty of time to leap from their vans. Running would simply blow their cover. Better to stay cool and walk out, hoping fright and foul air wouldn't deck them first.

Natalie's safety glasses had slipped to the tip of her nose. From the bottom of the stairs Mark watched her lift a voluminously gloved hand and push them back, pausing about midway down. In her sagging cuffs and drooping eyewear, it was a miracle she could walk at all.

As she resumed her descent, some clamor on the warehouse floor made her look up. In rapid succession her glasses slipped, her hand let go of the rail, the rubber sole of her left shoe caught the flapping cuff of her right leg, and she tumbled head-first down the stairs.

Mark saw her coming but couldn't do a thing from below except shorten her fall. The thud of her body against the open metal stairs reverberated through the warehouse. She came to rest in Mark's arms on the bottom step, curled and motionless within the white tent labeled *RUDY.*

Mark touched her gently. "Natalie?" Beyond the edge of his hood he saw several white-clad figures look in their direction. "Can you hear me?" He couldn't tell for sure how her body was arranged within the bulky folds of fabric, or even whether her limbs bent the right way. Sweat ran down his back. A worker in white started toward them.

"There's nothing wrong with my hearing, you nincompoop," Natalie whispered from the depths of her hood, slowly uncurling her legs. With one eye on the person approaching, Mark stuffed her hair out of sight and quickly straightened her glasses. "Can you walk? Someone's coming."

"I think so." She ignored Mark's helping hand, pulled herself up by the rail and waved to the interested person who hesitated, still watching. "I'm Rudy, remember," she snapped, squaring her shoulders. "Stop fussing." The observer regarded them a moment longer, returned Natalie's wave and went back to work.

Mark looked around. No one else in the vicinity seemed concerned. Ahead and to the right loomed a grid of Dumpster-like containers that could offer partial concealment during their walk through the warehouse. If he and Natalie kept their faces low, they could circle behind the receptacles halfway back to the outbound docks without too much exposure to the people in the control room. Mark peered tentatively up at the brightly lit, glass enclosed booth. He saw the back of a man's head, someone standing perhaps, but was still too close underneath to see very much.

Natalie followed him between the high metal bins that snaked across the warehouse. Mark heard her groan a time or two but all of her appendages appeared to function. The oversized suit that had caused her fall also apparently shielded her from serious injury.

Mark raised a gloved hand to his nose. Up close, the metal containers looked and smelled ugly. Smeared with grime of unknown origin, they exuded an oily, knock-out perfume that made the fragrance in Fred Dunn's locked metal box seem like eau de cologne. No wonder Shand hung out in a sealed skybox. Mark tried not to think about the waste products that were consolidated and transferred in that grisly place. His innards lurched.

They turned right and moved quickly, heads down, directly in front of the control booth. Mark felt eyes—the functional variety—boring into the back of his hood. Was Shand watching them? Without warning a man in white overalls stepped into Mark's path.

"Lou?" the man said, sounding surprised. "I thought you left."

Mark started, then remembered the name sewn above his pocket. "Uh, hi," he mumbled. The man's suit read *BO*.

"Rudy?" Bo said, looking warily at Natalie.

Natalie tossed her shrouded head and hurried past both men. Mark followed her, stepping sideways to block Bo's view of his suspiciously diminished colleague. Natalie was walking fast now, not waiting to test Bo's curiosity. Mark looked over his shoulder and saw the man still standing there, frowning. Like the observant worker who saw Natalie fall on the stairs, Bo appeared to be a prime candidate for the elite outbound fleet.

Beyond the last Dumpster stretched twenty yards of open space, rolling carts, and busy workers in jumpsuits who might or might not be interested in the odd pair labeled *RUDY* and *LOU*. The crossing would be tricky. Natalie paused to consider their rush to the end zone. Mark turned his head inside his hood. Bo had vanished. Mark decided to take a chance, and looked cautiously upward.

From his vantage point behind the Dumpster he could see the entire expanse of the control booth. A white-coated female technician worked on the side next to a small bank of computers. Near the middle of the booth stood none other than Julian Shand, resplendent in a three-piece suit. Shand sucked on a cigar and appeared to be listening to another person who sat in a centrally positioned, high-backed chair turned away from the window. Mark couldn't see the seated person's face. Once or twice he glimpsed a hand that rose from the arm rest, gesturing, and the flash of a silver watch.

The scene baffled him. Who except Shand would be parked in that throne?

Natalie nudged him. "See the bay on the far right? Dock One?" Her head dipped toward the last loading dock on the west end of the outbound row. In that wide-open space, swayed a slender youth who leaned precariously over a rolling cart. He looked as though he might bliss out before the end of the shift. "Let's take the stairs down from there."

"Past the chemically altered individual?"

She nodded.

"Right. Be careful. Shand is upstairs."

"I know. I looked too. Who's in the chair?"

"I was hoping you could tell me." Mark watched Natalie steal another glance toward the control booth. Behind the glasses slipping down her nose, her blue eyes widened in disbelief.

She jerked her face away from the scene as though she had been slapped. "They're looking this way."

"Who?" Mark lowered his head, prepared to grab her and run.

"Shand and the one sitting down. I don't think they saw us."

"Do you know who the other person is?"

Mark watched while fury contorted her face.

"Yes. And so do you."

CHAPTER 32

▼

Rick shifted his weight to ease the cramp in his leg, and looked anxiously at his watch. Mark and Natalie had been inside Biovak nearly an hour. It was a promising sign, he told himself. They must have found the file room unoccupied, nicely incriminating, and worthy of a good long look. Photographing the documents would take a while.

He glanced toward the guardhouse where Jefferson slumbered quietly out of sight on the liquor-dappled floor beneath the flashing electronic console. Did those blinking lights require a response? Rick hoped not. He shivered in the nighttime chill and shifted his weight again.

After Mark and Natalie went inside, Rick stationed himself at the northwest corner of the property where he had unimpeded views of both the guardhouse on the north side of the block and the Jeep parked in darkness on the west. Crouching next to Biovak's steel mesh security fence, he tried to appear nonthreatening and inconsequential, a rootless waif finding comfort against a chain-link backrest.

Headlights occasionally grazed his rumpled form, crooked beams from the white rattletraps that clanked around the corner to their lucrative assignments as part of Biovak's outbound fleet. Rick watched the truckloads of Burton-Abbey disposables cruise into the night, and gnashed his molars. Illicit dumping went against everything he and his eighty-year-old company stood for. He was the corporate spokesperson for ecological responsibility, with the biggest speech of his career in just a week. The knowledge that the slimeball whiz kid, Julian Shand, had gotten rich from this disgusting enterprise made his teeth throb.

Another van rounded the corner loudly dragging a loose exhaust pipe. The sound of metal scraping asphalt echoed from the concrete walls. Rick lowered his head and sat as gray and unmoving as the lead boulder in Lindsey Grant's second grade play. Lindsey. Thinking of Mark and Andrea's daughter and the risk they were taking while she remained in the hands of the kidnappers made his heart pound.

He stared at his running shoes, and suddenly became aware how big and bright they appeared, stuck there between the charcoal of his sweat pants and the brown packed earth. At night in that mournful, soulless slice of Los Angeles, shoes meant for healthful pursuits seemed garish and incorrect. He tried to tuck his feet under him and out of sight.

When the headlights and noise had passed, he scratched the ground for dirt to rub into the white shoe leather. The bone-dry particles fell over his toes like rosin. He spit on his hand and tried again, working up a dark paste that streaked the surface commendably. He should have thought of this earlier. Hadn't people been killed for their shoes?

In a couple of minutes another vehicle approached. Rick ceased the spit shine and sat still and bowed, listening while the screeching van drew near and slowed to turn the corner. Something about that particular wreck disturbed him. He peeked from under his hood and glimpsed a rusty tailpipe clacking against the pavement. That van had gone by once before. Rick caught a fleeting look at a vulpine face inspecting him through the side window.

He held his breath, kept his head low, and fingered the keys in the pocket of his sweatshirt. If the driver stopped, should he sprint for the Jeep? No—better to divert attention from the getaway car and, if necessary, make use of the potent arsenal in his medicine bag. He slid one hand slowly out of his pocket and touched the leather pouch on his belt.

The van and its clattering exhaust system dragged around the corner a few feet in front of him. Acrid fumes made Rick's eyes water. He watched, poised to scram, while the noxious vehicle proceeded noisily up the block toward Biovak's main entrance. But instead of stopping, the thing crept slowly past the guardhouse to the corner and turned right. It was circling the block again.

Rick sprang to his feet guessing he had a minute, maybe two, until the van reappeared around the opposite corner. He looked up and down the empty street wondering where he could hide in that barren stretch of concrete. If he simply ran from the vicinity he would risk botching Mark and Natalie's escape. The two of them could rush out the door at any moment and find him gone. Then what?

He darted across the pavement and turned up the street, listening for the nerve-jangling sound of dragging metal. The van was probably about halfway around the block. He racewalked until he was opposite Biovak's main entrance, scanning the guardhouse for Jefferson and the doorway for his friends. No sign yet of Mark and Natalie.

From a distance came the screech of the killer wreck gunning its broken parts around a curb. Dream on, Leadfoot, Rick sneered, hurrying past a trash-filled viaduct. He would have enjoyed taking on that outbound heap in his Porsche. Unfortunately, he found himself vehicularly challenged at the moment, an on-duty getaway man with no wheels to call his own. In light of the situation, he supposed he should look upon the van and its felonious, possibly drug-crazed, shoe-craving driver with a tad more respect. He accelerated his pace. Ahead, near the end of the block, burned the surreal blaze in the bathtub.

Rick reached the little campfire and dropped to his knees at the same moment headlights flashed into view around the corner he had just vacated. The driver of the crippled van was looking for him, no doubt about it. Biovak's finest slowed to a crawl, then nearly stopped in the intersection next to the vacant corner. Disappointment oozed from the cracks in the windshield. When another outbound vehicle, another muffler-impaired model, rumbled up behind him, Rick's assailant gunned the engine and dragged his sorry tail on up the street. Breathing hard, Rick crouched low behind the fire and watched the skunked stalker screech past, turn the corner, and drive toward juicier prey.

"Noisy, ain't they," declared a gravelly voice.

Rick jumped. He squinted into the darkness behind the flames and made out a gaunt face squeezed between a pair of fuzzy earmuffs. A man? No, a woman; someone swathed in a blanket was hunkered down on the opposite side of the blazing bathtub.

"Uh, yes," Rick answered, eyeing his companion warily. If he shifted his gaze a little to the right, he could see Biovak's guardhouse and front door, but not the Jeep parked around the corner. He wondered whether the pipe-dragging van would return.

The apparition across the campfire wore a benign expression, staring at him with deep set, dark blue eyes that were startlingly handsome in a smudged and world-weary face. Rick thought of Natalie and glanced surreptitiously at his watch. Ten forty-five.

"Ever drive one?"

The rough voice did belong to a woman. Rick regarded her with interest.

"No. Have you?"

"Yep."

His eyes widened. All appeared calm at the guardhouse. Biovak's entrance remained brightly lit and vacant. Rick decided he would spend a few more minutes conversing with the amiable outlaw.

CHAPTER 33

▼

"It's Sam Folee," Natalie hissed. "The one in the chair is Sam Folee."

Mark felt the floor dip beneath his feet. A seismograph attached to his ribcage would have swung off the charts. *Sam? Of Folee's Nursery?*

As Mark absorbed the aftershocks of that stunning information, an officious teenager wearing regulation overalls unzipped to the navel rolled a cart into his shins.

"Dock Three," the boy barked. A gold cross dangled against his bare chest.

Snapped painfully to attention, Mark winced and nodded at the Young Turk who turned on his heels to torment someone else. Mark shot a look at Natalie, who wore a murderous expression behind her plastic eyewear. She had never been a fan of the Folees. Now no doubt she could cheerfully murder Sam.

Mark was ready to help her. Sam Folee had been his chief competitor in the bid for Hancock's Landscape Services. Folee must have obtained Mark's purchase proposal, the one Mark found in Biovak's file room, from Rudy Vale, who had ample opportunity to raid Maggie's records. Armed with crucial insider information, Sam had played Mark like a puppet. If Folee ever truly wanted to purchase Hancock's, he must have changed his mind—and written that ludicrous proposal for Beth—when he got a look at the financial statements of Mark W. Grant.

There, in stark black and white, was the fiscal portrait of a middle-aged, mortgage-strapped, out-placed banker who couldn't wait to spend his last two cents—the perfect *schlemiel*. Once Mark dumped his career in finance and pledged everything he owned to buy Hancock's Landscape Services, Folee and Shand would have him—and Hancock's Landscape Services—right where they wanted. Or so they thought.

Natalie touched Mark's arm. "Let's concentrate on getting out of here."

Mark nodded, acutely aware that not one but two people in the control booth could recognize them if they weren't careful. Shand and Folee. Mark shuddered at the idea of their partnership. A medical waste hauler and the owner of nine huge garden centers. The havoc they could cause was unthinkable.

Natalie removed one glove and jammed it into the top pocket of her jumpsuit so that the fingers stuck up over the incriminating red *RUDY* on her chest. Mark tried to appear casual as he tossed the black trash bag containing his briefcase onto the pile of nearly identical plastic bags in the loaded cart. He wondered where his leather attaché case would end up. In a garbage can on someone's front lawn? Or maybe the gardener paid to plant that particular load of trash would appropriate the briefcase for hauling around the cash Sam Folee paid him. Inside his Biovak issue work suit, Mark seethed.

Together he and Natalie rolled their heavy cargo into the wide-open space beyond the metal Dumpsters. The cart made a useful and literal prop, Mark realized, still reeling with indignation at Folee's involvement with Shand. He simultaneously pushed and braced himself against the waist-high tubular frame, guessing that Natalie, for all her bravado, needed to steady herself too.

Bent forward with exertion, Mark kept his head down while surveying the dozen or so workers in the vicinity of the loading docks. They were a motley crew in various stages of protective dress, from fully shrouded in white to hoodless, gloveless, sockless, and unzipped. So much for OSHA standards, he thought, worrying that his and Natalie's regulation attire might actually look out of place. But no one on the floor seemed to pay them the slightest attention. The most urgent question remained how to get out of that asylum and into the Jeep without stirring up all the inmates.

Shoulder to shoulder, Mark and Natalie pushed their load as ordered toward Dock Three. Twenty-nine rolls of film and a small camera jostled in the pockets on Mark's thighs. The odor that had gagged him earlier seemed almost tolerable now. He wondered if his sense of smell had been irrevocably traumatized. Or did the cold air in the warehouse simply dull the senses? Sniffling, he eyed the black bags in his custody.

Inches from his fingertips, beneath a mil of plastic film, sat what variety of hazardous material he did not know. Contaminated lab equipment? Surgical specimens? Autopsy waste? Whatever brand of medical scrap the bags contained, Mark knew that anyone in his right mind wouldn't go near it unless he or she were dressed for the occasion.

He slipped one hand into the top pocket of his jumpsuit and removed the silver pocketknife Natalie had given him.

"Open this," he said without looking at her.

She took the knife in her ungloved hand and returned it, open, a moment later under the cover of her wide sleeve. Mark leaned into the cart as if to steady the load, and deftly cut a long surgical slash along the equator of the largest bag within reach. Straightening up, he closed the knife smoothly against the rim of the cart and replaced it in his pocket.

"Grandpa would be proud," Natalie murmured, looking away.

"I hope so."

As they approached the loading docks, the unsteady youth in Dock One hoisted a bag from the cart parked beside him, teetered on his toes, and swung the parcel sloppily in the general direction of the driver standing below on the pavement outside.

"Gravity is that guy's only asset," Mark observed in a low voice. "Let's finish our assignment and scram."

"Roger."

Dock Three's version of the addict in Dock One seemed more inclined toward the upper ranges of mood alteration. Mark watched the wild man grab three large sacks from the nearly empty cart in his purview and hurl them in quick succession at the outbound driver who had the bad luck to be at the head of line three. The name sewn on the man's jumpsuit was *BUZZ*.

When Mark shoved the cart full of fresh ammunition near Dock Three, Buzz quickly torpedoed his hapless target with the last of his old supply and pulled the new bombs into his fort. Through the open bay Mark could see a frantic driver in the lot below scramble to load the fallen bags into his van before the next barrage began. Buzz was the model maniacal dockworker. Flushed, frenetic, and focused, he no doubt led the pack in productivity.

Mark backed slowly away from Dock Three, casting sidelong looks for the inquisitive Ike, the infamous Amp, and the teenage tyrant who had put Natalie and him to work. Hoping no one watched from the skybox, he and Natalie edged sideways toward Dock One. Near the exit and poised to flee, Mark calculated the odds for one last risk.

He slipped his hand into his pocket and fingered the camera nestled deep among the canisters of film. Sam Folee's curly head and the dark pinstripes worn by Julian Shand were clearly visible through the glass upstairs. No one nearby showed the aptitude or the initiative to question *LOU* and *RUDY*. In front of Mark, Natalie was approaching Dock One. He decided to chance it.

Cradling the Minox in his hand, he withdrew the tiny, light-sensitive camera from his pocket, raised it to his face, and quickly snapped a sequence of flashless exposures in the general direction of the control room. Shand turned toward Mark at the same instant Mark dropped his hand to replace the camera in his pocket. Mark did not wait to find out the boss's reaction. He turned his back on the control room and made tracks for Dock One.

The discombobulated dockworker in the first loading bay seemed to barely register Natalie and Mark in his watery vision as they hurried past him, down the concrete stairs and into the parking lot. Natalie descended the steps by holding up her pant legs, but her glasses fell off. Mark tried to keep the film and the camera from clanking in his pocket. Deep within the warehouse the loudspeaker crackled and a voice paged Rudy Vale.

The van driver parked in the lot beneath Dock One stood with his hands on his hips like a driver at LAX enduring an interminable wait for luggage. Behind him, other drivers in line tooted their horns. "This guy's hopeless," the man in front said, exasperated.

"*Si*," answered Mark, hoping to discourage chitchat while he and Natalie backed toward the corner of the building. Up the row, around Dock Four, Mark saw Amp's white T-shirt moving quickly in their direction.

"Hey you two! Get back to work!" the foreman yelled.

Amp stormed past Dock Three at the same moment Buzz launched a preemptive strike on a new driver who had just driven up to receive cargo. Fortunately for Mark and Natalie, the missile Buzz selected was defective, big time. Slashed across the middle. The bag flew from the doorway and burst in a torrent of tubes, bandages, bottles, and splatterings of shapeless, unidentifiable matter that exploded into the air like shrapnel. Amp ducked in fear and covered his head with his clipboard. Mark and Natalie slipped around the corner of the building and into the darkness, unseen.

"Way to go, Buzz," Mark said, listening to the sweet clatter of toxins on the Tarmac. He whipped off his plastic glasses and tried to control the sheer joy he felt as he and Natalie dashed toward the Jeep. They would have to either scale the fence or run to the gate. Had Rick spotted them yet? Mark strained to hear the sound of the engine starting, ready to roll. Maybe he could signal Rick to meet them in front.

As his pupils adjusted to the dim light, he began to make out the Cherokee through the fence ahead of him and—movement? Someone—no—two or three people suddenly scampered away across the street, climbed the wall on the neighboring property, dropped over the side, and vanished.

Natalie gasped.

Outside Biovak's chain-link fence the Jeep—or what was left of it— sat awkwardly on one tire and three naked hubs. Rick was nowhere to be seen.

CHAPTER 34

▼

"Keep running!" Mark shouted in Natalie's direction. There was no way to go but forward, away from the bright lights and appalling appetites of the outbound docks. He hardly paused to survey the remains of the Jeep. One glance told him their getaway car had been relieved of its radio, battery, license plates, and three sets of tires and wheels. The mechanics in that neighborhood were efficient. Mark hoped they hadn't also dismantled Rick. Where was he?

Mark sprinted with Natalie toward the north side of the building, still dressed in white Biovak overalls. Natalie stumbled on the cuff of her jumbo jumpsuit and managed to recover without falling. Twenty-nine canisters of film jostled in Mark's pockets. Near the northwest corner of the property he suddenly noticed the air. Compared to the pungent aroma of the warehouse, the air outside smelled as sweet as Yosemite in the spring.

The guard, Jefferson, appeared to doze peacefully where they had left him. Mark could make out a couple of dim forms hunched over the campfire that burned farther up the block. The rest of the street was deserted. He stepped cautiously around the corner and motioned to Natalie to follow. A long strand of dark hair had escaped from her hood. Almost instantly Rick shot out of the blackness across the street and ran to them, grinning.

"Am I glad to see you," he panted. "Did you get the files?"

Mark nodded.

"Great." Rick threw an arm around Natalie's shoulders and dangled the Jeep keys in his hand. "Let's take a powder."

"In what?" Natalie snapped. "Most of the Jeep is halfway to Guadalajara."

Rick cast a stricken look in the direction of the carcass parked around the corner. His jaw dropped.

"A fine getaway man you are," Mark said, torn between relief at the sight of his friend and homicidal impulses at Rick's failure to protect the vehicle. He unzipped his jumpsuit and fished inside the pocket of his blazer. "Fortunately we've got an upgrade. Come on."

Walking at a fast clip, Mark entered the pool of light that marked the area between the guardhouse and the double front doors of Bio-vak's main entrance. Jefferson had shifted a little; one shiny black shoe protruded from the guardhouse door. To his right, Mark caught a glimpse of the Muzak-playing receptionist seated at the desk in the lobby, absorbed in a magazine. Mark wondered if the DJ had repeated his page to Rudy Vale, and how soon the search for Rudy would begin.

With Rick and Natalie close behind, Mark hurried across the circular drive and into the shadows where all three of them broke into a run. Mark reached the far corner of the building first. He poked his hooded head around the cinderblocks and found the east side of the property nearly deserted.

The inbound docks remained as closed and dim as they had been when the three of them circled the block in the Jeep almost two hours earlier. Next to the inbound bays opened a brightly lit garage. Mark couldn't see inside from his vantage point, but the smell of fresh paint and the white tracks leading out onto the asphalt told him Natalie had been correct about the vehicle-painting booth. Facing the docks and the garage in perfect rows sat the immaculate inbound trucks and their hypocritical red crosses. Beyond the trucks stood the other vehicles Mark remembered: the employee parking lot.

It didn't take long to spot Rudy's Land Cruiser, license PLANTS2. Mark raced toward it with Rick and Natalie right behind. *PLANTS TWO? PLANTS TOO? PLANTS TU?* Anger shook his hand as he fumbled with Rudy's key ring. How long had Hancock's foreman been in cahoots with Shand and Folee? Since Fred hired him? Possibly; the way Rudy threw money around, he could be their partner.

"Hurry up," Natalie urged, watching a raspy outbound van chug up the street beyond the fence. Inside the open garage two men could be seen spraying white paint on an old van.

Mark located the silver Toyota key and turned it in the door lock. A deafening shriek sliced through the night. Mark's heart leapt against his ribs. He groped on the key ring for the alarm button. The device shrieked again, echoing nauseatingly against the cement. A third salvo had just begun when Mark found the remote and managed to interrupt the alarm mid-shriek. One of the men in the garage stood squinting into the darkness. In the sudden silence, the three friends piled into the vehicle. Rick, the designated getaway driver, slid into the back seat without comment, still mortally embarrassed by the demise of the Jeep.

"Tuck in your hair," Mark commanded Natalie who sat next to him in front. "We're not out of here yet."

He swung the Toyota out of its parking space at the same moment Amp and two figures in white suits rushed around the southeast corner of the warehouse. In the rear view mirror Mark saw the foreman break into a run. He gunned the Land Cruiser northward, past the inbound docks and trucks, and careened around the corner to the front of the building. Ahead stood the guardhouse, and next to it, a guard.

Jefferson was on his feet. Guessing that the drugged security man remained unarmed and woozy, Mark stepped on the gas pedal, intending to drive right past him. Jefferson, however, took a wobbly step forward, tripped on the curb and fell directly into the path of the oncoming vehicle. Mark slammed on the brakes. Even with pursuers closing in he wasn't ready to run over a man. He turned the wheel sharply and jumped the curb, missing the guard's body by inches.

"Look out!" Natalie screamed. The path across the dirt between Jefferson and the guardhouse might have accommodated a smaller car but the Land Cruiser was not going to make it. Mark gripped the wheel with his chewed hand and prepared to take a chunk of Jefferson's guard station with them.

"Oh, oh," Rick said just before they crashed.

The right headlight hit the corner of the prefabricated structure and exploded in a spectacular spray of glass and particle board. Natalie braced herself against the dashboard while debris rained down. The Toyota had come to a halt, but the guardhouse appeared to have lost the contest. Most of two walls and windows were crushed and the entire structure had been moved from its moorings like a phone booth in a riot.

Mark shifted into reverse. By changing direction slightly, he might be able to clear the dislocated station and make a U-turn out the front gate. He backed up, looking in the rearview mirror, and saw the receptionist emerge from Biovak's front door with a gun clutched in his hands.

"Duck!" he yelled, slamming the gear shift into drive. A shot rang out. The rear window of the Toyota went opaque with a thousand cracks. Scrunched down in the front seat, Natalie squealed. From the floor in the back, Rick uttered a string of expletives. Where the bullet lodged, Mark didn't know.

He kept his head low and gunned the Toyota around the flashing remains of Jefferson's electronic console. Accelerating sharply to the right, he sped out the gate and laid two long streaks of rubber on the road in front of the fire in the bathtub. A dark silhouette raised a hand and waved in their direction.

"That's Wanda Juju," Rick said, peeking out the side window. "She used to make drops at your house."

Twenty-five minutes later the Land Cruiser was headed north toward Wilshire on San Vicente, and Mark resumed breathing normally. He had taken a circuitous route out of the warehouse district, avoided freeways, and worked his way west on side streets. Olympic, Pico, Venice. Glass and debris dropped from the damaged vehicle at every sinkhole. But nothing in Mark's sideview mirrors gave cause for alarm. Apparently Shand's henchmen did not think a car chase worth the risk.

Through the white light of the dashboard, Mark eyed Rudy's mobile phone and wished he could call Andrea. Committing their home number to Rudy's cellular bill, however, would be crazy enough for Biovak's second string. In the rear, Rick unloaded film from his camera.

"That woman drove for Biovak?" Mark asked, picking up where Rick had left off six or seven miles earlier.

"Zone eleven, West Side. Distribution at Biovak is highly organized. Wanda Juju said she retired from the fleet when her craving for crack outdid her desire to please her boss. She still works in the warehouse when she's low on cash."

Rick passed five canisters of film over the seat to Mark, who slid them into his nearly full pockets. That made thirty-four rolls altogether, more than twelve hundred exposures of premises, papers, and perpetrators.

"How are you, Nat?" Rick asked, placing his hands on her shoulders. "What happened in there besides the fashion show?" He sniffed. "And what's that smell?"

Natalie unzipped her formalin-doused jumpsuit. Reaching across the seat back, Rick helped her wriggle out of the suit's cavernous depths while she told him about their encounter with Rudy Vale.

"Rudy Vale?" Rick exclaimed, looking in the rear view mirror at Mark. "Hancock's foreman?" When that news sank in he processed the rest of the story. "You decked him with a peck of pickled peepers?"

Like a slip of tectonic plates, the tension that had gripped them gave way. "It could have been worse," Natalie said. "It could have been a peck of pickled peckers."

"Or a pack of puckered posteriors," Rick put in.

Relief had made the two of them giddy. Rick and Natalie hooted helplessly, while even Mark managed a smile. He flexed his stiffening hand. "Do you have a tetanus shot in your little doctor's bag?"

When they came to a halt in front of Rick's building in Westwood, Rick inoculated Mark against a few of the pathogens that could be touring his bitten flesh. Natalie said, "You can drop me here, too." She looked at Mark, and a soft expression beatified her features. "I'll say a prayer for Lindsey's safe return. Please keep us posted."

Natalie and Rick. Rick and Natalie. Mark was beginning to like the idea. He looked at them gratefully. "Thanks for the fun evening. Let's do it again sometime."

"In a pig's patootie, pal."

CHAPTER 35

▼

When Mark turned up Palm Street, the clock on Rudy's dashboard read eleven twenty-eight. Andrea would be frantic by now, he realized. He sped around the corner, past Helen Woodley's, and into view of his own brilliantly lit house. Lights shone from every room. A police van sat under a lamp post in front. *Police?*

Fear prickled his scalp. Had something happened to Andrea? Or Lindsey? Heart pounding, Mark drove the Land Cruiser several blocks past his own property, turned left, continued two more blocks, and parked in the million dollar shadows near a half demolished tear-down. He jumped out, peeled off his jumpsuit and the Biovak visitor's pass, and balled them up under his arm. Keeping watch for inbound trucks, outbound vans, and any other conveyance that might contain a big shot from Biovak, he jogged home, and stuffed the white wad and its cache of film under a dense growth of azaleas near the police vehicle.

He crept quietly around to the back of the house. Lights blazed from the kitchen window. Through the glass in the door Mark saw two uniformed officers sitting at the table. He blinked. They were eating spaghetti.

Before he could process the bizarre scene, Andrea stepped into view wearing oven mitts. In her hands rested a flute of bread. Her face looked as pale as the Parmesan on the policeman's plate. Mark climbed the steps and pulled open the door.

"Mark!" Andrea exclaimed, placing the bread on the table. She hurried to him. The two officers wiped their mouths with napkins and rose.

Andrea hugged Mark fiercely, then stepped back to introduce Officers Olson and Zeeb, a veteran and a rookie by the looks of them. "The police received a call from Dr. Broder about the bones you gave her to identify," Andrea explained with commendable composure. "Remember, the ones Wiggles found?"

Mark nodded slowly. After the veterinarian told him Wiggles had been poisoned he neglected to follow up on the bones. He knew what was coming next.

"Mr. Grant," Officer Olson said somberly. "Two of those bones were human. As a formality we obtained a warrant to search your property, but we prefer to speak with you first."

"I see," Mark said gravely, looking at Andrea. He wondered how much she had told them.

Andrea took Mark's arm and steered him to a vacant chair at the table. The way she squeezed his wrist told him there was more. He dropped into the seat and looked at her expectantly.

"These two gave me quite a scare," she said, pouring him a glass of water. "You know how much I hate being alone at night."

Untrue, he knew. The men scared her because she thought they might be connected with Biovak.

"When we finally got Mrs. Grant to open the door," Officer Zeeb explained, "she told us you were due before midnight and invited us to wait."

She also invited them to dinner, Mark noticed, wondering how many rules the officers had bent by eating it. Suddenly parched, he drained the glass of water.

"That was the least I could do," Andrea said, observing Mark's glance at the meal on the table. "When I didn't answer the door,

Officer Olson called me on his cell phone, but I made him park the police van in front before I would consider letting them in. Even then I telephoned Dr. Broder to confirm their story, although I only got her answering service." Andrea smiled. "After they held their badges to the window, I felt I owed them some hospitality. Spaghetti, darling?"

Mark looked at the slippery red mess on Officer Olson's plate and felt his stomach clench. "Uh, no thanks."

"Mark," Andrea said, leaning toward him. "They also escorted our daughter to the door. She's upstairs, asleep."

Mark's chin dropped. He looked quickly at both men and waited for Andrea to continue.

"During the interminable wait for me to decide what to do, the officers saw Lindsey walk up the driveway. She told them a ridiculous story about a scavenger hunt. We really must speak firmly with her about sneaking out after dark."

Without a word Mark bolted from the table. He took the stairs two at a time. Lindsey was sleeping peacefully in her bed, just as Andrea said. She looked so serene and trusting; Mark wanted to cry.

Evidently the kidnappers had treated her well, acted as though her incarceration were a game, and then brought her home a little past bedtime, unharmed. Mark refused to feel grateful. Lindsey's kidnappers knew they didn't have to hurt her to accomplish their goal—scaring the wits out of her parents. He gently tucked her favorite stuffed animal, a sea lion, into the crook of her arm and left the room.

"If it's not too late, Mr. Grant, I would be glad to take your statement now," Officer Olson said when Mark returned to the kitchen. "Just tell us how you came into possession of these remains, and anything else you might know about them."

Mark lowered himself into the fourth chair at the table without taking his eyes off Andrea. The relief they both felt was almost palpable. She had managed to ease Lindsey into bed and detain the officers until he returned without revealing a morsel of information. If his foray into

Biovak had failed, Mark would remain free to plead ignorance about the origin of the bones until his case against Shand was air-tight.

But his foray had not failed. Shand and Folee were as good as cooked. They were no doubt also seriously alarmed by the imposters who had nosed around in their file room. Who knew what they would do next? Lindsey was safe. The officers could help her stay that way. And Mark had less than a week—six days—to execute the rest of his rapidly evolving plan. He needed allies.

He regarded the two earnest, armed, and able public servants sitting at his kitchen table and made up his mind. Now was as good a time as any to begin cleaning up the colossal mess he had stepped into when he bought Hancock's Landscape Services. He smiled at Officers Olson and Zeeb, cleared his throat, and started talking.

He began with the bones Lindsey presented at Wiggles's funeral, and filled in the story to the events of that evening, right up to his hasty job of hiding the film in the bushes outside. It felt good to unburden himself, to share the ingenious plot he had uncovered, and test the nightmarish story on two sensible, uninvolved individuals. Telling Officers Olson and Zeeb made him feel like he had reentered the real world.

Andrea stared at Mark, barely moving, while he related the discoveries he and Natalie had made inside Biovak. The personnel files on Fred Dunn and Mark himself. The huge discrepancy between the waste Biovak collected and the waste it disposed of legally. The perfidious involvement of Rudy Vale and Sam Folee, and their almost certain intention to implicate Mark.

"Guess who talked Lindsey into leaving the airport," Andrea interrupted. "Rudy Vale."

The policemen looked at Mark, expecting a reaction. He sat with his jaw clenched, absorbing the full treachery of Hancock's trusted foreman.

"Lindsey told me she recognized Rudy, of course," Andrea continued. "She thought he was part of some elaborate game you and I and

Ellen had planned. She's been out with one of Rudy's crews all after-noon, swimming in the pool at an estate they tend."

Mark could only shake his head. Rudy was a confident bastard. He probably owned a truckload of laborers who would swear he spent the entire evening with them. Rudy's so-called job at Hancock's didn't worry him because his real employers—the ones who paid the big bucks—were Shand and Folee. And if Mark tried to threaten him directly, Rudy could always recall the little hand-holding scene he had witnessed in Mark's office. The lunch with Natalie was hardly a federal offense but the intimacy was, in retrospect, indiscreet—a mistake Mark would prefer to leave in the past. Mark regarded Andrea and hoped the jar of eyeballs he had smashed into Rudy Vale's skull gave the traitor a permanent headache.

The two policemen listened intently, absorbed, learning much more than they had come to find out. Officer Olson got out a pen and jotted notes on a pad. Young Zeeb, whose bulk barely fit on the kitchen chair, started to fidget, restless, looking as though he'd like to get his mitts on the meatheads who would snatch a little girl.

"We'll have to talk to your friends," Olson said. "Natalie Dunn and Rick...?"

"Edwards," Mark filled in. "You'll find them both at Rick's condo on Wilshire." He recited Rick's address while Olson wrote down the information. Andrea raised her eyebrows. Natalie and Rick. That sur-prised her too.

"Now, Mr. Grant," Olson said. "If you will go get the film you left outside, please, I have a few more questions to ask your wife." He glanced at the blood trailing up Mark's wrist. "First I suggest you wash that hand."

Andrea's gaze fell on Mark's wound and she looked at him with concern.

"Someone tried to have me for dinner," he explained, examining the teeth marks across his palm. Already Biovak's shower room seemed a distant memory. He got up and went to the kitchen sink, grateful for Olson's solicitude.

While he gingerly soaped his hands, Andrea told the officers about her circuitous trip to the airport—which no doubt gave Lindsey the idea that a great game had begun—Lindsey's kidnapping, and the real reasons for her caution when the men first arrived at the house. She sounded as relieved as Mark had been to finally speak about their ordeal. Olson brushed aside her earlier subterfuge and praised both of them for their candor. For the first time in weeks, Mark felt they had regained control of their lives. He stuck a bandage on his palm, exchanged a cautious, hopeful smile with his wife, and hurried out the kitchen door.

The wadded up jumpsuit remained exactly where he had stashed it. He knelt on the grass next to the police vehicle and reached deep into the azalea bushes, inhaling the sweet fragrance of greenery and blossoms—and something else. He sniffed. The jumpsuit?

Pulling the canvas overalls from under the bush seemed to mask rather than intensify the odor in the area. The suit gave off a pungent, meaty mix Mark remembered all too well from the warehouse. What he smelled near the bushes seemed more like chemicals, a solvent.

It didn't matter. He gripped the bunched up fabric with its load of film canisters, placed a steadying hand on the police van, and rose from his knees. The mission into Biovak had succeeded beyond his expectations. He and Natalie collected more incriminating material than he had dared hope. Neither of his friends had been hurt. Lindsey was home. And soon he would have the entire police force on his side. Maybe his luck was changing.

He glanced absently at his hand, the good one he had pressed on the vehicle. The hood felt tacky, gummed up, as though it recently sat beneath some juicy tree. But the nearest jacaranda grew halfway down the block.

Curious, Mark touched the side panel again, wondering what plant could weep so profusely that time of year. He brought his fingers to his nose and inhaled, expecting the sweetness of sap. Slowly, like a waft of poison gas, a different odor pulsed through his system. The smell he had detected moments earlier. Paint.

He rubbed a forefinger across the blue letters on the side door and watched the crisp dark edges smear. For a long, dark moment he stood perfectly still. Then, clutching the jumpsuit and its load of film, he stepped to the back of the van, glanced toward the house, and quietly turned the handle on the rear door. Unlocked. The panel swung out. Instead of a security grill and a back seat, the van contained a flimsy cardboard partition behind the driver's seat, and an open, flat area from the partition to the rear. In this space, piled almost to the roof, sat a heap of fat, black plastic bags.

Mark stared at the load while a cold, mechanical calm iced his gut. From the top pocket of the canvas overalls he extracted the silver knife. Snapping back the blade, he reached toward the nearest sack and, feeling a nightmarish sense of déjà vu, sliced a long slash around the middle. He stepped aside to let light from the street lamp fall across the dark plastic. What tumbled out sank his soul. Ampoules, syringes, fragments of plastic and cord, dark-stained gauze, a paper cup. Biovak cargo in a Biovak van.

CHAPTER 36

▼

"Lindsey thought our route to the airport was a game," Andrea explained to the two officers, pouring coffee into mugs. "I came home the same way. By cab, foot, and car. Wearing sun glasses. Darting looks left and right. I was suspicious of everything that moved, but of course Rudy Vale, Mark's foreman, got to Lindsey anyway and convinced her the 'game' wasn't over. That was clever. Lindsey has been taught not to speak with strangers."

Andrea sighed with a mixture of chagrin and relief. "I doubt I could get a job in your detectives division."

Zeeb ran his eyes down her soft linen skirt. "We would be thrilled to have you, Mrs. Grant," he drawled.

"Your caution was understandable," Olson interjected, casting a severe look in Zeeb's direction. "You had reason to be frightened." He turned a page in his note pad. "Now if you will let us know exactly where you planned to send your daughter, I'll notify our local bureau and make sure the location remains a safe haven."

Andrea stood motionless, holding the coffee pot. Safe haven? She felt grateful to Olson for taking her precautions seriously, but after what happened to Lindsey she had no intention of sending her daughter away again for a long, long time. She said so.

Olson nodded again. "Okay, I understand. It makes sense to sit tight until the major players—the people who threatened your daughter—are behind bars." He sat forward. "Nonetheless, it is important for us to know Lindsey's planned destination. The information will remain strictly confidential, of course. To ensure her continued safety and complete the record."

Andrea looked at the officer. She and Mark agreed to tell no one where Lindsey was going. Why involve Ellen and Eddie now? She turned toward the blackened window, considering. What was keeping Mark?

"Mrs. Grant?"

Andrea swallowed. He was only trying to help. Not long ago she would have given major appendages for police protection for her daughter. "You're right," she said, flushed. What had she been thinking? "Lindsey was going to stay with my sister, Ellen Peterson."

Officer Olson lifted his pen and wrote.

"Mrs. Edward Peterson," Andrea continued. "Three Wren Lane, Hooper, Wisconsin."

The phone in the kitchen began to ring. Andrea looked at the clock on the wall. Past midnight. Puzzled, she reached across the counter and lifted the receiver. "Hello?"

"Andrea?" said a female voice. "This is Fran Broder."

For one blank second Andrea couldn't think who Fran Broder was. When the identity of the caller came to her, she wondered why their veterinarian would phone in the middle of the night. "Er—yes, Doctor?"

"I'm sorry to call so late," the voice apologized. "But I just got your message and it's tagged urgent. Oh, excuse me one moment please."

Over the line came the sound of dogs barking. Andrea thought of Wiggles with a pang. She heard footsteps, a stern command, silence. Dr. Broder returned to the phone.

"My apologies," she said. "I'm training a pair of delinquent Dobermans."

Andrea shifted her weight, impatient to reach the point. Officer Zeeb had risen from the table and was peering out the window.

The vet continued. "Actually I'm a little confused by this message. It says you want to know what I told the police about the bones your husband brought me for analysis. Is that right?"

"Well, yes," Andrea replied. "But now I don't think it's necess—"

"Uh, Mrs. Grant," Dr. Broder interrupted. "I haven't called the police. I wanted to be sure of my findings, so I sent the bones to another lab for verification. The results aren't due for several days."

Andrea felt the blood drain to some far depth of her anatomy. The words "haven't called the police" marched across her mind like a firing squad at an execution. She stared at the hulking form of Zeeb with his nose to the kitchen window, not daring to meet Olson's eyes. From his chair at the table, the older man watched her closely.

"I see," Andrea croaked into the mouthpiece, clearing her vocal cords. "Well, um, you're sure about this?" Her throat had dried up.

"Of course. As you know, it's quite a serious matter."

Uniforms, badges, guns. Out front, a police van. Who were these men? Sickened, Andrea knew. And she and Mark had told the so-called officers everything, including the location of Lindsey's last, best chance for safety. She took a deep, exhausted breath.

"Yes, extremely serious," she said into the mouthpiece, struggling to find the correct tone of voice. She gripped the receiver and made herself stay calm. Out of the corner of her eye she saw Zeeb turn to face her.

"What you've described sounds like her allergies," Andrea continued, dredging up facts from a recent *Healthy Times*. Frowning, she continued, "My mother-in-law reacts severely to a number of allergens, and is susceptible to anaphylactic shock." She allowed a measure of the genuine panic she felt to enter her voice. "Yes, it certainly is an emergency. I'll go tell my husband right away."

She held her breath, waiting for word that Dr. Broder understood something was terribly wrong at Andrea's end of the line. But she heard only silence.

"Doctor?" Hot tears had gathered behind her eyes, storm clouds on the horizon. She could not let them loose.

Behind her Olson spoke. "Since when do veterinarians take care of old ladies?"

Andrea turned to find him standing behind her. In one hand he held the unplugged phone line and in the other, a pistol.

Zeeb stepped forward and took the receiver from her hand. Swiftly, before he could stop her, Andrea picked up a crock of wooden spoons and heaved it at the window above the sink. "Run, Mark, run!" she screamed toward the pane of glass. The jar bounced off the window frame and shattered in the sink. Spoons clattered in several directions.

Zeeb smacked her across the face with the back of his hand, a blow that sent her reeling into the corner.

"Just shut her up, Zeeb. You don't have to hurt her," Olson said, squinting through the window. "I doubt he heard that, but I'll go out and make sure."

Olson looked at Andrea, now crumpled over the countertop, and replaced his gun in the holster on his belt. "Your husband and I are going to pay a visit on your friends Rick and Natalie. I suggest you behave yourself while we're gone. Don't forget," he glanced at Zeeb, "your kid's upstairs."

Leaning on her elbows, Andrea watched a drop of blood splatter on her forearm. The blow had made her nose bleed. Out of the corner of her eye she saw Olson speaking in a low voice to Zeeb. She felt sick, knowing she herself had invited these men into her house. She had fallen all over them with gratitude for returning Lindsey. And then she had let Mark reveal everything he and Natalie had learned about Shand and Folee and the criminal enterprise they ran. Between gulps of air she swallowed, blinking with shock and humiliation. Slowly, like an animal stalking prey, she eased her palm across the counter and closed her fingers around the handle of a paring knife.

Olson went out the door. Zeeb sashayed in her direction, hitching up his trousers. When he was close behind her, she spun around and lunged, thrusting the knife with all her might into his ample belly. Blood spattered the front of his shirt and he stopped in his tracks, astonished.

Wide-eyed, still holding the knife against him, Andrea watched Zeeb drop his gaze to the crimson stains down his front. For what seemed like an eternity neither of them moved. Through the silence in the kitchen came the sound of an engine in front of the house, revving into gear. Andrea's heart sank as the noise faded down the street. Mark and Olson had departed.

Suddenly Zeeb's hand shot up, clamped on her wrist, and yanked her fist away from his body. Andrea's stare followed his. The knife in her hand was shiny, clean, and bent at an acute angle. She had struck his belt.

Blood dripped from her nose, down her chin, and onto the white T-shirt she had worn all day. The corners of Zeeb's lips curled into a leer. "Want to get physical? I'm happy to oblige."

Before she could resist he jerked her right arm behind her, sending a riptide of pain through her shoulder. She cried out. He pushed her roughly across the room until the backs of her thighs pressed hard against the edge of the kitchen table. With a sweep of his free arm, he brushed dishes, silverware, and food to the floor.

Throwing the weight of his upper body upon her, he slammed her backward until her spine lay flat on the crumbs of his dinner. With lips so close she could feel his breath in her seeping nostrils, he uttered words no weapon could match.

"Cooperate or I'll try this out on your little girl."

Pinned to the table, her shoulder screaming with pain, Andrea stared at a crack in the ceiling and felt him fumble for the hem of her skirt. Jagged fingernails dragged a path across the flesh above her knee.

Hot tears pooled in her eyes. She lay on the table like a stick of wood, and prayed that Lindsey wouldn't hear them and come downstairs. Please, Lord, let her sleep.

Panting with power, Zeeb tightened his grip on the arm bent behind her and muscled against her thighs. "That's nice, real nice," he drooled, knuckling aside her inconsequential underwear. A reedy noise like the wail of a small animal rose from her throat. And then the kitchen door burst open. Zeeb half rose from the table in time to receive the full force of two snarling, fifty-pound Dobermans who had recently learned the meaning of the words *sic 'em!* Behind the dogs, holding a cellular phone to her ear stood Dr. Broder.

CHAPTER 37

▼

Mark closed the door on the incriminating black bags, fighting a mighty urge to tear into the kitchen and beat the shit out of Olson and Zeeb. His capacity for staying cool under pressure was just about exhausted. The night so far had been interminable, now this.

As he stood next to the recently painted van his anger almost eclipsed the panic that was rising in him like a moon. Were they cocky or what? Pretending to be cops while a load of illicit cargo festered right here in their so-called police van. Acting like heroes for returning the child they themselves probably helped kidnap. What colossal arrogance. He had fallen for their performance like a first class clay-brain.

He buried his fingers in his hair and stared at the cheery, mocking wattage that shone from every pane of glass in his house. Welcome to the party, it seemed to say. Bring your own costume, side arm, and seven-year-old abductee.

This party was about to end.

With the zeal of a born hoodlum, he circled the van, opened the driver's door, and groped inside. In a moment he located the compartment he was looking for. Closing the door without a sound, he laid the jumpsuit on the pavement and went to work on the van's left front wheel.

The lug nuts were badly rusted. He applied the wrench and strained, clenching his teeth. After a few hard cranks, one of the ancient parts rotated slowly on its threads. In moments he had loosened all five fasteners counterclockwise just enough to make them lethal.

Based on the condition of the lug nuts, Mark guessed the rust around the wheel's center hole had corroded the wheel to the hub. That meant the wheel might remain in place on the axle of the moving vehicle even after the lug nuts fell off. But only until the van rounded a few sharp corners or hit a good-sized sink hole. Then, watch out.

Mark looked at the brightly lit house, knowing his minutes alone wouldn't last for long. He gathered up the pockets of film, ran across the lawn, and tossed the wrench into the bushes. Sidling past the hedge that bordered Helen Woodley's restored and verdant landscape, he dug deep inside the overalls and threw handful after handful of precious, incriminating film across the tangled quarter-acre that hosted his neighbor's renowned zucchini patch. Soaring through the dark of night, the sealed plastic containers scattered, fell, and disappeared beneath Helen's rich canopy of vegetables and greenery.

He knelt and quickly refilled the canvas pockets with wood chips from under Helen's neatly groomed Eugenia bushes. Then he heard it. A crash? Coming from the direction of his house. As his pulse soared, he balled up the jumpsuit and its load of cedar and sprinted around the hedge. He loped across the grass, making a sharp right turn at a plausible path from the azalea bushes to the kitchen door. At that moment, Olson stepped outside.

In one stride Mark decelerated to a walk and tried to control his breathing. His only chance to free his family was to keep Olson thinking he still viewed him as a savior. "I found it," Mark said, managing a crooked grin while holding the canvas bundle tightly under his arm.

Olson approached warily. "Let's see."

"Uh, sure." Mark fumbled with the garment, keeping himself a distance from the man he wanted to suffocate. Shapes were difficult to discern through the heavy fabric. He smiled sheepishly, pretending clumsiness. When he located the pocket he wanted, he slipped his hand inside. In the dim light on the outskirts of the glow from his house, he turned his palm upward and uncurled his fingers. Between the bandage on his wound and the shine of his wedding band sat a single plastic canister of film, the one he had decided to keep for just such an emergency.

"All the proof we need, right here in these pockets," he said, trying to sound triumphant.

Olson nodded while Mark returned the film to a pocket and screwed the suit into a wad. He started toward the house.

Olson stepped into his path. "Thank you, Mr. Grant. I'll take it right here." He reached for the bundle. "And if you wouldn't mind, I'd like you to come along while I question your friends, Natalie and Rick."

"Now?" Mark looked toward the house, still worried about the noise he had heard. More than anything he wanted to alert Andrea to the reptile in her kitchen, call the real police, and get these two out of there.

"Now," Olson affirmed, bunching up the canvas. "It shouldn't take very long."

Reluctantly, Mark turned away from the house, telling himself Andrea and Lindsey would be okay as long as the men continued their bid for Academy Award nominations. Zeeb and Olson had nothing to gain by blowing their cover. They no doubt wanted to keep things cool until they figured out a way to silence Rick and Natalie. At the moment, Rick and Natalie needed him more.

Mark followed Olson toward the fake, booby trapped police van. His empty stomach began to roil. Olson opened the passenger door, laid the overalls on the floor in front, and waited for Mark to get in. At the door Mark hesitated, then sank onto the vinyl seat. He moved the overalls carefully aside with his foot. The air in the van reminded him of the stink inside Biovak. He cranked the window on the passenger side all the way down, locked his door, and buckled his seatbelt. Tight.

In the pale light of the street, Olson failed to notice the minor alteration to his left front wheel. He climbed into the van, slammed the door, and turned the key in the ignition. Headlights on. Brake off. Then, almost as an afterthought, he felt around for his seat belt and buckled up.

"Take a left at the corner," Mark said.

"Right." Olson maneuvered the van in the general direction of Wilshire Boulevard. Mark guessed he wasn't too familiar with streets on the West Side. "There is construction in the next block so turn right here," he said, bracing himself.

Olson executed the second turn without mishap. Rick's condominium was only five blocks away. A trickle of sweat ran down Mark's temple. "Go right again."

"Right? Are you sure?"

"Yeah. Wilshire's over there." Mark gestured vaguely and let his left hand fall near the buckle on Olson's seatbelt. "See, straight ahead, then turn right."

As the van rounded the corner onto the six broad lanes of Wilshire Boulevard, Mark felt the first wobble. Traffic was light at that hour of the night, and Olson responded by stepping on the gas. A man on a mission, he appeared oblivious to the erratic performance of his vehicle. The van bobbled precariously along the rows of glittering condos while Mark kept his eyes on the pavement. Then he saw it, straight ahead.

"Get over now!" he ordered. "Turn left here!"

Startled, Olson jerked the wheel toward the left lane, driving his left front tire straight into the deeply lacerated gouge of a sink hole. Mark simultaneously grasped his door handle, braced his head against the headrest, and squeezed the release button on Olson's seatbelt. A split second later, the van's left front axle slammed against the pavement in an ear-splitting screech of metal on cement. In rapid succession the vehicle spun out, teetered, and rolled, throwing Olson and quantities of medical waste into the path of oncoming traffic. A panicked driver in a black Lexus swerved away from the flying debris, then tried without success to avoid hitting the man in blue.

When the badly dented van lurched to a halt on its three wheels and broken axle, Mark found himself peppered with glass but not seriously hurt. He extricated himself from his seatbelt, crawled through the open window, and stood dizzily next to the creaking wreck. Without wasting a moment, he eyed an opening in the rapidly building gapers' block and sprinted across three lanes of traffic to the opposite side of the road. As he jogged down Wilshire Boulevard he passed the left front wheel of Olson's van, still rolling toward Beverly Hills.

CHAPTER 38

▼

One week later, on Thursday, June 14, at 5 AM, four police units simultaneously arrested Julian Shand, Sam Folee, George Alder, and a hospitalized and recuperating Rudy Vale on charges of fraud, conspiracy, racketeering, kidnapping, environmental mayhem, and the suspected murder of Frederick H. Dunn.

Julian Shand requested permission to smoke a cigar in the squad car that took him to jail. Permission was denied. Sam Folee left home without his toupee and was unrecognizable to many of his landscape customers who saw him later on the nightly news. George Alder tried to slash his wrists with a barbless fish hook but was discovered before he lost more than a pint of blood. In his hospital bed, Rudy Vale heard the charges against him and passed out.

The four arrests launched a carefully calibrated plan of damage control designed to stem panic in the community, short circuit misinformation, and generate a concerted, rational response to the environmental crisis caused by the illegal dumping. Not incidentally, the plan would also save Hancock's Landscape Services from extinction.

Mark knew timing was critical. Already reporters were swarming over the story about Olson and his fake police van full of biohazardous waste. Zeeb's apprehension had been less spectacular because the badly mauled man went straight from Mark and Andrea's kitchen to the hospital in police custody. But when the newshounds got wind of that morning's predawn, high-profile arrests, they would chase the details all day long. If Mark's plan went as expected, by the time the cameras rolled for the evening news, the reporters would have an even bigger story to tell.

*   *   *   *

At 9 AM, Rick Edwards got up from his chair on the dais in the ballroom of the Biltmore Hotel to deliver the keynote address to some eight hundred pharmaceutical executives gathered for the Second Annual International Conference on Sustainable Development. His topic: *The Responsible Life Cycle of Products.*

As he took his place at the podium, a large screen descended into view behind him. Applause rose and fell; coffee cups rattled in saucers; someone coughed. Rick surveyed the audience, and began.

"I am truly honored to stand here this morning among my colleagues in the pharmaceutical industry who share a common concern for saving and improving human life."

His gaze swept the sea of faces and stopped on a distinguished wavy-haired gentleman a few tables away. "I see, for example, Mitch Roos, chairman of Pfipps-Crabbe, a company that is charting new paths in genetically engineered blood proteins, membrane oxygenators, and other technologies that are advancing the treatment of hemophilia, heart disease, asthma, and cancer." The chairman dipped his head graciously.

"And over there," Rick pointed to the opposite side of the audience, "is Susannah Tenor of Hauser, the company that recently introduced a needle-free IV therapy system to protect health care workers from potentially life-threatening accidents." Susannah Tenor sat up in her chair and smiled.

"I am also glad to see the president of Jacque Lezarde, a pioneer in antiviral, anti-AIDS, and cardiac resuscitation drugs. With us too is

Martin Bates of American Research Products, a premier maker of clinical and research lab equipment. And—what do you know—right over here is a large contingent from my own company, Burton-Abbey—"

Laughter ripped through the audience.

"—a leader in the manufacture, marketing, and distribution of single-use products for diagnosis, surgery, and patient care."

Rick waited while the conferees settled, nicely warmed by his remarks.

"This meeting is a testament to our shared commitment to improving human life in yet another important way: by resolving the environmental challenges we face as our businesses grow and prosper. We have gathered here to ask what we can do through better emissions controls, more environmentally aware purchasing, packaging, transportation, and systems to promote a cleaner, healthier environment."

He paused. "The conference, I might add, is also a testament to the growing proliferation of government regulations." Nods and grunts from the audience supported his statement.

"Twenty years ago federal environmental regulations filled 450 pages. Today those rules cover more than 10,000 pages. And that's not counting environmental controls imposed on industry by individual states. Every person in this room knows that mere compliance with government regulations is not enough. Compliance today is a moving target. We in the pharmaceutical industry need the foresight to get ahead of the rules or we will be forever trying to catch up." Murmurs of agreement sounded across the room.

Rick signaled to an aide, and the lights slowly dimmed. On the screen behind him appeared an enlarged view of an earth-encrusted vial. A second slide showed another dirty vial, then a beaker, an ampoule, miscellaneous scraps and shards in rapid succession, slide after slide, as the images flashed and the camera backed away to show a dozen gritty containers half buried in a vegetable garden. The next startling sequence moved in, close up, to focus on the labels clearly visible on several of the items. Pfippes-Crabbe.

A few people in the audience exclaimed. Others tittered nervously. At the table near the podium Mitch Roos's expression froze on his face.

"My talk this morning is going to focus on the disposal of the products we produce," Rick said in a strong voice. "How we can help our customers reduce, recycle, and responsibly manage medical waste."

More slides appeared on the screen behind him. Grimy syringes, soil-streaked IV bottles, fragments of petri dishes, a coil of tube. The trash was shown strewn across a lawn from an opened garbage bag. Dumped from a clay pot. Freshly dug from a flower bed. Resting against a manicured edge of grass. Many of the items bore labels, logos, or an unmistakable design that made the audience stir. Hauser. Jacques Lezarde. American Research Products. Burton-Abbey. The noise level in the ballroom rose.

"I don't need to remind you that volumes of regulations govern the disposal of medical waste," Rick said in a louder voice as the offensive images continued their assault. "But as I will explain—and as you can plainly see—the regulations can and have been circumvented. These pictures are authentic. They were taken this week in Bel Air, Beverly Hills, Brentwood, Holmby Hills, Pacific Palisades, San Marino—communities in and around the city of Los Angeles."

"Good lord," said someone near the podium.

"Before we as an industry are slapped with more severe regulatory controls—not to mention an outbreak of infectious disease and a public relations nightmare—I propose we take action now, today, to clean up this mess and figure out how to keep it from happening again."

*   *   *   *

At 11 AM, twelve miles from Rick's pharmaceutical conference at the Biltmore Hotel, Natalie Dunn stared across the podium in Ajax Hall at an auditorium packed with local luminaries. In addition to many of her former university professors, the audience for the annual Silas K. Udahl Lecture included a galaxy of business owners, chamber of commerce presidents, mayors, city council members, and officers of neighborhood homeowners associations from Westwood to Westlake Village.

Natalie knew these people hadn't come merely to see her. They had come to be seen, to network, to rub shoulders with other invited guests who could be useful to them. The annual lecture and reception had become prestigious in these circles, boosted even more in the previous week by a monsoon of last-minute publicity. Natalie's announced topic—*Business in the 'Hood The New Symbiosis*—struck a chord.

She adjusted the microphone. Student volunteers stood in the aisles waiting to distribute handouts stacked neatly on a table in front. Natalie smiled at those assembled. In the rear of the auditorium, a video camera began to roll.

"Silas K. Udahl was a business professor who believed leadership is the heart and soul of management," she began. "Leadership—not theories, organizational charts, or formulas. Nothing, in fact, that can be spelled out in a textbook. As you might imagine, Professor Udahl was something of an anomaly in academia."

Laughter sounded in the hall, followed by expectant silence. Natalie's low, silken voice had entranced her listeners already.

"The professor would be pleased that so many notable leaders are present today for an event that commemorates him. He might regret, however, that your purpose for being here is to sit and be lectured." More chuckles. "As many of you know, Silas Udahl was a gifted teacher who believed leadership could not be taught. He did believe, however, that leadership could be learned. His classes were famous for running overtime because his students were so engrossed in brainstorming, team building, and the resolution of business problems drawn from real life that they didn't want to leave. Professor Udahl gave them the chance to learn leadership by leading."

Natalie paused, and looked around the room. "Which brings me, in a roundabout way, to my topic, *Business in the 'Hood: The New Symbiosis*. I'd like to illustrate this symbiosis as Professor Udahl might have done, by presenting a case study, a portrait of a small entrepreneurial company that has benefited in innovative ways from its neighborhood and its neighbors, and made a significant impact in return."

She gestured to the student volunteers, who began to distribute the first handouts from the table.

"These are financial statements from the company in question for its first two years of operation. While you're looking them over I'll give you a brief overview of the business, its market, and some of the reasons for its success. We're talking about a medical waste hauler I'll call Company X."

For the next ten minutes Natalie described "Company X" as she first perceived the phenom called Biovak—a paragon of entrepreneurship that provided jobs, gave hope and meaning to the people in its vicinity, and found creative ways of working that cut costs and increased productivity in the delivery of a needed service. She mentioned the company's homeless and rehabilitated warehouse workers, its incentives to remain clean and sober, and its unorthodox outbound fleet. Then she waited while her audience absorbed the information on Company X's balance sheet.

Murmurs rose from various parts of the hall. Admiring, incredulous. A few people laughed. Profit margins like that for a start-up?

"The numbers are accurate," Natalie informed them. "They amazed me too." She took the microphone in her hand and stepped away from the podium. "How do you suppose Company X was able to make so much profit in its first two years of operation?"

She walked to the edge of the stage and looked into individual faces in the front rows. Guests at these lectures were not accustomed to speaking out.

"It had to be illegal," someone near the back shouted jokingly. The audience laughed.

Natalie nodded and smiled. "I knew this was a smart class." She waited for the laughter to subside. "He's right. It was illegal."

What? Heads turned. People shifted in their seats. In the front row the dean of the business school scowled. This was not the speech he had expected.

Natalie stood her ground. "The owner of Company X, his two principal partners, and a top official from the Department of Environmental Health were arrested this morning on multiple charges including environmental mayhem. Company X is Biovak, Inc., of Los Angeles, California. And, ladies and gentlemen, there is strong evidence that for the past two years Biovak, Inc., has been dumping medical waste in our backyards."

A din arose. Natalie walked to the podium and hammered the gavel. She signaled to the students to pass out the second packet of information. It had been assembled that week with the help of Wanda Juju and other residents of the warehouse district—whose loyalty to Biovak was superseded only by cash up front. The material included detailed maps of Biovak's prime dumping districts, illustrated descriptions of the objects in a typical drop, and a list of likely places the medical waste might be found on a landscaped property. The packet also contained a guide for the safe removal of the trash; a list of recommended protective clothing, tools, and bagging procedures; and proposed consolidation sites for collection by legitimate haulers.

"The information presented here will help you understand the scope of the problem and what needs to be done about it," Natalie continued in an even voice. "As I speak, the same materials are being printed and sent to thousands of your neighbors, customers, and constituents across southern California. Other concerned parties are now devising a financial framework for the cleanup, using seized assets of the culpable parties as well as corporate contributions from the pharmaceutical industry.

"But the solution to this problem—yes, I assure you, it's a very real problem—is going to require more than information and money." Natalie paused for several beats. "It's going to require leadership."

One by one, she leveled her gaze on the faces in front of her. "Starting today, this afternoon, people in our communities are going to be afraid. They're going to wonder if it is safe to walk in their own backyards. They're going to worry about protecting themselves and their families. They're going to need reassurance and guidance as well as goods and services. We in this room can help meet those needs by recognizing the symbiosis that exists between our businesses and our communities. We can stock and distribute protective clothing, scoops, bags, and other needed supplies, and make our stores centers of vital information. We can develop new services specializing in cleanup and hauling. We can encourage our political leaders to facilitate the recovery by easing certain fee and permit requirements. We in this auditorium can innovate, motivate, and inspire. We can, in short, lead."

Natalie leaned forward on the podium. "In the days and months ahead, meeting the needs of our communities is going to be good business—very good business. And I suggest we start now, here, this very afternoon to lay the groundwork for a concerted and effective response."

Some people were writing notes on the pages in their laps. Dozens had opened their cell phones. Two or three got up and hurried out the door. Several hands shot up.

"Good," Natalie responded. "Now let's hear what you have to say."

*   *   *   *

At noon, not far from the pandemonium in Ajax Hall, Andrea Grant scrawled her initials on the revised blueline for *Healthy Times,* sat back in her chair, and sighed with relief. A technician snatched the blue and gray proof from her hand and rushed from the tiny office to the great iron machinery of Pico Press.

She had done the unthinkable. Substituted at the very last minute an entirely new, full-page cover story in each of the four newsletters scheduled to go to press that day. Bad, bad form in printing circles—

schedule-busting work and expensive too. Both of her printers had conniptions. At Alpha Print the crew told Andrea not to expect any fruitcake next Christmas. Who could blame them for being cranky?

The good news, as far as the printers were concerned, was that the hastily revised bluelines did not have to go back to their respective editors for approval. Andrea could—and did—sign off on them herself.

She shifted in the old wooden office chair and rubbed her shoulder. The truth was, none of the newsletter chiefs had the slightest idea their cover stories had been changed.

Two days earlier the editor of *LA Business Report* signed off on a press-ready proof that featured job cuts at major banks. The lead story in *Property Line* was about Saturday's grand opening of Glenwater Place. Andrea moved that article to page two. *Garden Works* led with *Drought-Proof Your Landscape.* And *Healthy Times* planned to run a front-page survey of LA's top gyms, fitness gurus, and personal trainers.

As soon as the editors released their bluelines for printing, Andrea took them to her studio, inserted the new cover story, and, today, exercised her time-honored privilege of approving the revised proofs herself. She had never before abused her editors' trust. Now she doubted she would ever have their trust, not to mention their business, again.

The blue pencil she had used to sign her business away rolled off the table and clattered on the linoleum. She leaned over and picked it up, calm now that the mutinous deed was done. Waiting for approvals on this explosive story would have meant waiting a month if not longer to go to press, when the need for timely and accurate information was now, today, before people throughout the region started to panic. And before the perpetrators of the dumping atrocity who were still at large took steps to cover up, distort, or minimize the extent of their crimes. Or silence the people who knew.

Andrea shivered and looked at her watch. In a few minutes she would go to the press room and check the first print run. Rick's speech had started at nine o'clock, Natalie's at eleven. Mark would be occupied the entire day. They all had agreed on the importance of acting fast, before the breaking news was likely to spin out of control. None of them doubted for a moment that Biovak's racketeers could manipulate at least a handful of influential newsmakers, editors, and reporters, possibly even from jail. Leaving the development of this story to chance was a far greater risk than the professional risks the four of them were taking that day.

Andrea picked up the carefully drafted manuscript on the table in front of her. Custom-written, rewritten, and revised with care for each newsletter, the new cover story began with a flag, a banner, and a sub-head:

Medical Waste in Your Backyard?

BIOVAK CEO ARRESTED FOR ILLEGAL DUMPING

Now the Cleanup Begins

In a few hours those headlines and the thirty-five detailed paragraphs that followed would be on their way to a quarter of a million subscribers throughout southern California. In no time the newsletters would reach at least twice that many readers, including reporters, editors, and publishers of larger newspapers in Los Angeles, Ventura, and Orange counties. Television and radio outlets would jump on the story.

Andrea's job as a graphics editor could be history. But her family and her friends would be safe from harm by Shand and his paid thugs. From that day forward, the Biovak cabal would have nothing to gain by dropping rocks on people's heads, poisoning dogs, threatening immigrants, or kidnapping children in order to torment their parents. Scattered like seeds through the words in those headlines, the truth could lodge, take root, and grow.

CHAPTER 39

▼

By lunchtime that Thursday, Maggie McBride's new fax machine had been working almost nonstop for four hours. Using her recently updated customer lists, Maggie spent the morning electronically transferring letters to Hancock's landscape clients for the preceding three years. Now she was in the process of faxing a similar letter to the company's entire roster of retail customers.

Maggie had typed Mark's gutsy letters carefully. In frank and forthcoming language, her boss spelled out the likelihood that plants and landscapes purchased from or installed by Hancock's during the previous twenty-four months were contaminated with medical waste. Biohazardous medical waste—glass, plastic, metal—and worse from health care establishments across the city; establishments which, by the way, played no part in the illegal dumping. The criminals responsible had been apprehended, Mark wrote. The time had come to undo the damage.

Hancock's, in effect, was recalling its work.

Clients could choose one of two options. Unearth the debris themselves at their own risk (using recommended protective clothing, equipment, and safety procedures spelled out in the letter) and return the bagged waste to Hancock's for cash compensation. Or request cleanup and removal services from Hancock's, free of charge.

Hancock's new owner expressed deep regret that the company and its patrons had been unwittingly exposed to the criminal distribution of hazardous material. He pledged to correct the matter safely, without delay, to the satisfaction of every customer. And, in a heartfelt tribute to Fred Dunn, Mark added that his predecessor knew nothing about the illegal activity.

"The contamination of landscapes and plant material goes against everything Fred Dunn and his father stood for during Hancock's impeccable fifty-year history," he wrote. "When I acquired the business less than a month ago, I pledged to maintain the Dunns' high standards. I intend to honor that pledge, beginning with the cleanup of your property.

"My employees and I stand ready to assist you in any way we can, to help the community as a whole recover, and to maintain the integrity of the landscape business."

Maggie punched in another fax number and brushed a wisp of hair from her cheek. Behind a pair of narrow pink reading glasses, her eyes sparkled. She couldn't tell what excited her more, operating the new electronic hardware in her office or helping short-circuit the crooks who had dumped all over Hancock's. She was sure of one thing: Beth Dunn made a smart move when she sold the business to Mark.

*   *   *   *

Outside Maggie's office, Carlos Hernandez stood before a sizeable group of trainees who were learning how to safely remove and bag buried biohazards. Buoyed by the news that he had passed his landscape contractor's exam, Carlos spent the previous six days becoming an authority in yet another field, the handling and disposal of medical waste. By the end of the week he could quote the Medical Waste Management Act almost as accurately as the Basic Plant Care section of the *Western Garden Book*.

Speaking careful English and Spanish, Carlos showed the new employees how to put on the OSHA-approved overalls, gloves, boots, and masks that Mark had special ordered in Hancock's trademark shades of green and yellow, and had rushed to the nursery. "We will give you clean protective gear for every job," Carlos promised. "All of these items are also available for sale at wholesale prices here at Hancock's, along with the scoops, bags, sharps containers, metal detectors, and other waste recovery supplies you will use at the sites." He grinned. "Please tell the gardeners you know to get their cleanup *equipamiento* here, okey-dokey?"

Carlos regarded the men and women standing in front of him, so eager and glad for their new jobs. He understood the warmth Fred Dunn must have felt for him in the early days. A skinny kid from Mexico with little to offer but a sunny disposition and an insatiable hunger to learn, Carlos had wanted more than anything to please his kindly boss. Did Fred know then what Carlos knew with certainty at that very moment? That among the earnest, expectant faces in front of him was Hancock's next young rising star.

*   *   *   *

While Carlos conducted his class at Hancock's, a small army of matronly figures wearing sturdy pink jumpsuits, gloves, and garden hats swarmed over the lavishly planted landscape of Glenwater Place. Trained, equipped, and quivering with indignation, this special task force searched for the most disgraceful litter they had ever encountered in the garden club's forty-two-year history of neighborhood beautification.

The troops were divided into three deadly serious battalions headed by Helen Woodley, Beth Dunn, and Ginny Grant. Trowels and maps in hand, Helen's unit patrolled the terraced gardens, efficiently dispatching the junk they found beneath the boxwood borders, the *Raphiolepis* bushes, and the recently planted begonia beds. Beth led her forces on a foray through the colonnades where the dainty dogwoods endured invasive blades of shovel and hoe. Ginny's pink-clad company took on the spectacularly blooming Camellia Court.

"You can't tell a book by its cover," Ginny declared in a muffled voice behind her pink OHSA-approved mask. She triumphantly lifted a broken IV bottle from the dirt beneath a verdant *C. japonica* Tiffany semidouble.

The club members dug out the surface debris manually and bagged it meticulously. When a probe near one of the deeply planted hedges, jacaranda trees, or fan palms indicated foul play in the root ball, the squad leaders called in the heavy artillery. A narrow gauge, fifty-horse-power dozer stood at the ready behind the front lines with a licensed operator in full biohazard dress.

By sunset the following day, the garden club expected to complete its most historic mission. They would peel off their pink uniforms and head for various Friday evening appointments with accommodating hairdressers, masseuses, and manicurists, secure in the knowledge they had not only done their civic duty, but also outdone forever their counterparts in sister clubs across the nation. Best of all, Glenwater Place would open at noon on Saturday in certifiably perfect condition, a credit to the garden club and a spectacular showcase for its creator, Hancock's Landscape Services.

*   *   *   *

As the garden club labored historically at Glenwater Place, Mark Grant sat in the boardroom on the fifty-second floor of the American Coastal Bank Building making history of his own. At his right sat Mel Beckman, lead banker to Biovak, Inc., the man who almost single-handedly brought the hot new entrepreneurial company through the doors, onto the record books, and into the stratosphere of American Coastal dealdom. The Biovak coup, on top of long and competent relationships with other middle-market businesses, including Folee's

Nursery, put Mel on the map in banking circles. When Mark informed Mel about the impending demise of both Biovak and Folee's, it became difficult to distinguish the supplicant from the savior.

Like Mark, Mel started working fast to recoup his losses, both real and potential. Having two key corporate customers crater at the same time was the least of Mel's problems, and Mark knew it. American Coastal's vast retail business relied largely on the goodwill of the community. In a high volume, low margin business where the difference between one competitor and another rested on little more than the color of their checkbooks or the location of their ATMs, public perception was all.

What would people think when news broke that American Coastal profited from the illegal actions of two of its corporate customers, a fraudulent medical waste hauler and the nursery it paid to bury the stuff? Worse, that the crud turning up in everyone's backyards was connected to the big bank downtown? The lender had no knowledge? How come?

Bankers had been fired for less, as both Mark and Mel were acutely aware.

They had worked on a way out for a week. Consulted with attorneys. Quietly drafted documents. Made and confirmed appointments. Reserved the bank's boardroom. Ordered vast quantities of coffee and food. At 5 AM on Thursday, June 14—the precise moment the police clamped cuffs on Julian Shand, Sam Folee, and the others—Mark and Mel put their plan in motion.

Over the next twelve hours the two men met with no less than forty-five individuals, including American Coastal's executive committee, senior corporate counsel, and entire loan review board. Administrative assistants who rushed in and out with processed documents, drafts, and photocopies would remember that Thursday their entire careers. VIPs, including their boss's boss's bosses, came and went all day. The executives put all other business on hold. They sweated like distance runners. And they ate. Three dozen blueberry muffins, two boxes of egg bagels, four platters of sliced fruit and cheese, twenty containers of low-fat yogurt, thirty-six chicken fajita sandwiches, and forty-two extra-large chocolate chip cookies, to be exact.

By 8 AM, Mark had spelled out to his former bank colleagues—in grim detail—the scope of the biohazardous dumping, the roles played by Biovak, Inc., and Folee's Nursery, the innocent involvement of the ownership of Hancock's Landscape Services, and Mark's proposed remedy for the dire situation. After their initial shock, the bank executives greeted Mark like a long lost treasure.

By 11 AM, Mel had gathered all the signatures he needed to execute material adverse change documents against Biovak and Folee's, rescinding all previous loan commitments.

Around noon an American Coastal committee met in an adjoining conference room with Rick Edwards and a group of prominent pharmaceutical executives who had hurried over from the Biltmore to get started on a corporate superfund to finance the recovery. About the same time, bank attorneys obtained a court order to freeze the assets of Biovak, Inc., and initiated proceedings to both recover bank debt and assign a large portion of the former hauler's liquid assets to the cleanup of the illegally dumped materials.

At 2 PM, Natalie Dunn arrived direct from Ajax Hall with the mayor of Los Angeles, who asked Mark to accept a position as honorary chair of a blue-ribbon task force, CleanUp LA. On the condition that no public funds would be spent on the task force or the cleanup, Mark respectfully accepted.

At 3 PM, eight of Sam Folee's stricken relatives filed into the boardroom accompanied by twelve attorneys. Except for Sam, who languished, toupee-less, in jail, the relatives constituted the entire board of directors and all the shareholders of Folee's Nursery. Although it was never mentioned directly, the question of the various Folees' culpability filled the room like a nasty odor.

Word came from the courthouse that Rudy Vale planned to turn state's evidence and finger all parties involved. News was also beginning to trickle in about widespread contamination in the Folees' land-scape portfolio. Dr. Broder called to tell Mark about several new stashes of bones unearthed by dogs. Neighborhood recycling centers reported bags turning up that contained medical waste mixed with the household variety.

If the Folees wanted to salvage anything of their investment in the nursery business, the time to deal was now.

In the middle of negotiations, Andrea Grant hand-delivered copies of four newsletters she had rushed from the presses on Pico Avenue: *Healthy Times, LA Business Report, Property Line,* and *Garden Works.* Mark introduced his wife, who passed the newsletters around the table. Everyone in the boardroom recognized at least a couple of the publications. American Coastal's chairman said his office subscribed to three of them. Eyes fell on the headlines, and conversation stopped. *Medical Waste in Your Backyard?* Some of the Folees squirmed in their arm-chairs. Mel Beckman wiped his forehead. The chairman tweaked his glasses. Several people cleared their throats and reached for water. They had danced around this subject for hours. Seeing the words in print brought the music abruptly to a halt.

By five o'clock, the deal was done. There had been little dissention. Mel and his colleagues wanted Folee's Nursery wiped off the record books, if not the planet. Already impressed by Mark's cleanup initiatives at Hancock's, the bankers were bug-eyed when the mayor walked in and shook his hand. For their part, the Folees wanted cash, presumably to finance their defense if not their relocation to some remote tropical island. And Mark?

Mark sat at the conference table with his necktie loosened, cuffs rolled back, elbows nestled in an intoxicating array of legal pads, documents, fountains pens, and calculators. He leaned back in his chair and gazed through the fifty-second floor windows at the panoramic view from downtown to the West Side. Winston Latour and the high-priced gurus of Webb, Watson, Latour and Meeks had been correct. Nearly two decades out of business school, he was still pumped and primed to become a captain of industry. Well, a lieutenant at least.

That day, with help from his new coterie of corporate bankers, he personally acquired the entire chain of Folee's Nurseries. Nine established and profitable locations, soon to be renamed Hancock's Landscape Services. The deal included all key assets including the Folees' buildings, inventory, equipment, software, and computerized mailing lists. In carefully crafted legalese, the written agreements ensured that none of the nursery's liabilities resulting from prior illegal activity was included in the sale. In return, Mark agreed to manage the cleanup of Biovak-infested properties throughout the Folee chain using capital from the corporate superfund and his own proven team-building skill. The chairman of American Coastal, the district attorney, and the mayor were going to explain it all when Mark joined them in a few minutes for a prime-time news conference scheduled to precede the evening news.

Mark met Andrea's sparkling eyes across the conference room, and felt a rush of indescribable pleasure. What he learned during his eighteen years in banking still held true. With a well-crafted loan agreement, everybody won.

CHAPTER 40

▼

Saturday dawned sunny and fresh, a clear June morning made for brides and baccalaureates and busy realtors with buyers in tow. Between the weddings, graduations, and house tours, much of West Los Angeles planned to check out the grand opening of Glenwater Place.

At half-past noon, Mark, Andrea, and Lindsey climbed out of their new green Jeep Cherokee near the entrance to Camellia Court. The pale stucco buildings of the brand new complex seemed to glitter with light and hope. Heat rose gently from the terra cotta sidewalks where opening-day visitors wandered in twos and threes, admiring the graceful architecture, the custom wrought iron, and the acres of elegant landscape.

"There's Grandma!" cried Lindsey, running to a geranium-decked table at the intersection of two sidewalks. "*Hola,* Grandma! *Hablas español?*"

Lindsey's day as an oblivious kidnap victim produced an unexpected result. She woke up speaking Spanish. "*Buenos dias mis amigos!*" she shouted as she jumped on Andrea and Mark's bed late the next morning. "*Me llamo* Lindsey."

It turned out her kidnapper, Rudy Vale, had entrusted her to the care of a recently arrived landscape laborer from Guatemala who spoke zero English, missed his own adored offspring, and thought he was tending Rudy's daughter. Lindsey, basking in the limelight, lost little time figuring out how to communicate with her indulgent caretaker. "*Vamos a la piscina!*" became her favorite new expression.

"Well hello, dear," Ginny replied. "*No hablo mucho,* unfortunately. When it comes to languages, I'm all thumbs."

"Hi, Mom," said Mark, approaching with Andrea. "*Que pasa?*"

Ginny rose from her chair. She wore a pretty flowered dress and the pleased expression of a person laughing last and best. "Welcome to Glenwater Place," she said, sounding like a tour guide. "This six-acre development was designed by the architectural firm of Jones and Clarke. Landscape by Hancock's Landscape Services. Litter removal and beautification by the garden clubs of Greater Los Angeles. We hope you enjoy your visit. How's that?"

She handed each of them a flyer that explained the garden club's role in the eradication of illegally dumped waste and offered guidelines for other gardeners to follow in the safe removal of buried debris.

"Your club has done an outstanding job here, Ginny," Andrea said, casting a glance around the immaculately groomed greenery of Camellia Court.

"Thank you, dear. You did a great job too. That terminally boring *Garden Works* knocked my socks off this issue. I'm writing a letter to the editor. So are all of my friends in the garden club."

"Maybe that man won't fire me after all," Andrea said. "He would trample his tiger lilies before he'd offend the garden club."

Ginny winked at Andrea. "There's strength in numbers, you know."

"Subscribers to the other newsletters are writing in too," Mark told Ginny. "Including the chairman of American Coastal. Andrea doesn't have to worry too much about losing her clients."

"I'm glad," Ginny said. She looked at Mark with a twinkle in her eye. "I understand you took my advice and went back into big business."

Mark smiled at his mother. "You could say that."

Helen Woodley and Beth Dunn trundled up carrying more boxes of flyers. "Well, if it isn't the couple of the hour," Helen exclaimed, setting her load on the table. "Beth just told me you bought Folee's."

"Fred would dance on these sidewalks if he knew," Beth said. A large bronze-colored orchid blossomed on the shoulder of her yellow dress. "I spoke with Maggie and Carlos. They're ecstatic about their new responsibilities. You know, Hancock's was ready for a change."

"Ten locations will be a stretch at first," Mark admitted. "Rudy Vale has sworn that Sam Folee's nine branch managers are clean. Most of the illegal activity took place at the foreman level with bribed day laborers doing the dirty work."

"Dirty work? Can't we talk about something else for once?" said Rick Edwards, approaching the little group at the garden club table. He was wearing faded blue jeans and a navy blue blazer, and was holding the hand of Natalie Dunn.

Rick and Natalie exchanged greetings all around. Natalie looked ravishing in red. She hugged her mother. "You didn't tell them my news, did you?"

"Of course not," Beth replied, appearing ready to burst with delight.

"UCLA offered me a teaching position," Natalie told them. "I'll be moving back to Los Angeles before fall semester."

"Actually, she couldn't bear the thought of leaving me," Rick burbled.

"It must have been that syringe you stuck in her neck," Mark commented.

"Congratulations, Natalie," Andrea said, smiling. "Evidently they liked your lecture."

"The dean of the business school told me it gave him the shivers," Natalie answered with a blush. "He thinks I'm the next Silas Udahl."

"This must be a common malady," Rick put in. "She gives me the shivers too, and I never met Silas Udahl." He stared past Natalie. "Isn't that Wanda Juju?"

Walking across the colonnade in the company of Maggie McBride was a tall, slightly stooped woman with cropped hair wearing a new blue warm-up suit. Maggie waved in their direction.

"Wanda is someone we met in the warehouse district," Mark explained to Helen, Beth, and Ginny. "She recently entered a drug rehab program on the West Side. Carlos is training her to work in Hancock's nursery, and Maggie sort of took her under her wing."

"Drug rehab?" Helen said pensively, squinting in Wanda's direction. "You're a good man, Mark. Tell Wanda she may work in my garden anytime. I'll need help rehabilitating the zucchini patch after the police finish harvesting your film."

Helen and Ginny got busy handing out flyers while Lindsey, hoping to snag a passing linguist, stood next to them calling, *"Buenos tardes!"* Beth and Natalie crossed the courtyard to speak with an old family friend. And Mark turned to see Dottie DeLuca tripping toward him on white high heeled sandals.

"Yoo-hoo. Mark Grant? Is that you? And Rick!" she said breathlessly. "I've been reading about both of you in the papers."

Air kisses all around. Mark introduced Andrea. Dottie murmured in her direction, then turned to Mark.

"Congratulations on your takeover of that behemoth Folee's. You know, I always did like Hancock's better. And I hear you're heading the mayor's blue ribbon committee, CleanUp LA?"

Dottie leaned her shiny cap of hair toward Mark conspiratorially. "Those clay pots weren't really defective, were they?"

Mark lowered his head. "Dottie, be glad we rounded them up when we did." He glanced at Rick. "Tell me, Dottie. Are you all wrapped up in a disease at the moment or would you have time to help us on the new corporate superfund? Rick and I are looking for a chairperson."

Dottie regarded Rick with interest. As Mark suspected, diseases excited her less than the process of extracting cash from corporations. Give her a cause, any cause.

"Why don't we talk about it?" she cooed.

While Rick high-beamed his charm on Dottie, Mark took Andrea's hand and strolled toward the banner-decked platform in Camellia Court. A band was tuning up in anticipation of the mayor's arrival. Under the fan palms, two clowns and a juggler entertained a throng of laughing children while their parents stood nearby. The crowd had thickened considerably. The sidewalk cafés were jammed. Browsers walked in and out of the newly opened bookstore. People studied the plant identification markers stuck discreetly in the soil. The opening-day celebrants appeared relaxed, interested in Glenwater Place, and, best of all, unafraid.

"Remember the day we walked around this courtyard for the first time?" Andrea asked, looking up at him with warm brown eyes. She was wearing a simple cotton shift and a string of amber beads that seemed wedded to her rich coloring. The sweetness of their triumph was already beginning to supplant the horror of her encounter with Zeeb.

Mark nodded and lifted her fingers to his lips. He remembered. Only seven weeks and several lifetimes earlier. He was glad that period in their lives was over.

"Mark," a voice said. He turned to see Mel Beckman and a fresh-faced young man walking toward them.

"Congratulations," Mel said. "The landscape is a blockbuster."

"Thanks."

"Hello, Andrea." Mel pecked her on the cheek. "I'd like both of you to meet Pete Allan. He got his master's at Kellogg like you, Mark, and recently joined American Coastal. He's going to work on our Hancock's team."

"How do you do?" Pete said to Andrea, who shook his hand. He turned to Mark. "It's a pleasure to meet you, Mr. Grant. I've heard a lot about you."

Mark regarded the bright-eyed MBA and felt a pang of recognition. A brand new graduate—pumped and primed to become a captain of industry? Perhaps. He gripped the proffered hand. It was going to be interesting to find out.

Author's Note

This is a work of fiction. The characters are inventions that grew into lively, unpredictable companions during the solitary process of writing the novel. Turning the manuscript into a book, however, required real people to whom I am very grateful. Editor Michael Hoffeditz applied encyclopedic knowledge of *The Chicago Manual of Style*, and commented helpfully on composition and content. Shelly Bell Eckerman designed a handsome, botanically authentic cover after visiting the Garfield Park Conservatory. Kristin Oomen, computer virtuoso, pulled everything together at iUniverse with patience and skill. My sincere thanks to all of them.

978-0-595-35660-7
0-595-35660-5

Printed in the United States
35466LVS00005B/55-63